# MARRYING HIS BROTHER

A Billionaire Arranged marriage Romance

Elara Long

Copyright © 2024 by Elara Long

All rights reserved.

No part of this book may be reproduced, distributed, or transmitted in any form or by any electronic or mechanical means, including information storage and retrieval systems, without written permission from the author, except for the use of brief quotations in a book review and certain other noncommercial use permitted by copyright law.

Resemblance to actual persons and things living or dead, locales, or events is entirely coincidental.

MARRYING HIS BROTHER:

Cover Designer: Raymond A. Barth

Editor: Diana Karanja

Proofreader: Lois Hall

# CONTENT

## Chapter 1: Emily

"Emily, we've got a problem at the Riviera Army Base." Amy's voice crackles through the line, urgency in her tone. "A pipe burst in the middle of the night. We've got flooded rooms, and the guests are furious. Again."

I groan. "How many rooms are affected?"

"Four, but the water's creeping into the hallway. Maintenance is already on-site, but the complaints are pouring in."

"Damn it. Not again." I glance around my cluttered office, stacks of paperwork and endless to-do lists glaring back at me. "Can you handle the angry guests? I'll send an email to the front desk to issue compensation."

I picture our older properties, their charm overshadowed by the never-ending maintenance issues.

"Got it. I'll keep you updated."

I hang up the phone, the weight of constantly putting out fires pulling at my shoulders. Just another day of damage control. It's all I've done since my father's stroke.

I barely have time to think about long-term strategy because every day, something falls apart.

Before I can even take a breath, my phone rings again. My heart skips a beat when I see Mom flashing on the screen. I fumble to answer.

"Is Dad okay?" The words fly out of my mouth before she can even say hello.

"He's the same," she says softly, and tension eases from my body. "I'm calling to remind you about tonight's dinner at the Bennett's'. We're finalizing the wedding arrangements today."

Right. The wedding. Because I don't have enough to worry about.

The Bennetts want a huge affair while my mother and I are determined to keep it small and intimate.

The invitations are going out next week, and we're still fighting over the guest list. I don't even know half the people they want to invite, but what does it matter? It's not like this is a real wedding anyway.

I let out a sigh which my mother immediately picks up on.

"Are you sure you still want to go ahead with this?" she asks.

"Yes," I say, not giving myself time to hesitate. This isn't about love or romance. It's about saving Dad's company. It's about keeping Riviera alive.

"I can't imagine living with a man I didn't love," she says after a pause. "If I didn't love your father, I would have left when he got sick."

"Not everyone is cut out for love, Mom," I reply, thinking back to my last relationship. Jaime had wanted a wife who didn't embarrass him by speaking out her opinion in public. A meek wife.

The criticism increased by the day. That was when I knew we weren't going anywhere. I started pulling away before he even realized what was happening.

But Daniel Bennett? Not a man I would have fallen in love with, if love even exists.

"I'll pick you up at six," I say, eager to change the subject.

"Okay, sweetie. See you then," she says before we hang up.

I sit back in my chair, staring at my phone. I should call Daniel but the thought is annoying. I'm the one always reminding him of these things.

I've barely heard from him this week, not that I've had time to care. Sorting out problems with the hotels has kept me more than occupied.

I scroll through my contacts, find his name, and hit dial. It rings, and rings and then goes to voicemail.

Typical.

"Daniel, it's Emily," I say after the beep. "Just a reminder about dinner tonight with my mom and your parents. It's important, so please don't forget."

I hang up, my irritation simmering just below the surface. It's bad enough I'm agreeing to marry him for the sake of our families' businesses. Now I'll have to nanny him, too?

By the time the clock hits 5:30 PM, my to-do list is only half-checked. Meetings bled into more meetings, followed by a constant stream of follow-ups on the Riviera Army Base disaster.

I'm still managing damage control. My inbox is a mess of complaints, updates, and financial warnings. Every time I think I've caught up, something else slips through the cracks.

I rub my temples, exhaustion seeping into my bones, but I can't afford to slow down. Not yet. Grabbing my coat, I shut my laptop and head out of the office. My phone buzzes with another notification, but I shove it into my bag. I'll deal with it later.

First, I need to see Dad.

As I pull into the driveway, sadness settles into me. It's been, what, four months and no change. The doctors tell us that he could wake up any time, but my hope is dwindling.

The second floor has been converted into a hospital suite for my father. It's hard to accept, even now, months after the stroke. A nurse stays with him 24/7, and yet, I still can't stop myself from worrying every time I walk through the door.

Inside, the house is quiet, except for the distant sound of the nurse moving around upstairs. I drop my keys on the table and head straight up.

Joan, one of his regular nurses, jumps when I fling the door open and we both laugh.

"How is he today?" I ask her.

"He's good. Go on in, I've just finished turning him."

"Thanks," I say and enter the room. The strong smell of antiseptic hits me as I shut the door behind me.

I sit down beside his bed, taking in the familiar sight of him. His face is peaceful, though it's hard to see him like this, so still, when he was always so full of life.

I take his hand, feeling its warmth, but it's the stillness that gets me every time. I blink back the sudden tears that fill my eyes. We were told to keep talking to him. That people in a coma can hear what is going on around them.

"I'm getting married, Dad," I say quietly, squeezing his hand gently. "In six weeks."

The words bounce back at me. *A marriage. To someone I barely know.* For reasons that have nothing to do with love. If that doesn't wake Dad up, nothing will. He'd be livid at what I'm doing.

"I know you'd hate what I'm doing," I continue, my voice cracking just a little. "But I have to do it, Dad. I'm doing it to save Riviera, to save everything you built."

My eyes sting, but I blink back the tears. He wouldn't want to see me cry, wouldn't want me to feel weak. So I stay strong. "I've been fighting to keep things together. I've been doing what I can. But without the Bennett deal, the hotels will crumble."

I lean closer, studying his peaceful face, hoping that his eyes will flutter open, that I might see some reaction. But there's nothing. Just the soft beep of the machines and the steady rise and fall of his chest.

The silence in the room grows suffocating. I let go of his hand and rub my own palms together. Unable to stare at him any longer, I kiss his dry, soft cheek and leave.

Joan glances up as I walk out, giving me a soft smile. "He's lucky to have you, you know."

"Thanks," is all I can manage, as I head down in search of my mother.

She's waiting in the foyer as I walk down the stairs. "I saw your car and figured you'd gone to say hello to Dad." She's dressed elegantly in a soft blue dress that brings out the color in her eyes, but there's an aura of sadness around her.

I get to bury myself in work and forget that my father is in a coma, but Mom has to live with it day and night.

"I did," I reply, adjusting the strap of my bag. "He's the same."

She nods and opens the front door. We step outside into the cool evening air. I unlock the car, and we both slide in.

"You look tired," Mom says gently, fastening her seatbelt.

"Long day." I start backing out of the driveway. "Issues at the Army Base hotel again. Burst pipes, angry guests, the usual chaos."

"You're working too hard," she says.

I force a smile. "We're both working too hard. But we do what we have to do."

She smiles. "Have you heard from Daniel?"

"Not today. Left him a message about tonight."

"You'd think he'd be more involved, considering..."

"Considering we're getting married in six weeks?" I finish for her, a hint of anger creeping into my voice.

"Yes," Mom says. "You let him off the hook too easily, Emily."

To be fair, I sort of understand Daniel's attitude. It can't be easy accepting your parents' choice of a bride for you. Daniel is still a teenager in his head and his parents think that marriage will make him grow up and take responsibility.

I'm not so sure that will work but I don't really care. All I care about is the injection of capital the Riviera group will get once Daniel and I are married. After that, he can do whatever pleases him. I won't be chasing after him.

## Chapter 2: Andrew

The guests have already arrived when I get home, but I don't see Daniel's car. No surprises there. Daniel will probably be late for his own funeral. I straighten my jacket, taking a moment before heading inside.

The air is cool, and I pull in a deep breath, steadying myself. This dinner is important. For once, Daniel is doing something that is completely selfless. Something good for the family.

I step through the front entrance, where voices are coming from the drawing room. I'm eager to meet Emily Young. Daniel's bride. The woman who agreed to a marriage of convenience for the sake of rescuing her family's business.

I step through the front entrance, the voices from the drawing room drifting down the hallway. The butler gives me a nod, and I offer a curt nod back, making my way inside.

I'm curious to meet Emily Young. Daniel's bride. The woman willing to marry for the sake of rescuing her family's business. I can respect that kind of pragmatism.

As I enter the room, my mother is the first to look up. She greets me with a small smile, though her jaw is tight. She's good at hiding it, but I know her too well. Daniel being late must be driving her up the wall.

"Andrew, darling," she says, rising gracefully from her seat to kiss my cheek. "I'm glad you're here."

"Of course." I glance at my father, who is nursing a drink near the window, his expression unreadable. "Evening, Dad."

"Andrew," he replies, giving me a brief nod. "You're just in time."

I turn back to my mother as she gestures to the two women seated beside her. "Andrew, I'd like you to meet Mrs. Young and her daughter, Emily."

Mother and daughter stand up. I exchange pleasantries with Mrs. Young. She resembles a delicate porcelain figure, fragile and graceful. Her smile is polite, but there's a certain weariness in her eyes.

I turn my attention to Emily. And then I stop. For a moment, I forget to breathe.

Emily Young is stunning.

Her simple black and white evening dress hugs her figure just right—elegant, but undeniably sexy. Her deep green, almond-shaped eyes meet mine, cool and assessing. Her oval face, framed by waves of chestnut brown hair, is serene, composed. She cuts a calm, collected figure.

Not the type of woman I was expecting to meet. I swallow and extend my hand. "Emily."

She reaches out, her hand cool in mine as we shake. "Andrew," she says, her voice smooth, polite, but distant. Her eyes, those green eyes, take me in, the same way I'm taking her in.

"It's a pleasure," I manage to say, though I'm still caught off guard.

She tilts her head ever so slightly, a flicker of something in her gaze—curiosity, maybe. "Likewise."

"Have you heard from Daniel?" I ask, turning back to my mother, though I already know the answer.

She shakes her head, the faintest irritation slipping through her otherwise calm exterior. "No."

Father looks at the clock. "We can't keep waiting for him," he says, doing a poor job of hiding his annoyance.

I'm irritated too. I hope this doesn't turn Emily off from my brother, but I'm pretty sure she's well aware of his tardiness.

We move toward the dining room, and I find myself walking beside Emily. Pinpricks of awareness light up my skin. I'll be damned. I'm attracted to my brother's fiancée. Anyone would be. She's a very attractive woman and her lavender scent doesn't help.

We settle into the dining room, the clinking of silverware and soft conversation filling the air. I can't shake the tension running through me as I sit beside Emily. The scent of lavender drifts over and it stirs something in me.

*Damn it, Andrew. Focus.*

The small talk flows, but I only half-listen, nodding when appropriate. My father clears his throat, shifting the conversation.

"Emily," he says, folding his hands on the table, "I was hoping your father would join us tonight. It would have been a pleasure to meet him."

The briefest flicker comes in her eyes before Emily responds. "Unfortunately, he couldn't make it," she says smoothly. "He's taking a much-needed sabbatical after decades of managing the family business. After years of relentless work, he decided it was time to step back temporarily and focus on himself."

My mother raises her eyebrows, her curiosity piqued. "I would think he'd want to be present for his daughter's wedding, especially one as important as this."

Emily holds her ground, her smile unwavering. "I insisted that he not cut his travels short. The wedding arrangements are under control, and I'll introduce him to Daniel when he returns. We thought it best he focus on his health."

I'm impressed by how well she handles the scrutiny from my mother. She doesn't flinch, doesn't crack under the pressure of the unspoken questions hanging in the air.

It's clear she's used to navigating difficult conversations. A skill that will no doubt serve her well in this marriage.

By the time the main meal is served, everyone is anxious and trying not to show it. Every few minutes, my mother glances at the door as if he might suddenly appear.

Finally, she leans over, keeping her voice low but firm. "Andrew, can you call your brother?"

I sigh, pushing my chair back as I stand. "Excuse me for a moment," I say, my voice neutral, though inside, I'm boiling.

This is Daniel's dinner party and he's treating it like a casual get-together he can skip. I step out into the hall, my phone already in hand, and dial Daniel's number. It rings twice before he picks up.

"Daniel," I say, not even bothering with pleasantries. "Are you on the way?"

There's a pause on the other end before he answers. "I'm in New York."

I blink, my irritation flaring into something hotter. "You're what?"

"I'm not coming," he says, his voice flat. "I'm not marrying Emily Young."

For a second, I'm stunned. My mind races, but the words feel like they've knocked the breath out of me. "You waited until six weeks before the wedding to say this?" My voice rises despite myself.

"Do you even realize what you're saying? This isn't just about you. We need a stake in Riviera, and this marriage is the only way we can get it."

There's silence on his end, then Daniel's voice comes back, cold and detached. "It's always business for father, isn't it? And now for you. I'm not doing it, Andrew. You can tell them the wedding is off."

I clench my teeth, fury coursing through me. "Don't be a fucking coward. Come here and tell them yourself. Face everyone, including Emily and tell them to their faces."

The line goes dead.

I stand there, phone in hand, seething.

This isn't just about the wedding. This merger was my shot. My chance to prove myself after everything—to show that I'm more than just an ex-soldier with issues.

I worked alongside my father before I left for my military tour, but it was always in his shadow. I wanted my own space to make decisions, to carve out something for myself. But leaving created a wedge between us that never healed.

My father never forgave me for abandoning the business when I left to serve.

Now, because of Daniel, that opportunity is slipping through my fingers. The deal with Riviera—something I could have spearheaded—is crumbling because my brother has suddenly decided he doesn't want to get married.

*Fuck!* I curl my hands into fists.

I take a deep breath and slide my phone back into my pocket, forcing myself to calm down. I have to tell them. Clearly, that coward of a brother, will not.

When I return to the dining room, all eyes turn to me.

I clear my throat, every step heavy as I make my way back to the table. "Daniel won't be coming tonight. He's called off the wedding."

The words drop like a bomb. Shock reverberates around the table. My father's hand tightens around his glass, the color draining from his face. My mother's mouth falls open in disbelief.

Mrs. Young looks utterly stunned, a gasp escaping her lips. And then there's Emily. She doesn't flinch, doesn't react immediately, just sits there for a moment, processing the words.

I pour myself a large glass of whisky and drown it in one go.

## Chapter 3: Emily

The drive home is silent except for the hum of the engine. I grip the steering wheel a little too tightly, trying to make sense of what just happened.

I should've seen this coming when he went quiet over the last few weeks, but I just assumed he was busy, partying up a storm as usual. I mean, that's what he does, right? He coasts; he's unreliable and selfish.

But this? This is worse than I expected.

"Maybe this is a sign," Mom says from the passenger seat, breaking the silence.

I glance at her. "A sign of what?"

"That the wedding was a bad idea to begin with," she says, rubbing her forehead. "I don't know how we would have explained this to your father. Selling off half his company..."

I scoff, shaking my head. "What will he say if he wakes up to no company at all?" My words are sharper than I intend, but I can't help it. I'm furious.

*Damn Daniel.*

*Damn everything.*

I bite down on my lip, trying to focus on the road ahead, but all I can think about is what this means for Riviera.

The problems we face. The endless problems. There's always something—the leaking pipes, the outdated infrastructure, the angry guests. Every day, it's another disaster waiting to happen, and now, without this wedding and the capital it would have brought in, what am I going to do?

I slam my palm on the steering wheel, my frustration bubbling over. "This was supposed to be the perfect solution. An injection of capital would've meant renovations, finally fixing all the damn issues.

"And we could've launched an aggressive marketing plan, drawn in more clients, filled those rooms. Now, it's all gone," I say, my voice filled with bitterness.

"And I'll just have to watch it all go downhill." I know that I'm ranting, and it's not fair to take it out on my mother, but there's no one I can talk to about this.

There's my best friend, Lisa, but it's late and unfair to call her now.

My mother's gaze pierces me, but I don't look at her. I can't. The pressure is too much, the disappointment too sharp. For a moment, neither of us speaks, the tension settling like a heavy fog between us.

We pull up to the house, and I put the car in park, but I don't turn to face her. Instead, I stare straight ahead, my mind already racing through contingency plans, none of which seem feasible.

"You've done everything you could, Emily," she says softly, reaching out to touch my hand. "No one could have asked more of you, including your father."

I turn to her and smile. "We'll think of something else." Empty words. I have no plan B or C. Or D for that matter.

As she disappears inside, I lean back against the seat and close my eyes. What am I supposed to do now?

***

I stand in the middle of the Riviera Army Base hotel, watching the repairs going on around me. The place is a mess. No matter how much patchwork we do, it's not enough. This hotel needs more than a few fixes. It needs a full renovation, and that takes money we don't have.

I walk past a section of piping they've torn open, shaking my head. The water damage stretches farther than I thought. I swallow the frustration bubbling in my chest, but it's a losing battle.

Every time I look at these walls, I get angry all over again. At the state of the hotel. At the never-ending problems. At Daniel.

Daniel and his damn cowardice. We were six weeks away from a solution. Six weeks from pulling Riviera out of the quicksand it's sinking into. And he couldn't even tell me to my face. Instead, he sent his brother.

As I try to focus on the contractors, my phone buzzes in my pocket. I pull it out and see a new number flashing across the screen. Probably more bad news. Don't they say that when it rains, it pours?

I hit answer, already dreading the call.

"Emily Young."

"Emily, it's Andrew Bennett."

I freeze for a second, caught off guard. Andrew. Of course. It's not like I wasn't expecting to deal with the Bennett's after Daniel bailed, but I wasn't expecting it this scene and certainly not Andrew. We barely know each other.

"I need to meet with you. It's important," he says, not even bothering with a greeting. His tone is blunt, curt.

I glance around at the chaos surrounding me—contractors, broken pipes, the never-ending list of problems at this hotel. The last thing I need right now is another Bennett to deal with. Still, I can't exactly ignore him.

"Meet with me? About what?"

"Preferably in private."

His words are clipped, professional. But the demand annoys me. "Alright, how about my apartment? Six o'clock?"

"Works for me." Before I can respond, he hangs up.

I pull the phone away from my ear, staring at it like it just insulted me. Great. No pleasantries, no explanation. Andrew could borrow some charm from his brother. At least Daniel knew how to talk to people, even if he was a spineless coward. Andrew's all business. Cold, efficient.

I text him my address, without expecting a response back.

I'm surprised when he texts back, *Thank you.* Not such an asshole after all.

I pocket the phone and turn back to the mess in front of me. My anger, which had been simmering beneath the surface, flares again. Andrew probably wants to meet and attempt to explain his brother's actions. Maybe even apologize.

What good will that do me? *Damn Daniel.* This is probably the hundredth time I've cursed Daniel since last night.

The coward couldn't even face me, and explain why he was bailing on a wedding that was more than just a union. It was the key to saving Riviera.

Now I'm left picking up the pieces, including talking to his older brother.

I spend the rest of the afternoon at the Army Base Riviera and finally leave in time to get home and take a shower before Andrew arrives. As I wash off the grime of the day, I remember Daniel mentioning that his brother had served on a military tour.

Soldiers are sticklers for time, and the last thing I want is for him to show up and catch me fresh out of the shower, wrapped in a towel.

I dress quickly, choosing something simple but presentable—a cream blouse and jeans. As I towel-dry my hair, nervousness takes root in the pit of my stomach.

At exactly six o'clock, the buzzer rings. Of course, Andrew would be punctual. I let him up, thankful I'd had the foresight to warn the doorman I was expecting a guest.

I stand by the door for a moment, taking a breath, trying to push down the tension swirling in me.

A knock on the door pulls me from my thoughts, and I open it to find him standing there, as serious as ever. Andrew steps inside, his eyes sweeping the room in that calculated way of his, like he's taking in every detail and filing it away.

"Andrew," I say, trying for casual as I lead him toward the living room. The tension between us is palpable, thickening with every step. "Can I get you something to drink?" I say when he sits down.

His muscled thighs barely fit into his jeans. I purse my lips, and realizing what I'm doing, I fake a cough to cover up my embarrassment.

"Just water," he replies curtly.

I'm shaken by my ogling, as I head to the kitchen to grab water from the fridge. I want to pour ice cold water all over my body to cool it down. Taking a deep breath, I carry the two bottles back to the living room.

I hand one to Andrew as I sit down across from him on the couch. He takes the water, his expression unreadable.

There's a long pause, and I can feel him studying me, those blue eyes too sharp, too focused. Finally, he breaks the silence.

"I want to apologize for what my brother did."

I exhale sharply, irritated. I was right. He wanted to meet me to apologize, something he could have done over the phone. "You don't need to apologize on Daniel's behalf. He's a grown man and can apologize himself."

Andrew doesn't flinch. "That's not why I came."

"Oh?" I raise an eyebrow, caught off guard.

"I have a feeling that you, unlike Daniel, understand how important that marriage would have been to both our family businesses."

I stare at him for a moment, processing his words. "Go on."

Andrew's gaze doesn't waver, his eyes locked on mine. "I have a proposition for you," he says, his voice calm but firm. "Let's go ahead with the wedding. Let's get married, Emily."

I blink, thrown by the bluntness of his statement. For a second, I think I misheard him. *Has he lost his mind?* Before I can even form a response, Andrew continues.

"We'll achieve what our families need, what we both need. One year, and then we can go our separate ways."

I set my bottle down, staring at him. I want to laugh but his expression is solemn. He's actually serious. "That's a ridiculous proposal."

"Why?" he asks. Then he tilts his head slightly. "Unless you actually loved my brother?"

That's personal territory and none of it's business. Rather than tell him so, I dodge it. "What would people think? Me jumping from one brother to another?"

Andrew leans back slightly, his gaze never leaving mine. "Which people? Only the two families were aware of the arrangement in the first place."

I open my mouth, but no words come out. He's right, technically. Outside of our families, no one knew about the business deal wrapped up in this so-called marriage. But still, there's something deeply unsettling about this entire proposition.

Andrew stands, towering over me for a moment as he straightens his jacket. "I know it's a lot to take in. Think about it." His tone is calm, composed, as if he's just proposed a simple business transaction.

Then, without waiting for a response, he turns and heads for the door. The sound of the latch clicking shut as he leaves echoes through the quiet apartment.

I sit there, frozen. The idea is preposterous, but as much as I want to dismiss it, I can't. The stakes are too high.

My mind flashes back to the crumbling walls of the Riviera Army Base hotel. The constant repairs. The never-ending problems. An injection of capital would solve everything. Renovations, marketing, stabilizing the company—all of it could be within reach. And all I need to do is say yes to Andrew.

But I don't know him. Not really. Even though I didn't love Daniel, I knew him. We went to school together. There was history, familiarity. Andrew, on the other hand, is a mystery—cold, calculated, and now offering marriage as if it's just another deal to close.

I pick up the bottle of water and take a sip, trying to clear my head. What kind of person makes a proposal like that? More importantly, what kind of person actually considers it?

## Chapter 4: Emily

"Well done, everyone. See you tomorrow," the yoga instructor says, signaling the end of class. I sit up slowly, rolling my mat and glancing at Lisa, who's already on her feet, her usual energy barely contained.

"You want to grab something to eat?" she asks, stretching her arms over her head.

I nod. "Yeah, let's go downstairs."

We head out of the studio and down to the deli shop on the corner. The nutty scent of freshly brewed coffee greets us as we walk in. We get two coffees and two salads, an early dinner for both of us.

The small table at the corner empties and we quickly make a beeline for it.

"You're not actually considering it, are you?" Lisa asks, picking up where we left off before class, her eyes widening as she leans over the table.

I sigh, tearing open the top of my salad container. "I am, Lisa. The company is in a bad state. You know that."

"You could bring in an investor," she insists, stabbing her fork into the salad. "Someone who'll be a silent partner. There's got to be a company willing to invest without tying you to... well, this."

I shake my head. 'It was an option at first, But most of the investors I've talked to want to completely restructure the hotels; some even suggested demolishing a few locations.

"They'd bring in their own teams, cut costs, replace our employees—people who have been with us since they were eighteen. They've built their lives with Riviera. Most of them hope to retire with us."

Lisa's eyes soften as she listens, her fork suspended midair. "I didn't realize it was that bad."

I nod, taking a sip of my coffee. "It is."

There's a pause, and then she says, "I could be an investor."

I blink, surprised by the offer. I know she means well—Lisa's always been the supportive, jump-in-with-both-feet type of friend.

She runs a cosmetics company that's already causing a buzz in the market, but they're still growing.

"Lisa, you've got your own business to think about," I say gently. "Your company is doing amazing, but you're not in a position to direct funds into saving Riviera. You don't need to take on that kind of risk."

She frowns, poking at her salad. "I hate seeing you like this, Em. You've worked so hard. Your Dad worked so hard. There has to be another way."

"I wish there was. But if we don't get a cash injection soon, we'll lose everything. The hotels need renovations, repairs, marketing... without capital, we're dead in the water."

Lisa leans back in her chair, studying me with her usual intensity. "So, what? You're seriously going to marry Andrew Bennett?"

I let out a breath, staring out the window at the cars passing by. "I don't know. It's insane, right? But I can't stop thinking about it."

"Of course it's insane," she exclaims, setting her fork down with a thud. "You barely know him. You don't even know if you can stand being around him for more than an hour."

"I know," I murmur, stirring my coffee absently. "But if we get married—even for just a year—the company survives. His family gets what they want, we get what we need, and then we can both walk away."

"And you're okay with that?" Lisa asks, her voice softer now, more concerned than shocked.

"Honestly? I don't know," I admit. "It's not like I dreamed of this kind of marriage. I didn't even love Daniel, but at least I knew him. Andrew's different. He's cold. Distant. But he understands the stakes. And right now, I can't afford to let emotions get in the way of what needs to be done."

Lisa's quiet for a moment, watching me. "Just promise me you'll think about this long and hard before you say yes."

"I will," I say, though in the back of my mind, I'm already thinking about how high the stakes are.

How quickly things are unraveling. How the solution might be sitting right in front of me, in the form of a marriage that neither of us wants, but both of us need.

After dinner with Lisa, I head home, still mulling over our conversation. It's crazy to think that marrying Andrew Bennett might actually be the solution to all of this.

But what other options do I have left? As I sit on the couch, my phone in hand, I stare at the screen for a long time before I finally open up a new message.

*Could you come by my office tomorrow?*

I hit send, my heart pounding a little faster than I'd like to admit. Almost immediately, the screen lights up with his reply.

*Andrew: Yes. What time works for you?*

I bite my lip, thinking it over. Mornings are usually chaotic, but better to get this over with than let it hang over me all day.

*How about ten?*

The response is quick, as always.

*Andrew: I'll be there.*

I let out a breath I didn't realize I was holding. There. It's done. I put my phone down and head to the bathroom, hoping a shower will clear my mind, but even the hot water can't wash away the worry of what's to come.

At least with Daniel, I knew to expect wild parties, never seeing my husband and possibly affairs. With Andrew, it's a complete blank. I don't know what to expect *if* we do go ahead with the wedding.

***

I sit at my desk, my eyes flicking to the clock on the wall. Ten to ten. Andrew should be here any minute.

I check over my notes again, not that I need to. The facts haven't changed: Riviera needs a capital injection, and fast. But Andrew's proposal is driving me crazy. One minute, I've made up my mind and in the next, I decide it's a completely stupid idea.

At exactly 10:00, the intercom on my desk buzzes. I can't help but grin as I press the button. At least he's predictable when it comes to time.

"Mr. Bennett is here, Miss Young," Catherine says.

"Please, show him in," I reply, sitting back in my chair.

Andrew's time keeping is refreshing, honestly. The first time I went for dinner with Daniel, he kept me waiting at the restaurant for half an hour, not even a text to let me know he'd be late.

I like that Andrew values my time.

The door opens, and he steps inside, his expression inscrutable as usual, all business. He's wearing a sharp suit, every inch of him put together, as if nothing could ruffle him.

His dark brown, slightly tousled hair that falls just above his collar, giving him a rugged, sexy look.

"Good morning, Andrew," I say, keeping my tone professional.

"Emily," he says, walking toward my desk. He sits down without hesitation, his movements precise, deliberate. He doesn't waste time with pleasantries, and for a second, I wonder if he ever does.

"I appreciate you coming in," I start, clasping my hands together on the desk in front of me. "I've had some time to think about your proposal."

His eyes narrow slightly, but he remains silent, waiting for me to continue. Those sharp blue eyes don't miss a thing, and I can feel him gauging my every word, every move.

"It's unconventional," I say, searching for the right way to phrase it. "But I'm not dismissing it outright."

"It is unconventional," Andrew agrees, as if we're discussing the sale of a property. "But we both know what our families need. It's practical, and right now, practicality is what matters."

I lean forward slightly. "And you're comfortable with that? With marrying someone you barely know for the sake of business?"

He shrugs, not missing a beat. "Comfort isn't part of the equation. This is about what needs to be done."

I stare at him for a moment, trying to read between the lines, trying to see if there's anything else behind his calm, calculated demeanor. But Andrew Bennett is an enigma, and I'm not sure I'll ever crack that exterior.

"And what happens after the year is up?" I ask, leaning back again. "What then?"

"We go our separate ways, as we agreed," he says simply. "No strings. Our families get what they need, and we move on."

It sounds so straightforward when he says it. So clean. Andrew seems to have worked out the whole thing in his head.

"What about living arrangements? Would we live in the same house?" I ask.

Andrew frowns. ""My house is bigger. It would make more sense for you to move in with me."

"No," is my instant response. "I'm not moving into your house."

He waves off my protests. "We can fight about that later," he says, like the logistics of where we live are a minor detail compared to the rest.

I take a breath. "What about sleeping arrangements?" My voice falters. I hate how unsure I sound, but this is the reality we're discussing—a marriage, even if it's just on paper.

That's when I see it. A smile. The first time I've ever seen him smile, and damn it, he's incredibly handsome when he does. The smile softens his otherwise serious face, making him look human.

For a second, I forget the stoic man who walked in earlier.

"Surely," he teases, his voice light for the first time, "You don't think this is a ruse to get you into my bed?"

Heat rushes to my face. "That's not what I'm saying," I protest, embarrassed, looking anywhere but at him.

"Relax," he says, the hint of a smile still on his lips. "Different rooms. We'll only be married in name, Emily. But don't do anything that will embarrass me or our families."

That wipes the away my embarrassment. The insinuation stings, and I can't stop a flash of anger. I lean forward, my eyes narrowing. "What do you take me for?"

Andrew's expression shifts, his smile fading. His eyes lock onto mine, serious again. "I don't know you, Emily. And you don't know me. I might have researched you, but there's only so much a search brings up."

I open my mouth to argue, but then I close it again. He's right. We don't know each other. Not really. The craziness of this entire proposal hits me all over again. We're talking about marriage—an actual marriage—and we're practically strangers.

I exhale, leaning back in my chair, trying to calm myself. "We really don't know each other, do we?"

## Chapter 5: Andrew

I like that Emily is asking all these questions. It shows she's cautious, practical. I want her to go into this marriage knowing exactly what it is and what it isn't.

Emily tilts her head to the side, and her thick, silky brown hair falls slightly over her shoulder. It catches the light, and for a second, I'm distracted. That annoys me. This isn't supposed to be about attraction or anything personal, but damn it, there's no denying she's an attractive woman.

Her eyes are searching mine, trying to find something in me, but I stay composed. I'm good at that.

"Why did you join the military?" she asks then follows it up with another. "And why did you leave?"

I shift slightly in my seat, my gaze still fixed on her. Of course, she'd ask. I almost expect it. "Like I said before, military service runs in the family, apart from my father. My grandfather served as did his father before him."

Not the entire truth but it's enough for Emily's purposes.

Her eyes stay on mine, quiet but curious, encouraging me to keep going without even having to say anything.

"As for why I left," I pause. "Let's just say it wasn't by choice. I was medically discharged due to an injury."

The words come out clipped, discouraging further questions. I don't want to elaborate. I don't need to. She doesn't need to know the details—that's not part of the deal we're making.

Emily nods again, her expression thoughtful. "I see."

There's a moment of quiet, then I shift the conversation back to what really matters. "All the legal documentation is done," I tell her. "As soon as we're married, the capital will be injected into Riviera, and 50% ownership will transfer to Bennett's. You'll have the funding to start the renovations immediately."

Emily's eyes light up at that, and I can see the wheels turning in her head. She cares about the business, about the future of the hotels. It's everything she's been fighting for.

I like that about her—she's not doing this just for show or convenience. She's in it because she cares about saving her father's legacy.

"We'll bring Riviera back to standard," I continue, leaning forward. "But I'll need an office here. I plan to work closely with you for the first six months, at least, to make sure the changes are implemented smoothly."

Her eyebrows raise slightly, but she's smiling. "Aren't you needed at BDG?"

"I'll split my time," I tell her. "I want to be hands-on. If we're going to turn this around, I need to understand the day-to-day operations. The weaknesses, the strengths."

"That's actually great," Emily says, looking genuinely pleased. "I didn't expect you to be so involved."

"I'm not Daniel," I say, a little more sharply than intended. Her face shifts, and I soften my tone. "I take this seriously, Emily. If we're doing this, we're doing it right. I want the hotels running smoothly, and I want our investment to succeed."

She nods, a bit taken aback, but I can tell she appreciates the seriousness of my tone. Her smile returns, and for the first time, I think we're on the same page—aligned, at least when it comes to business dealings.

"This is everything I've wanted for the hotels," she says quietly, almost to herself. "The repairs, the marketing strategy, stabilizing the staff. It's everything."

There's relief in her eyes.

Her eyes meet mine again, and there's something unspoken between us—a moment of understanding, maybe even respect.

This is my chance to prove I can take control, turn something around. Prove to myself, and my family, that I can do more than follow orders.

"I'll do it," Emily says, with a huge grin on her face.

For a moment, I almost can't believe she's said yes. Then, relief washes over me, a genuine smile pulling at the corners of my mouth. I let out a breath I didn't realize I was holding. Fuck yes. She said yes.

But I can't linger in the satisfaction too long. I reach down to my briefcase and pull out the folder I had prepared ahead of time. I slide it across her desk toward her, knowing this is the next necessary step.

Emily's smile falters. She glances down at the papers, her brow furrowing slightly. Then she realizes what it is.

The contract.

Annoyance flickers across her face. Bringing the contract with me was a risk I had to take; the military taught me about preparation. My father taught me to seal the deal. Fast.

Her lips press into a thin line, her eyes flicking up to meet mine, irritation simmering behind them. She doesn't need to say it, but I can feel it—*arrogant bastard*. I can bet my last dollar that's what she's thinking.

But I don't flinch.

"Were you this sure that I was going to say yes?" Emily says in a sharp tone.

I meet her gaze evenly. "I prefer to be prepared."

"Prepared?" She raises an eyebrow, incredulous. "Or presumptuous?"

I lean back slightly, keeping my hands resting on my knees, my body language calm but firm. "Emily, this is a business arrangement. It's what we both need. I'm not here to play games and I'm sure, neither are you."

She reaches for the contract. ""Is there anything in here that's going to surprise me?"

"No, of course not," I say.

Emily's eyes flicker down the pages, the irritation still simmering but contained. There's something about the way she handles herself—composed, smart, always thinking. I can tell this is all a calculation for her, just like it is for me. But still, Daniel was a fool.

I sit back, studying her while she skims the contract. Emily is a rare kind of woman. Brains and beauty, both.

I find myself comparing her to Chloe, my ex-girlfriend. On paper, Chloe had seemed perfect—polished, stylish, the kind of woman everyone expected me to settle down with.

But it didn't take long for the boredom to creep in. All she cared about was shopping and lunch dates, filling her days with meaningless gossip about people I didn't know and couldn't care less about.

I wasn't about to spend my life listening to stories about who wore what and which sale was going on.

Emily, though, she's different. She's got fire and purpose, something that drives her. She's not just along for the ride—she's steering the ship. I can respect that.

She flips through the last few pages of the contract, her expression serious, then finally reaches for the pen on her desk.

My breath suspends in my chest. But before I can dwell on it, she signs both copies with a swift stroke and slides one across the desk toward me.

"There, all done," she says, her tone dry but with a hint of disbelief. She leans back in her chair, shaking her head slightly. "I can't believe I just agreed to this."

I take the contract, glancing down at her signature for a moment before meeting her eyes. "You're a very persuasive man, Andrew," she adds with a small, ironic smile.

I smile back, folding the contract carefully and tucking it into my briefcase. "I'm not persuasive, we just happen to want the same thing."

Emily waits until I look at her again, then says, "Are we really going to keep the same wedding date?"

I shrug, keeping my tone light but matter-of-fact. "I don't see why not. Everything's already in place, and it's not like we have much time to waste."

She nods, but there's a flicker of something in her eyes—uncertainty, maybe? Then something dawns on me. This is her wedding, after all, and I can't expect her to feel entirely comfortable when everything was originally set up with my brother in mind.

"But," I add, the idea coming to me as I speak, "You should get another wedding dress if it'll make you more comfortable."

"You think so?" she says.

I nod, completely lost when it comes to wedding dresses. I'm going with logic here and my knowledge of human nature. "Look, this is a new arrangement. I don't want you walking down the aisle in something that was meant for a different situation. This wedding should be on your terms now, not Daniel's."

"That's very thoughtful of you," Emily says. "Maybe I will."

I'm about to leave when one more thing occurs to me. "I should invite you home to see where I live, then you can decide if you'll be comfortable moving in after the wedding."

She nods. "Sounds fair."

"And you can meet Bruno and Bear. They have the final say," I say with a straight face.

A stricken look comes over Emily's face. I fight to stop from bursting out laughing. "Who are they?"

Finally, I can't hold the laughter in any longer. "They're my dogs."

Emily takes a paper, crunches it up into a ball and tosses at me. It misses by a mile, landing somewhere near the corner of the desk.

We both pause for a second, and then, at the same time, burst into laughter. The tension between us evaporates, and for the first time, this whole arrangement feels almost natural.

"You have terrible aim," I tease.

"Don't make me get another paper ball," she warns, her eyes twinkling with humor.

I hold up my hands in mock surrender, grinning. “Noted.”

## Chapter 6: Emily

"Have you completely lost your mind?" my usually mild-mannered mother screams into the phone, her voice so loud I instinctively flinch, even though she's on Bluetooth.

This is definitely not the conversation I wanted to have right now. I've been putting off telling my mother for as long as I could, but when Andrew mentioned today that he told his parents and they were on board with it, I realized I couldn't wait any longer.

The last thing I need is for her to hear it from someone else—like Andrew's mother. So here I am, driving to Andrew's house, having the worst possible conversation at the worst possible time.

My fiancé—I have to get used to thinking of Andrew as my fiancé—hadn't even flinched when he broke the news to his parents. The word fiancé still feels strange on my tongue, even if this marriage is purely business.

Not that my mother cares but I must admit that telling her over the phone was probably not my best idea. But here we are.

"Mom, calm down," I say, gripping the steering wheel a little tighter as I navigate the streets. "It's the same thing I was going to do with Daniel."

Even as the words leave my mouth, I cringe internally. I know it's a weak defense. My mind scrambles for something better, but what else am I supposed to say?

At the end of the day, it is the same arrangement—it just happens to be with a different Bennett.

"That's your defense?" she snaps, her voice still elevated, disbelief laced through every syllable. "Andrew is Daniel's brother."

"For the record, I was never intimate with Daniel." The very idea makes nausea swirl in my belly. "I never even kissed him." I can't believe I'm saying all this to my mother. Too much information.

But I care what she thinks and I'd hate to go around thinking she has a sick husband and a slut for a daughter.

"That is not what is worrying me," Mom says. "They are brothers at the end of the day."

I wince, knowing she's not wrong. "It's a business arrangement, Mom," I say for what feels like the hundredth time. "Andrew's family needs this just as much as we do. It's practical, and it's the only way to save the hotels."

"You're playing with fire."

I bite my lip, trying to stay calm as I merge into traffic. "I'm not playing with anything. It's a simple agreement, nothing more. We both get what we want, and that's it."

"And what about your happiness?" she presses, her voice gentler now but no less worried. "Are you really willing to marry someone for the sake of the business? What would your father say?"

I feel a pang in my chest at the mention of my dad. I know exactly what he'd say—he'd want me to find another way, a better solution that doesn't involve sacrificing my future. But the reality is, I don't have time for that.

"I'm doing what needs to be done, Mom. I don't have any other options. If I don't go through with this, everything Dad built will crumble." We've had this conversation so many times that the words just flow seamlessly from my mouth

There's a long pause on the other end of the line, and I know my mother's struggling with what to say next. She's always been protective, always the one to tell me to think about my choices. But right now, there's no other choice, and the ink on the paper is already dry. We're having this wedding.

"I just don't want you to lose yourself in this, Emily," she says finally, her voice quiet, but I can hear the pain in her voice. "Don't let him change who you are."

I swallow hard, forcing myself to focus on the road instead of the knot tightening in my stomach. "I won't. Andrew knows this is business. He's not trying to change anything. We're in this together, and we both know what we're getting into."

"Alright," she sighs, the sound heavy with reluctance. "Just promise me you'll take care of yourself. And if it gets to be too much, don't be afraid to walk away."

"I promise, Mom," I say, my voice softer now. "I'll be okay."

I end the call just as I turn onto Andrew's street, his house coming into view. It's large and imposing.

As I pull into the driveway, I take a deep breath. I can still hear my mother's words swirling around in my mind, her concerns lingering in the air like a shadow. But I push them aside.

This is business. Nothing more. I can handle this. I have to handle this.

The gate opens automatically, gliding aside as if expecting me. The front lawn is impeccable, manicured to perfection, with lush green grass and flowers that look like they were arranged by a professional. Of course, they probably were.

Everything about this place screams control, order, and wealth—just like Andrew himself.

I park the car just as the front door opens.

Andrew steps out, and before I can even process what's happening, two enormous dogs bound out after him. They're huge, barking excitedly, and circling my car with such energy that fear surges through me.

I tense up, gripping the steering wheel as I watch them, my heart racing. I expected tiny, white, huggable dogs—the kind you could cuddle on a couch—not these gigantic beasts with enough muscle to knock over a small tree.

Their barking echoes around the quiet lawn as they circle my car. My breath catches in my throat. Are they trained? Are they going to attack?

Then, Andrew strides over, completely unfazed by the chaos his dogs are causing. He knocks on the window, his expression calm but amused.

With trembling fingers, I lower the window a few inches, just enough to speak to him but not enough for those dogs to stick their snouts inside.

"Are you coming in?" Andrew asks.

I glance at the two massive dogs circling the car, their tails wagging but their sheer size making my heart race. "Do they bite?" I ask, my voice smaller than I intend it to be. I'm trying to sound calm, but the panic bubbling up is hard to suppress.

Andrew chuckles, shaking his head. "No, they don't bite. Bruno and Bear are harmless—big, friendly giants."

I eye the dogs warily, still not convinced. "They don't look harmless."

"They're just excited to meet you," he says, with a smile that almost makes me want to believe him. "Come on, Emily. They're good boys, I promise."

I take a deep breath, glancing at the dogs one more time before slowly lowering the window the rest of the way. "If you say so," I murmur, still not entirely convinced as I prepare to step out.

As I open the car door, Bruno and Bear immediately bound over, their tails wagging so hard it's like they're going to knock something over. I tense, unsure, but then Andrew whistles, and just like that, the dogs sit.

"They're trained," he says. "You'll be fine."

I slowly step out of the car, feeling a little ridiculous for being so nervous, but the moment both dogs lean in and give me a friendly nudge, I relax—just a little. They're huge, but I can tell they're just trying to be friendly.

"See? Harmless," Andrew says, patting Bruno on the head. "Now, come on. Let's head inside before they overwhelm you any more."

As we step inside, the first thing that hits me is how unexpectedly warm the house feels. I don't know what I imagined—maybe something ultra-modern, cold, and sleek—but this? This is cozy. It's the last thing I expected from Andrew.

The entryway opens into a spacious living room bathed in soft, natural light, with exposed wooden beams stretching across the ceiling. The walls are a soft, muted gray, creating a calming atmosphere, while the hardwood floors add a natural warmth to the space.

There's a large stone fireplace against one wall, the kind you'd expect in a cabin retreat, and on the mantle are a few framed photographs. Personal touches I didn't expect.

A plush, oversized couch dominates the room, with cozy throws draped over the back and cushions that look so comfortable it's hard not to want to sink into them. There's a bookshelf along one wall, filled with what looks like a collection of classic novels, history books, and a few military memoirs.

The room smells faintly of pine, mixed with the scent of fresh coffee lingering in the air, giving it a homey feel. The large windows let in just the right amount of light, and outside, I can see a glimpse of the backyard, which looks just as meticulously maintained as the front.

"You have a beautiful home," I say, surprise in my voice.

Andrew closes the door behind us, looking slightly amused by my reaction. "What, expecting something different?"

I shrug, glancing around again. "I don't know, maybe something more, minimalist? Sterile?"

He smirks, walking past me toward the kitchen, which is open and inviting, with a large farmhouse sink and granite countertops. "I'm full of surprises."

I can't argue with that. The house is a mix of rustic and modern, but it feels like a home. A real home.

Andrew hands me a bottle of water, his expression softening for just a moment. "Thanks. It's home."

He leads me through the house, giving me a grand tour. I trail behind him, still taking in every detail. Each room we pass through surprises me more—there's so much personality in them.

We make our way downstairs, where he opens a door that leads to what must be every fitness enthusiast's dream: a fully equipped gym. Rows of dumbbells, a treadmill, a punching bag in one corner, and sleek, modern machines fill the space.

"You really don't mess around," I say, genuinely impressed.

"Gotta stay in shape," he replies with a shrug, though I can see the pride in his eyes.

I can't help but smile. Maybe moving in won't be so bad after all. Andrew's home is nothing like I imagined. It's warm, inviting, and full of character.

We continue the tour, and I find myself liking everything I'm seeing. The backyard is large, with a fire pit and a view that stretches far beyond the yard, giving the space a peaceful, almost secluded feeling.

And then I remember what Lisa said when I complained about moving in with Andrew. She pointed out that this was an opportunity—an opportunity I should take advantage of.

I've been wanting to sell my apartment for a while now, upgrade to something bigger and more practical. But moving is such a hassle, and finding the right place has been more stressful than I'd like to admit.

Maybe Lisa's right. Living here for a year could give me the space I need to figure out my next step. This house has more than enough room, and with the added convenience of being closer to work, it's starting to feel like a win-win.

Andrew pauses at the last stop of the tour, turning to face me. "What do you think?"

I glance around, nodding slowly. "It's a lot nicer than I expected. I can see myself living here."

Andrew smiles, and I get the feeling he's relieved to hear it. "Good. I want you to be comfortable."

I let out a small laugh, feeling the tension in my shoulders ease just a bit. "Well, you've certainly made a convincing case. And if Bruno and Bear approve of me, I guess I'm in."

Andrew chuckles, gesturing to the two dogs lounging in the corner. "They're already sold. Now it's just up to you."

## Chapter 7: Andrew

I step into the lobby and head straight for the building's private garage, where Robert, my driver, is already waiting by the car. He's been with the family for years, always punctual and dependable—just the way I like things.

"Morning, Robert," I say, giving him a brief nod as I slide into the backseat.

"Good morning, sir," Robert replies, closing the door behind me before getting into the driver's seat. "Where to today?"

"The Camellia Condos site," I say, glancing at my watch. "I need to check on the progress."

We pull out of the garage, merging into the busy streets of downtown Boston. The drive to Camellia Condos is short, but the traffic always manages to stretch it out.

I settle into the backseat, my mind already running through the issues Don mentioned earlier. The structure's already several stories high, but there's always something cropping up—today, it's the windows and the electrical wiring.

That's the nature of construction.

As we move through the city, I keep my gaze on the passing buildings, a mix of old Boston charm and new, gleaming structures.

Camellia Condos is supposed to be our latest standout project—a blend of luxury and modern comfort. It's something I've poured a lot of time into since I got back.

We pull up to the construction site. Cranes towering above, workers bustling around. Camellia Condos is coming together, but there's still a lot left to do. I get out of the car, Robert giving me a quick nod before pulling away to park.

Outside, the sun bounces off the surrounding skyscrapers, and I pull my sunglasses on as I approach the site.

The sound of heavy machinery fills the air, mixed with the constant hum of voices. Workers in hard hats are scattered around, all focused on their individual tasks.

I nod to the site manager, as I make my way toward him. "Morning, Don."

"Morning, Andrew," he replies, wiping the sweat from his brow with the back of his hand. "As I was telling you, we've hit a few snags on the electrical for the upper floors and some of the window fittings. They don't match the specs we were given."

I frown. "The windows? How bad are we talking?"

"Not too bad. The frames are slightly off, and we've already sent word to the supplier. Shouldn't set us back more than a day or two if they fix it on time. But it's still a pain."

I glance up at the towering structure, mentally running through the timelines. We can't afford too many delays. "Make sure the supplier knows we need that correction ASAP. What about the electrical?"

Don shifts, looking over at the wiring team on the upper levels. "Turns out a few of the plans didn't account for the structural beams in certain areas, and it's causing trouble with the cabling."

"Has the architect weighed in?"

"He's supposed to be here later today meanwhile, we're trying to reroute without losing too much time."

I nod, absorbing all the details. The project is moving, but these issues need to be smoothed over quickly. "I'll talk to the architect when he gets here. Make sure the wiring crew doesn't waste time while we wait."

Don gives me a nod, already moving to handle it.

As I pull out my phone, I notice the time. Still a while before I need to meet Jack. I scroll through messages and stop at one I sent Emily this morning.

My mother insisted I tell Emily about one of the best bridal dress shops in town—an upscale place with a long waiting list, but apparently, I could pull some strings. Emily had only replied with a quick "thanks."

I dial her number and wait as the phone rings. She picks up after a few rings.

"Hey," I say, keeping my tone casual. "Just wanted to check in. Did you get the dress?"

Emily's voice is cool but polite. "I've been busy with work, but I made an appointment for later this week."

The words hit harder than they should. *Busy?* This is our wedding—even if it's for business, it's still important. A strange feeling of jealousy creeps in. Did she take this long when she was supposed to marry Daniel? Why does it feel like she's pushing this aside?

"I see," I say, trying to keep the edge out of my voice. "It's important to get this done, Emily."

She lets out a soft sigh. "I know. I'm handling it."

There's a pause, before she speaks again. "Your mother called me yesterday," she says, her tone changing slightly, sounding a little uncomfortable. "She offered to go dress shopping with me."

I pinch the bridge of my nose. "What did you say?"

Emily hesitates. "It didn't really feel like I had a choice. And, well, I didn't invite her the first time around, so I said yes."

My mother has good intentions, but she can come off as overbearing, abrasive even, without meaning to.

"I'll talk to her," I say, my jaw tightening. "She means well, but I don't want you feeling pressured."

"It's fine," Emily replies, though her tone says otherwise. "I'll manage."

We exchange a few more words before I hang up. My mother bulldozing her way into Emily's dress shopping? Not what we need right now. This situation is already awkward enough. I dial her number quickly.

"Andrew, darling," she answers, her voice cheerful.

"Mom, did you push your way into dress shopping with Emily?" I ask, cutting to the point.

There's a pause before she responds, not quite defensively but close. "I should be there, Andrew. She's going to be my daughter-in-law, and I've never had a daughter. This is my chance to have one."

I sigh. "I get it, but go easy on her. Let her choose her own dress. Don't force your opinion."

"I would never do that," she says, sounding offended.

I smile to myself, knowing full well how she takes charge of events. "Of course, you wouldn't," I say, sarcasm thick in my voice.

Then, as if flipping a switch, her tone softens, concern lacing her words. "Have you had any more episodes?"

The question makes my stomach drop, and the lightness in my mood disappears. My family treats my PTSD like it's something they have to monitor constantly. It pisses me off.

Most of the time, I'm fine. It only bothers me at night, when the nightmares come. I don't need everyone hovering over me, waiting for me to crack.

"I'm fine," I say curtly, not wanting to discuss it. "I've got to go."

I end the call before she can dig any deeper, clenching my phone in my hand for a moment before slipping it back into my pocket.

I take a few more minutes to oversee the work at Camellia Condos, talking to a few contractors, making sure the project is still moving despite the setbacks.

By the time I finish at the site, it's nearly time to meet Jack. I text Robert to meet me at the front. The ride to the boutique gives me a chance to go over my email and respond to the ones my PA has marked as urgent.

The front of the boutique on Newbury Street has frosted glass windows that give nothing away as to what kind of store it is.

Inside, shelves of meticulously folded fabrics line the walls, ranging from rich wools to luxurious silks. Jack is lounging in a chair, his rugged form looking out of place among the refined fabrics and measuring tapes.

"Took you long enough," Jack says, standing up. "Thought I'd have to go through this tuxedo torture alone."

"Yeah, right," I mutter, rolling my eyes. "You wouldn't last five minutes."

The tailor, an older gentleman named Luciano, approaches us as soon as we enter. He's taken care of the male members of my family for as long as I can remember.

"Mr. Bennett," Luciano greets me before turning his attention to Jack, who stands next to me. "And your companion?"

"This is Jack," I say, gesturing to him. "We're both getting fitted."

Luciano nods, gesturing for us to follow him toward the back of the boutique, to the private fitting area awaits.

Jack whistles, taking in the espresso bar in the corner, a cart with high-end whiskey on offer, and a full-length mirror framed in dark wood that reflects the soft lighting of the room.

"Please, make yourselves comfortable," Luciano says as he gestures toward the plush leather chairs, his voice smooth and practiced. "Would you care for an espresso or something stronger?"

I shake my head, but Jack grins. "I'll take that whiskey, thanks."

"So, this is how the other half lives," Jack says as he settles into one of the chairs.

I can't help but grin at that. Jack and I come from completely different worlds—he grew up in a modest home, while I've lived in the thick of wealth and privilege my whole life. But it never seemed to matter much, especially when we served together.

Out there, in the military, none of this luxury, tuxedos, whiskey carts—made a difference. It still doesn't, at least not to him. But he enjoys watching me squirm in settings like this.

Luciano returns with the whiskey, handing it to Jack. "Are we thinking classic black tie, or would you prefer something with a modern twist?" he asks.

"Classic," I say, my tone firm. The wedding may be unconventional, but I'm not. No point in complicating things. "No flash, no embellishments. Just sharp."

Luciano hums in approval. "Excellent choice, Mr. Bennett."

Jack watches the exchange, shaking his head in disbelief. "Man, this is something else. Back when I got married, we rented our tuxes from the shop down the street."

I grin. "You mean they didn't serve you whiskey and take your measurements like royalty?"

"Hell no." Jack grins, then takes another sip. "I guess I'll live vicariously through you for today."

Luciano motions for me to step onto the platform in front of the mirror, and I do so, holding myself still as he works efficiently, measuring every angle and jotting down notes.

"Would you like any adjustments to the classic cut?" Luciano asks as he moves around me, measuring the breadth of my shoulders. "Perhaps a slimmer fit?"

"No," I say. "Keep it traditional."

Jack chuckles from the chair. "Look at you, all business even when it comes to a tux."

Luciano finishes with me, and Jack takes his turn on the platform, still grinning as the tailor starts taking his measurements. Jack is dressed in a T-shirt that reveals the tattoos on his arms.

He works for a private security firm now as a personal bodyguard and he seems to thrive in it.

As the tape moves around him, Jack looks over his shoulder at me, eyebrow raised.

"You really stepping into your brother's shoes just like that?" Jack asks.

"It's not about filling his shoes," I say evenly. "It's about business. We both know this marriage isn't about love."

Jack whistles low, shaking his head. "Man, I still don't get it. This is your life we're talking about. I can't imagine marrying someone I wasn't in love with. You're missing out."

"Not everyone has the luxury of waiting for love, Jack," I say, the words coming out fast, like a defense. I see the way Jack and his wife Sarah, are together. But that's not in the cards for me.

Jack looks at me for a moment, something serious in his eyes. "Maybe you should think about it, man. You're making it sound like a job, but marriage should be based on love."

I don't expect him to understand. Jack found the perfect woman for him. Sarah is quiet where he's loud, steady where he's impulsive. They're happy. I see it every time we hang out.

But not all of us get that, and not everyone has the option to wait. Some of us have a larger responsibility towards our families.

"Have you heard from Daniel?" Jack asks.

"Not a word," I say. "Nor do I expect to. Cowards have a way of disappearing when the pressure's on."

"It was cowardice not to tell Emily to her face that the wedding was off, but he probably figured out that he wanted real love. I don't blame him for that," Jack says.

I scoff. "Daniel wouldn't know real love if it bit him in the ass."

Jack raises an eyebrow but stays quiet, letting me continue.

"Look, I get it. Everyone wants that ideal, the perfect connection. But Daniel? He doesn't even know what he wants, let alone what love looks like. He ran because it was easier. No commitment, no responsibility."

"And you think you're the opposite," Jack says, half a statement, half a question. "Doing what needs to be done, even if it's for the family and not for you?"

I've already made my decision and I'm not in the habit of second guessing myself. I'm marrying Emily and that's that.

Luciano finishes taking the measurements and steps back. "I'll have the first fitting ready for you in a week, Mr. Bennett. As always, we strive for perfection."

## Chapter 8: Emily

The boutique is stunning. Rows of pristine white gowns shimmer under the soft lighting, each more elegant and intricate than the last. A pang comes over me. A part of me wishes that this were for real. That I was actually getting married for love and not to save my father's company.

The dress I'd picked for my wedding to Daniel had been more of an evening gown, but Andrew seemed keen for me to wear a traditional gown. It's a small price to pay for what we're getting in return.

My mother trails behind me, a distant look on her face. Lisa and I exchange a glance. We all know that it's a business marriage but a wedding is a wedding. I may never get married again and a bit of enthusiasm from my mother would be nice.

"Good morning, ladies," The saleswoman greets us as we step inside. "I've pulled a few dresses based on the details you shared. Shall we get started?"

"Of course," I reply, trying to sound more enthusiastic than I feel.

Before I can take another step, Andrew's mother, Mrs. Bennett, bursts into the room like a whirlwind. She's dressed to the nines in a tailored cream suit, accessorized with bold jewelry and a scarf that's almost as vibrant as her personality.

"Emily, darling," she exclaims, sweeping toward me with open arms. Before I can react, she plants a kiss on both my cheeks, her perfume strong and floral. "I can't wait until we're officially mother-in-law and daughter-in-law. We're going to have so much fun planning this wedding together."

She wasn't this enthusiastic when I was getting married to Daniel. Maybe Andrew is her favorite son.

I smile, feeling a little overwhelmed. Lisa stands behind me, stifling a laugh, and my mother sits quietly, looking even more detached than before.

"It's wonderful to see you, Mrs. Bennett," I manage to say, my voice polite.

“Oh, please, call me Barbara,” she says, grabbing my hands and giving them a squeeze. “We’re going to be family soon. None of this ‘Mrs. Bennett’ business.”

She turns to Lisa and my mother, greeting them with the same enthusiasm.

“Oh, darling, look at this place. It’s absolutely exquisite, isn’t it?” She rushes toward the racks of dresses, immediately picking out gowns, holding them up, and then putting them back faster than I can even process.

“Emily, sweetheart, you must try this one,” she calls, pulling out an extravagant gown with layers upon layers of tulle. It looks like something straight out of a royal wedding. “It’s bold, and grand.”

I glance at Lisa, and she arches an eyebrow in silent communication. This is going to be a long day.

Mrs. Bennett floats around the boutique, her presence loud and almost overwhelming. Meanwhile, my mother, in contrast, is quiet and subdued.

She’s flipping through a bridal magazine with a complete lack of interest.

I pull out a dress that’s much simpler, an A-line gown with soft lace detail. Something classic, not too fussy.

“Oh, that’s lovely,” Lisa says, running her hand over the fabric. “It’s very you.”

But before I can even get the dress fully into my hands, Mrs. Bennett swishes over, her eyes widening dramatically. “Darling, no, no, no. You don’t want something simple. This is a Bennett wedding. You need grandeur. Something that makes a statement.”

What statement? Has she forgotten that this is a marriage of convenience, not a real marriage?

I glance at my mother, hoping she’ll chime in, but she just gives a weak smile and goes back to flipping through the magazine. I bite back a sigh. I don’t know what I expected, but certainly not this.

"Emily, try this one first," Mrs. Bennett insists, holding out a ball gown dripping in beaded embellishments.

"Okay," I say, though it's more to placate her than because I actually want to wear it.

I step into the fitting room and slip on the gown with the help of the saleswoman. As soon as I see myself in the mirror, I know it's not me. The dress is beautiful, sure—sparkling and voluminous, but it's too much.

It's not the kind of dress I want to get married in. But when I step out, Mrs. Bennett gasps, her hands flying to her chest.

"Perfection," she exclaims, clapping her hands together. "Oh, darling, you look breathtaking. Andrew will be floored when he sees you in it."

*Andrew*. I don't even know what his taste is in women's clothes, let alone wedding gowns. Not that it matters what he thinks. As long as we both sign the marriage certificate. I could probably walk down the aisle in a sack and he wouldn't care.

Lisa gives me a subtle look, clearly trying not to laugh at the absurdity of it all. I catch her eye in the mirror, and we share a silent, knowing exchange. I feel like a cake topper, all frills and no substance.

"What do you think, Emily?" my mother finally asks, sounding as tired as I feel.

"I think it's a lot," I say, keeping my tone polite. I glance at Lisa, who's biting the inside of her cheek, trying to hold back a smirk.

"You look like Cinderella," Lisa mutters under her breath, just loud enough for me to hear.

"Not exactly the vibe I'm going for," I whisper back.

I head back into the fitting room, eager to get out of the dress. The next gown is more my style—a sleek, satin number with a low back and minimal embellishments. It's elegant and timeless, the kind of dress that feels like me.

When I step out, Mrs. Bennett's face falls slightly, though she tries to hide her disappointment. "Oh, it's very understated," she says, carefully picking her words.

My mother barely glances up. "It's fine," she says, flipping another page in the magazine.

I feel a pang of irritation. Lisa stands and walks over, adjusting the dress slightly on my shoulders.

After a few more dresses—none of which spark joy—I finally throw in the towel.

"I haven't found the dress yet," I say, forcing a smile. "I'll keep looking."

Mrs. Bennett looks slightly crestfallen, but my mother barely reacts. "I have to get back to work," I say quickly, giving myself an out.

I can't stand it anymore. I'm touched by Mrs. Bennett's enthusiasm, really, I am. But all it's doing is stirring up emotions I'm not ready to deal with.

I expected to come in, quickly pick a dress, and move on with our lives. This wasn't supposed to be an all-day event or a dramatic ordeal.

Mrs. Bennett's taste is certainly not mine, and this whole charade that Andrew and I are in love is frankly exhausting. I'd rather we treated this wedding for what it is—a business arrangement.

A practical solution to a practical problem. But that's not how she sees it. She's acting like this is some grand love story.

Barbara and my mother's drivers are waiting on the curb.

I walk toward the door, feeling a wave of relief at the sight of the exit. Outside, Barbara and my mother's driver are waiting on the curb.

Before she enters the car, Barbara touches my arm. "Emily, darling, we'll keep looking together, alright? I just know you'll find the perfect dress."

I force another smile. "Of course. Thank you, Barbara." No chance. There's no way I'm going through this again. I'll come back alone, get the dress I liked and avoid another circus like today.

Lisa and I walk a few blocks until we find a coffee shop, where we grab two lattes and collapse into chairs.

Lisa leans back, letting out a low laugh. "I don't envy you, you know. Your mother-in-law can be a bit overbearing."

"A bit?" I say, rolling my eyes, exhaustion settling into my bones. "I don't know how I'm going to handle her. She wasn't like this when it was Daniel I was getting married to."

"She probably doesn't want this chance to slip again," Lisa says.

We sip our coffees in silence for a few moments before my phone buzzes. It's Andrew.

"Did you find a dress?" His voice is casual, but I can hear the interest there.

"No," I say, leaning back in my chair. "But I'll keep looking. They're getting new stock next week, so..." I can't exactly tell him that I did find the perfect dress for me but it wasn't good enough for his mother.

"If you like, we can fly out over the weekend. Try some other locations. I hear New York is a fashion center," he says.

I'm touched by the suggestion. "No, it's fine. I'll find one. I promise, I won't get married in a denim dress."

He chuckles. "Good to hear."

Then, after a pause, he adds, "How about dinner next week?"

I hesitate, my mind going back to my dad. "I'll be quite busy between now and the wedding."

There's silence on the other end, but he doesn't press. We end the call soon after, and I let out a long sigh.

Lisa watches me carefully. "You're avoiding him."

"It's not that," I admit. "I just want to spend as much time with my Dad as I can before the wedding. It won't be the same after I'm married. I can't keep sneaking out to check on him like I do now."

"Maybe you should tell Andrew about your dad," Lisa suggests gently. "He'll understand. He might even help."

That's not even an option. "I can't. Dad was adamant that no one find out about his illness. If I tell Andrew, he'll tell his family, and from there... who knows? The company could take a hit if word gets out."

Lisa gives me a sympathetic look but doesn't push. "When are you moving into Andrew's place?"

"After the wedding, for sure." The thought of living in the same house with Andrew terrifies me.

It's odd but I didn't feel this way with Daniel. There's something in the air when I'm with Andrew. A pull. Something I don't want to feel for anybody, let alone a man marrying me for business purposes.

"Sounds like a plan," Lisa says, smiling as she sips her coffee.

A sigh escapes my lips. "What a wasted day. No wedding dress and not exactly the kind of day I had envisioned."

Lisa contemplates me, a thoughtful expression on her face. "It doesn't have to be a wasted day, you know."

I raise an eyebrow. "What do you mean?"

"You really liked that dress, didn't you? The simple satin one?" she asks, a mischievous glint in her eyes.

I nod slowly, unsure of where she's going with this.

"Why don't we go back to the store and get it? You'll have your dress, and Barbara won't know you snuck back and made the purchase," she says, a grin on her face.

I blink, then a grin starts to spread across my face. "That's the best idea you've come up with today."

Lisa laughs and clinks her coffee cup against mine. "Let's do it. You'll feel better once you have your dress, not one Mrs. Bennett pushed on you."

Guilt comes over me. I know my mother wouldn't care but Barbara would be terribly hurt. I swallow down my guilt. Our tastes are vastly different and no wedding dress I pick, today or any other day will please her.

Besides, I need to feel like I still have control over something even if it's as simple as my wedding dress.

"Let's go," I say, excitement bubbling up inside me. "Before I change my mind."

Lisa downs the last of her coffee, and we head out of the café with a new sense of purpose. Back to the boutique, back to my dress. No over-the-top suggestions. Just me making a choice for myself.

## Chapter 9: Emily

As I pull up to Andrew's house, the gate opens automatically and I take a deep breath, the knot of nerves in my stomach tightening. This is it. Moving day.

The moving van follows closely behind me, its rumble barely noticeable over the pounding of my own heart.

As I park, Andrew appears at the front door, and before I can even step out of the car, Bruno and Bear bound out, their tails wagging like crazy. I can't believe that I am frightened of them.

They are huge and friendly. I laugh as they sniff and lick my hands as if I'm a long lost loved one.

Andrew steps forward, giving me a small smile. "Hey, you made it." He's dressed casually in jeans and a gray T-shirt, looking far more relaxed than I've ever seen him.

"Working from home?"

"I thought you might need some help settling in," he says with a shrug as if it's no small matter to sacrifice staying home rather than going in to work where I'm sure he's needed.

"You didn't have to," I say. I can't imagine Daniel would have bothered to show up, let alone help. "But I appreciate it."

"You're welcome," Andrew says, brushing it away.

Warmth settles in my chest. This is so different from what I had with Daniel. Andrew texts me every day to check if I'm okay. It's a new experience that I don't know what to make of.

The last week has been a whirlwind of activity, figuring out what will go to storage and what I'll bring with me. Then the usual daily disasters at the hotels.

Thank God Barbara is taking care of the wedding arrangements. I feel bad leaving everything to her, but then I remind myself that everything is in place.

The only thing that is missing is the groom.

I can't wait for this wedding to be over.

"They missed you," Andrew jokes, gesturing at the dogs. Then he glances over at the moving van. "Let me show the movers where to put everything."

He opens the front door wider and heads back inside, motioning for the movers to follow. It's strange to think of this as home, even for a short while.

I follow him inside, and up the stairs, where he directs the movers to a room at the end of the wide hallway.

"Just let me know if there's anything specific you don't want in your room," Andrew says over his shoulder.

"They all go in there," I say, taking a deep breath and stepping into the space that's about to become my temporary home.

He shows me to my suite, and I'm blown away. The room is gorgeous, with large windows that overlook the sprawling backyard, the trees swaying gently in the breeze. The bed looks so comfortable I almost want to collapse on it.

I run my hand along the window frame, taking in the view. "This is beautiful."

"I'm glad you like it," Andrew says, standing a few feet behind me. There's a calmness about Andrew. He doesn't act as if he's in a rush to be somewhere else.

I turn to him, smiling. "Thank you. For everything. The movers, this room, all of it. I know it's not easy for you, either." I've been so focused on the changes that I have to make but it can't be easy to have to share your home with a relative stranger.

Andrew waves it off with a smile. "It's no trouble."

"I'm heading to my parents' house after this," I tell him. "I'll stay there before the wedding."

Andrew nods, understanding in his expression. "Makes sense."

"Yeah."

He's silent for a moment before asking, "So, what will you do with your apartment? Keep it or rent it out?"

"I'm going to renovate it and then sell it," I reply. "I've been wanting to do that for a long time."

My father's illness has put a lot of things that I wanted to do on hold.

Andrew nods. "If you need any help with that, let me know. Renovations and real estate are kind of my thing."

I smile at that. "I'll keep that in mind." But inside, I know I won't ask for help.

This arrangement has an expiration date, and the last thing I want is to start depending on Andrew. A year from now, he won't be in my life. It's best if I continue doing things the way I always have—on my own.

"I'll be in my office downstairs if you need me," he says, before shutting the door behind him.

I finish unpacking a few essentials, and once everything is in its place, I turn to leave.

Andrew's been kind. In ways I didn't expect. But as much as I appreciate it, I have to keep reminding myself about the boundaries.

Downstairs, I head to his office and peer in through the slightly ajar door. He looks up from his laptop.

"I'll see you on Saturday," I tell him.

"See you on Saturday," he says solemnly. "Oh and before I forget, I got you spare keys for the house along with the gate remote."

I cut across the room and as I take the keys he's holding out, our fingers brush and a jolt of awareness goes through me. I quickly take the keys and flash him a quick smile.

"Thanks," I say, a little unsettled by my reaction to his touch. But then it dawns on me that it's the first time that Andrew and I have ever touched. The tension between us is bound to make things awkward when we come into contact.

I shut the door behind me and head toward the front, where Bruno and Bear are lazily sprawled out. I give them each a quick scratch behind the ears before I step out.

This is really happening. I'm moving out of my apartment, stepping into a life with Andrew—a man I barely know. We're going to share a home, a life together, for a whole year. It feels surreal, and not in a good way.

The sadness I've been trying to suppress all day creeps up on me. I'm getting married for practical reasons. Not for love, not for some magical, romantic connection.

And as much as I've convinced myself that this is the right decision, there's a hollow ache at the thought of it. How would it feel to be truly in love? To marry a man who loved me, someone I loved back?

The thought lingers, unwanted, and I push it away as quickly as it came. There's no point in dwelling on what if's. This marriage is about responsibility, about saving my family's business.

My family are the most important thing in my life. I'd do anything for them. Even this.

As I pull up to my parents' house, the familiar comfort of home settles around me, Though my thoughts are far from being settled.

I park and walk inside, my mind still swirling with feelings I don't have the energy to process. The house is quiet, and I head straight to my father's suite.

The door is partially open, and I see my mother inside with the nurse, both of them standing by my father's bedside. The sight makes my heart clench. My mother looks worried, her brow furrowed as she watches the nurse take Dad's temperature.

"What's wrong?" I ask, stepping into the room, my voice laced with panic.

"He's got a bit of a fever," my mother says quietly, not looking away from my father. "The doctor said we should keep an eye on him."

I move closer, feeling a wave of worry rise in my chest. I reach out and touch his forehead—it's warm, too warm. My pulse quickens with fear.

The nurse, sensing my anxiety, offers a calm smile. "He'll be okay. It's happened before, and the fever went right back down. We'll keep monitoring him closely."

I nod, trying to ease the tension inside me, but it doesn't work. Seeing my father like this, so still and vulnerable, always tugs at something deep inside me.

I kneel beside his bed and take his hand, squeezing it gently, even though I know he can't feel it.

"Please be okay," I murmur.

My mother stands beside me, her eyes filled with the same unspoken worry. We've been through so much together, but moments like this remind me how fragile everything is.

*What if he doesn't make it? What if he never comes out of this coma?*

I can't think like this. I can't lose hope. I push away all the what if's that seem to haunt me these days. This is what I'm doing it for—my family. And I would do it all over again, no matter how hard it gets.

I lean over and press a soft kiss to my father's cheek, the warmth of his skin sending another pang of worry through me. But I straighten up, forcing myself to stay strong. He needs me to be strong. We all do.

I step away from the bed and give my mother a reassuring nod. "He'll be fine," I say, trying to convince myself as much as her.

"I hope so," she whispers, her eyes still focused on my father, worry etched into every line of her face.

The self-indulgent thoughts I had on the way here now seem like a mockery. I don't need love. What I need is to get married to Andrew, and have Bennett Construction come in and save my father's company. All that matters is that when my father wakes up, he's beloved company will be up and running.

## Chapter 10: Emily

The Bennett Estate has been converted into a wonderland. My mother has held my hand all the way from the house to here. As the driver parks the car in front of the house, she tightens her hold.

"It's going to be fine, Mom," I tell her.

""I know," she whispers, though her voice is laced with the exhaustion we've both been feeling.

The past two days have been a blur of sleepless nights, watching over my father as his fever finally broke. We're both drained, but at least he's stable now.

My phone shrills from my purse, and I gently loosen my mother's hold before digging it out.

It's Lisa. "Where are you?" she asks.

"We're coming in right now," I tell her, amused at the note of panic in her voice. I might be dead tired, but there's no chance that I would not show up at this wedding. My family's future is depending on it.

As the car comes to a stop, my phone shrills from my purse. I gently loosen my mother's hand and dig it out.

Barbara, Andrew's mother, opens the front door just as we step out of the car, her face lighting up as she hurries down the steps. "We thought you'd never get here."

I manage a smile.

"Go on up, Emily," Barbara says, gesturing toward the house. "I'll keep your mother company until it's time."

Lisa appears at the top of the staircase inside, her eyes widening with exaggerated impatience. "Finally," she says, throwing her hands up dramatically. "Come on, let's get you dressed."

I laugh, a real laugh for the first time in days. Lisa's organized the whole thing, making sure people are here to do my hair and makeup—because she knows there's no way I would have had the energy to pull this together.

As I make my way up the stairs, I take one last glance at my mother. She smiles at me, a weary but reassuring look in her eyes as she moves toward Barbara.

"Go on," she mouths silently.

I nod and follow Lisa up, my nerves kicking in, but at least I know I'm in good hands.

Lisa's already in full maid-of-honor mode by the time I step into the room. "I've got everything ready," she says, motioning toward the small vanity where a team is waiting to get to work. "You're going to look stunning."

I smile, touched by how much effort she's put into today. It's a relief to sit down and let other people take care of me.

An hour later, my hair and make-up are done and Lisa is helping me wear my wedding dress.

"I've never met a woman who switched her grooms and kept the same wedding date," Lisa says, shaking her head in disbelief.

"Why should we waste all the arrangements?" I retort, then suddenly burst out laughing. The absurdity of the situation hits me full force. It is ridiculous, and for a moment, we both laugh.

"You know, I really admire you," Lisa says after a moment, her voice softer now. "The way you go for what you want, not a single thought or worry for consequences and somehow, things always work out in your favor."

I do worry about the consequences but this is not the time to go into that. "Let's hope this one does. I want to see my father's company prosper."

Lisa raises an eyebrow. "Still on business, even on your wedding day."

"That's the only reason we're here," I say in a light tone.

Before Lisa can respond, my mother enters the room, waving a hand and scrunching her face at the overwhelming smells of hair spray, makeup, and perfume that fill the air.

"You look beautiful," she says, tears pooling in her eyes.

Lisa's team did a fantastic job camouflaging my tired eyes and skin. The dress is gorgeous, an elegant A-line gown with soft lace detail running along the bodice and sleeves.

The fabric is light and delicate, the lace just the right touch of femininity without being too fussy. The skirt flows to the floor, classic and understated. It's simple, yet timeless. Exactly what I wanted.

"I just wish your father was here," Mom says.

I swallow hard. I don't wish the same. If my father were well, none of this would be happening. I wouldn't be marrying Andrew for convenience, wouldn't even consider it. And I know my father would never have agreed to something like this.

The thought makes my own eyes burn, but I push the emotions away. I need to be strong—for my mother, for my family. The reality is harsh, but I can't let myself wallow in it now. So I step forward, wrapping my arms around her, trying to buoy her up as best as I can.

"I know, Mom," I say gently. "But he's with us in spirit."

She nods, wiping away her tears, and gives me a brave smile. She reaches for the veil made of soft tulle and tiny lace appliqués; it complements my dress in its simplicity.

I sit down and she carefully places it over my head, adjusting it gently. The veil falls into place, framing my face, making the moment feel suddenly very real.

"I'm getting married," I say, sudden joy coming over me. For today, I'll pretend that this marriage is real and I'll enjoy every bit of it.

My mother and Lisa laugh.

"You look perfect," Mom says, stepping back to admire me.

"You're glowing," Lisa says.

A knock comes on the door. Barbara peers in. "It's time."

I smile at her. "We'll be down shortly."

I stand up, and Lisa and I lock gazes then she reaches for me and wraps her hands around me.

"It's going to be an awesome day," I tell her.

"It will," she murmurs back.

The three of us make our way downstairs, the sound of our footsteps muted by the soft carpet. The moment we step outside, I'm greeted by the sight of the backyard, now transformed into a stunning wedding venue. Barbara has outdone herself.

White roses and soft greenery cascade from tall floral arrangements that line the makeshift aisle. Fairy lights twinkle from above, strung between trees. The Bennett Estate's sprawling lawn stretches out beneath us, now a picture-perfect setting.

Each chair has a small bouquet of white flowers tied to it, facing a beautiful wooden arch draped in more roses and sheer, flowing fabric. The petals scattered along the aisle create a soft, romantic path, leading toward Andrew, who's already standing at the altar.

Lisa squeezes my hand once before she steps forward, her dress shimmering as she moves down the aisle.

I turn to my mother, who stands beside me, and she links her arm through mine. We begin our walk down the aisle together, and for the first time today, I let myself breathe deeply, taking in the beauty of the moment.

The few guests gathered for the ceremony are mostly from Andrew's side, less than twenty people, none of whom I know.

Thank God Daniel isn't here. Now that would have been awkward. I can't imagine exchanging vows with Andrew while his brother, the original groom-to-be, stood watching. At least that's one uncomfortable situation I've been spared.

As we move down the aisle, I steal a glance at Andrew. He's standing tall, dressed in a sleek tuxedo, his gaze locked on me.

My mother squeezes my arm gently, and I glance at her. She's smiling, her eyes bright with emotion. We reach the end of the aisle, and she leans in, kissing my cheek softly before letting go.

Andrew steps forward, offering me his hand as I take the final step toward the altar. The officiant begins speaking, but my mind drifts as I stand beside Andrew.

I catch glimpses of the guests—strangers, mostly, save for Lisa and my mother. Everyone is watching, but it's almost as if I'm not truly present, like I'm walking through a scene in a play.

The vows come next.

The officiant's voice rings out, "Andrew, repeat after me."

Andrew says his vows with no hesitation whatsoever, his eyes on me as if he means every word. I hope I can pull off the same sincerity even though we both know that our marriage is certainly not until 'death do us part'.

The officiant turns to me, and my heart clenches slightly. It's my turn.

I take a breath, my hand tightening around Andrew's as I speak. "I, Emily, take you, Andrew, to be my lawfully wedded husband."

I swallow down the panic rising in my chest. This is a lot harder than I imagined it would be. "To have and to hold, from this day forward, for better or for worse, in sickness and in health, to love and to cherish..."

I stumble slightly over the last words, feeling the hollowness of them in my chest. "... until death do us part."

The officiant smiles, unaware of the turmoil inside me. "By the power vested in me, I now pronounce you husband and wife."

Andrew turns to me and leans in. His lips brush my lips in a soft kiss. The guests clap and a few people cheer.

It's done. The vows are said, the formalities over. I exhale, relieved to have made it through.

There's lunch and dancing to get through, but that feels like a breeze after the ceremony. The hardest part is behind me.

## Chapter 11: Andrew

"Congratulations," Jack says, leaning across the table toward Emily, his signature grin plastered on his face. "I'm Jack. You know, I usually meet the bride before the wedding, but I'll make an exception for today."

Emily laughs and I find myself staring at her. I've done a lot of that today. She looks stunning, more beautiful than I've ever seen her.

As Emily and Jack continue chatting, my eyes are drawn to her perfectly shaped lips. I remember how it felt to kiss her after the vows—how I had wanted to linger, to deepen the kiss, to hold her tighter and closer.

I take a deep breath and remind myself that this is business and Emily's lips are not part of the contract.

We're seated at a long head table, facing the rest of the guests who are laughing, chatting, believing that they are here to witness a couple in love wanting to spend the rest of their lives together.

I glance at Emily again. The way she carries herself with such grace, even with all the awkwardness of this situation is admirable.

And distracting.

The MC's voice cuts through the buzz of conversation. "Ladies and gentlemen, it's time for the best man's speech."

I turn to Jack, giving him a look that says, *I told you this wasn't necessary*. But Jack, being Jack, just winks at me. He insisted on giving a speech, claiming that if one thing had to be real about this wedding, it was the best man's toast.

He stands up, adjusting his tuxedo jacket, and clears his throat dramatically. "Alright, folks, I'll keep this short, but not too short," he says with a grin, the room quieting down as all eyes turn toward him.

"Andrew and I go way back. We served together, and let me tell you, there's no better way to get to know a man than to serve with him. You see them at their best, their worst, and everything in between."

As soon as he says it, my chest tightens. The room fades, the sound of clinking glasses and soft laughter drowning in the surge of noise in my head. The memories come fast and hard.

*Cover! Get down! The shout echoes in my ears, gunfire cracking through the air. Dust, heat, chaos. The blinding flash of light as an explosion goes off nearby.*

My heart races. My skin feels too tight, my hands curling into fists as the panic claws at me, threatening to take me under.

I try to pull myself back, but it's like being trapped underwater, my breath coming in short, shallow gasps. Sweat trickles down my neck. I fight to stay here, to stay present, but my memories are winning.

A hand grips my arm.

"Are you all right?"

I blink, focusing on Emily's face. Her deep green eyes are full of concern, her grip on my arm tightening.

Still caught between two worlds, I take a deep breath, forcing myself to nod, even though my heart is still hammering in my chest. Slowly, the world around me comes back into focus.

"I'm fine."

Emily watches me for a second longer, her eyes searching mine. She lets go of my arm, but the worry is still etched on her face.

I force my focus back on Jack.

"I've seen Andrew in some pretty intense situations. I've seen him lead with bravery, I've seen him stay calm when everything around us was falling apart. There's no one I'd trust more to have my back—and today, I can see he's going to be that for Emily too."

My heart is still hammering in my chest. That was too close. Too fucking close. I was a step away from a full blown episode.

"Emily," Jack continues. "You're in good hands. I've never seen Andrew step up the way he has for you, and that says a lot. I know he's going to give you everything he's got, because that's the kind of man he is."

The room is quiet, save for the soft clinking of glasses and the occasional murmur. Jack grins, lightening the mood again. "So, here's to Andrew and Emily. To a lifetime of laughter, strength, and maybe a little patience—for each other and for life's surprises."

The speech ends, and there's applause. I join in, but I feel like I've just come out of a battlefield, not a wedding reception. Emily leans in again, her voice soft.

"Are you sure you're okay?"

I nod again, this time more firmly. "Yeah. Thanks."

Jack raises his glass, and the guests follow suit, toasting us. I lift my own glass, avoiding Emily's eyes. What did she see? Did I give anything away? Fuck. It's our wedding day and I've already fucked up.

As Jack sits back down, I lean over and whisper to him, "Thanks man, that was great."

Jack just grins and clinks his glass against mine. "Anytime, brother."

As the applause for Jack's speech fades, the MC steps forward again, a bright smile on his face. "And now, it's time for the maid of honor to give her speech."

Lisa flashes a wide grin, tapping her glass lightly to get everyone's attention. "Hi, everyone. For those of you who don't know me, I'm Lisa, Emily's best friend. We've known each other since high school, and let me tell you, this girl has been my partner in crime for years."

Her speech, like Jack's is interweaved with seriousness and light moments.

"Andrew," Lisa says, turning toward me with a mischievous grin. "You've got yourself one amazing woman here. And remember, if you ever need advice on how to keep up with her, I've got years of experience."

The crowd laughs, and so do I, the tension in my shoulders easing. My breathing is easier now and my mind fully present.

As Lisa wraps up her speech, everyone raises their glasses to us, and I follow suit, clinking mine softly against Emily's.

The MC takes the microphone again, and his voice booms across the room. "Alright, everyone, let's give a round of applause for our wonderful speeches! And now it's time for the bride and groom to take their first dance as husband and wife."

I suppress a groan. Dancing. Not exactly my strong suit, and I've been dreading this part since the beginning. But it's a wedding, and I'm the groom. I don't have much of a choice.

We walk together to the center of the dance floor as a love song fills the room. Emily's hand is cool against my palm, and as I place my other hand gently on her waist, I catch the faintest hint of her lavender perfume. The same scent from when I first met her.

It stirs something in me, something I can't quite push away.

We start to move, slowly at first, swaying to the rhythm. It's surprisingly easy, the way we fall into step with each other.

As the song nears its end, I catch sight of movement near the back of the room. There's some commotion—a shifting of bodies, the scraping of chairs.

My senses heighten, my body going on alert, but before I can fully register what's happening, a voice rings out, loud and angry, cutting through the soft melody.

"You bastard!"

Everything freezes. The words are venomous, dripping with rage, and they claw their way through the air, making my pulse spike.

Hands grab my shoulders, spinning me around so fast that Emily's hand slips from mine. The faint scent of alcohol hits my nose just before my instincts kick in. My body tenses, reflexes sharp, as I come face to face with Daniel.

His eyes are wild, bloodshot, and filled with fury. The scent of whiskey wafts off him in waves, overpowering my senses.

"What the hell?" I growl, yanking his hands off me, but the anger in him is like a live wire. His face is flushed, his jaw clenched so tight I can see the muscle twitching.

"You stole my bride!" Daniel spits, his voice raw and loud.

"Daniel, this isn't the place," I say, my voice low and steady, trying to defuse the situation. My breathing comes out rapid and fast.

"Not the place?" Daniel says with a bitter laugh.

"This is between you and me," I say, my voice hardening. I grip his arm firmly, moving him to the side, away from the center of the room. "Let's take this outside."

But Daniel yanks his arm away, his eyes blazing. "You think you're the better man, Andrew? You think you can get away with this?"

I lock gazes with him, my patience snapping. "I already have."

From the corner of my eye, I see his hand fold into a fist. I'm prepared for it but before I can do anything, Jack grabs Daniel and yanks him back, his grip firm as he steps between us.

"That's enough," Jack says, his voice calm but laced with authority. "Walk it off, Daniel. Now."

Daniel's eyes are still burning with fury, but with Jack in the way, he hesitates. He knows he's outnumbered, out of his depth. His gaze flickers between me and Jack, breathing heavy, nostrils flaring like a cornered animal.

"This isn't over. I'll make sure of it," Daniel growls, his voice shaky now, less defiant.

His threats don't bother me in the slightest. "Leave before you embarrass yourself further." Heat simmers beneath the surface, the need to lash out, but I clamp it down. Daniel's not worth it. Not here. Not in front of Emily.

He glares at me for another long, tense moment, then staggers backward, pushing Jack's hand off him with a wild, drunken swing. He stumbles toward the door, his footsteps uneven, muttering curses under his breath.

The room is dead silent. All eyes are on us, the shock of the scene still hanging in the air. My heart is still racing, my chest tight, but the adrenaline is fading.

"Are you okay?" Emily says, stepping toward me cautiously. Her face is pale and her eyes wide with shock or fear.

Protective feelings come over me. "I'm fine. And you?"

She nods but she looks tense.

I nod, forcing a smile. "Yeah. I'm fine." I don't want her to worry about me. I can handle Daniel.

She stares at me for a moment longer, then takes my hand again, her fingers cool against mine.

Jack, still standing close, surveys the room, to leans in, his voice low. "You good?"

"Yeah. Thanks." I should have expected Daniel to show up but I'd been sure he wouldn't be returning home anytime soon, after what he had done.

"Anytime," Jack says, slapping my back lightly before turning to the rest of the room, offering a nod that signals it's safe to go back to normal.

The tension eases, conversation picks back up, and the music begins to play again, though the air is still thick with the aftermath of what just happened.

"Let's get through the rest of this, okay?" I say to Emily, trying to lighten the mood, but my voice feels hollow.

She nods, giving me a small smile in return.

The evening resumes, but it doesn't feel the same.

## Chapter 12: Emily

I smile so hard, my cheeks hurt as Andrew and I step into the car, waving at the small group of guests still lingering outside. The second the door shuts behind me, my whole body relaxes.

The car starts to move, and I slump into the seat, letting out a long breath. "Thank God. I thought that was never going to end."

Andrew chuckles softly, but there's tension in his voice. "Yeah, I'm relieved, too." He pauses for a moment, then adds, "I'm sorry about what happened back there."

I turn to him, my brows furrowing. I know exactly what he's referring to—Daniel. The way he stormed in, full of rage and whiskey, ruining what little joy we'd managed to scrape together for this sham of a wedding.

My stomach clenches at the memory of his voice, his wild eyes, the accusations he threw at Andrew.

"You couldn't have known," I say quietly. But even as I say the words, I can't shake the lingering embarrassment. Most of the guests were Andrew's family, his friends. Watching it all unfold, watching Daniel hurl his drunken anger at his own brother, was humiliating.

"I should have," Andrew mutters, his tone sharp. "It's Daniel. I should've known he'd pull something like that."

I glance at him, noticing the way his jaw tightens, his fingers curling against his knee. He's upset. Maybe even more upset than I am.

"I'm just glad it's over," I admit, letting my head fall back against the seat. "It was beyond embarrassing."

Andrew exhales roughly, his frustration barely concealed. "He embarrassed you. On our day." His voice is low, filled with an emotion I can't quite place.

"He embarrassed both of us," I correct, though I can't deny how raw it felt. How personal. This wedding, this deal was supposed to be business. But it didn't feel like business when Daniel barged in, all fury and accusations. It felt like a betrayal.

Daniel and I were supposed to get married. He was the one who left me, and now here I am, married to his brother. It's hard not to feel a twinge of guilt, even though I'd pick Andrew any day. Daniel just proved it today, what a mistake it would have been to get married to him.

"It's over. We move forward," Andrew says after a while. "That's all we can do."

I look at him, surprised by the calm certainty in his words. "Just like that?"

He meets my gaze, his expression firm. "Just like that."

"You're a lot calmer than I thought you'd be," I say, watching him carefully.

He shrugs, the corner of his mouth lifting into a faint smile. "I'm used to handling things like this."

He's right though. There's no point in dwelling on what happened. We have a lot to do. Now, The Riviera group can start recovering. Excitement courses through me. I can't wait to get started on the renovations.

The upgrades and the plans I've had to put on hold for so long. It's finally going to happen.

The car slows down in front of the gate before it slides open. We're home.

Andrew steps out and holds the door open for me. I gather the folds of my dress, careful not to let the fabric drag as I step out onto the driveway.

"Welcome home," he says at the door, stepping aside to let me enter first.

As I enter, the reality of our lives hit me. *A year*. One year of living together, working together, being married in name only.

Bruno and bear run around us in circles, their large paws skidding across the wooden floor. They bark, tails wagging as they circle around us in a happy frenzy. We both laugh.

Andrew crouches down to pet them, his expression softening as Bear licks his hand. "I think they've missed us more than anyone else today."

I smile, reaching down to pat Bruno, who's eagerly nuzzling against my legs. "At least we know who the real welcoming committee is."

Andrew stands up, brushing off his hands. "I can already tell they're going to follow you around like shadows. They've got a thing for people who smell nice."

I laugh at that, but the ease between us is fleeting. As we stand in the entryway, tension sprouts between us. *Now what?*

"Do you want to grab something to eat or just call it a night?" Andrew asks.

I shake my head. "I think I'll just call it a night. It's been a long day."

"Yeah," he says, his gaze lingering on me for a moment before he nods. "It certainly has."

With that, I start to head upstairs to my room, the sound of Bruno and Bear padding behind me fading as I climb the stairs.

I make my way to the suite Andrew showed me when I first moved my things in. The room is warm and inviting, but there's still that undercurrent of unfamiliarity.

I catch my reflection in the mirror as I start to take off my veil and dress. I look like a bride but I don't feel like anyone's wife. Standing in front of the mirror in my black lace bra and matching panties, I can't help but wonder how the night would have unfolded had we married for love.

I close my eyes and imagine Andrew standing behind me, hands wrapped around my waist, his lips nuzzling sweet words.

I can almost feel the touch of his hands, his lips grazing my skin as he pulls me closer, the electric charge between us undeniable. Dampness gathers in my panties and an ache forms between my legs.

I imagine Andrew's hand snaking between my legs, his fingers running over my soaked panties, teasing...

A soft moan escapes my lips, jerking me back to the present. I open my eyes, startled by the sound and by the thoughts swirling in my mind. What am I even doing? This is insane.

I take a deep breath, trying to steady myself, to calm the racing thoughts. My reflection stares back at me, flushed, with eyes gleaming with desire. For a man who was a stranger less than two months ago. A man I shouldn't be lusting after.

"Get it together, Emily," I whisper to myself, shaking my head as if to clear the thoughts away.

It's the stress of the day. That's the only reason I'm lusting after Andrew. The wedding, Daniel's outburst, the tension in the air, it was all too much. Tomorrow morning, I'll be well rested and back to my senses.

I take off my underclothes and step into the shower. The hot water runs over me, washing away the tension, but my mind refuses to fully relax.

Stepping out of the shower, I dry off, slipping into a nightgown before crawling into the massive bed. The sheets are cool against my skin, and as I sink into them, I reach for my phone and call my mother.

"How's Dad?" I ask as soon as she picks up.

"He's stable," she replies, her voice reassuring. "The fever hasn't come back. He's resting."

I exhale, relief washing over me. "That's good. Thanks, Mom."

"Don't worry about us, sweetheart," she says. "You just focus on settling in."

Settling in. I glance around the room that still feels foreign. But I don't dwell on it. Instead, my thoughts drift to Monday—the day Andrew and I start working together. The idea of diving into the work we have ahead fills me with a strange kind of excitement.

I can't wait to see the changes, to start taking charge and making things happen. That alone makes this marriage worth it.

I say goodnight to my mother and set my phone on the nightstand, turning over in bed, my thoughts still buzzing but slowly fading. Eventually, exhaustion overtakes me, and I drift off into sleep.

A sudden noise jerks me awake in the middle of the night. My heart races as I sit up, straining to listen. There's a sound—faint but unmistakable. Like someone screaming.

I throw off the covers and slip out of bed, my feet quiet against the cold floor. The noises are coming from down the hall. My pulse quickens as I creep toward the source, each step slow and cautious.

I stop outside Andrew's door, my breath held.

It's coming from his room.

The sounds are muffled now, but I can hear them clearly—low, guttural noises, almost like someone fighting in their sleep. Panic grips me for a moment. Is he hurt? Is someone in there with him?

I press my ear against the door and realize that Andrew is having a nightmare.

The sounds grow quieter, fading into silence. I wait, listening, but the house falls still once more. I pull back, stepping away from the door, my heart still pounding in my chest.

Should I check on him? No. It seems like an invasion of privacy. I turn and tiptoe back to my room.

Back in bed, I lie awake for a while, the image of Andrew—strong, composed Andrew—fighting something in his sleep sticking with me.

***

I wake up feeling unusually well-rested. I stretch, glancing at the clock. It's nine. I can't remember the last time I slept this late.

After a quick shower, I throw on a comfortable pair of jeans and a loose blouse, feeling relaxed as I head downstairs. The smell of coffee reaches me first, followed by the rustle of paper coming from the kitchen.

As I walk in, I spot Andrew at the table, his hair slightly ruffled, looking surprisingly casual as he sips his coffee and reads the paper.

The sight of him like at ease and unguarded, makes my face heat up, a blush creeping across my cheeks as I recall the thoughts that had run through my head the night before. I push them away quickly, trying to focus on the moment.

"Good morning," I say, grabbing a mug and pouring myself a cup of coffee. The rich aroma fills the room, and I take a sip, enjoying the warmth that spreads through me.

"Morning," Andrew replies, glancing up from his paper. "How did you sleep?"

"Really well, actually," I say, feeling the blush deepen. I busy myself by stirring my coffee, hoping he doesn't notice. "How about you?"

"I slept fairly well."

But I remember the noises from last night, the sounds of his nightmare. I hesitate, unsure if I should bring it up. Then, before I can stop myself, I ask, "About last night. I heard some noises. Were you having a nightmare?"

His face closes off immediately, the easygoing expression replaced by a guarded look. "It's nothing," he says, his tone cool and dismissive. He takes another sip of coffee, clearly not wanting to continue the conversation.

Suits me. I sip my coffee, wondering what to talk about. "So, how do you usually spend your Sundays?"

He relaxes a little, his shoulders easing. "Most Sundays, I have lunch with my parents. It's sort of a tradition."

I take another sip of coffee, thinking about my own Sundays. "I usually spend Sundays at home too." It's the one day where I can spend time with my Dad without feeling rushed. I read and talk to him about work.

Andrew is quiet for a moment, then he says, "I was hoping you'd come with me to my parents' house today."

I pause, feeling a wave of conflict. Sunday is sacred to me. But I also know Andrew's parents will expect me to be there. I'm his wife now, at least in the eyes of his family.

"They'll expect to see you there," he adds, watching me carefully.

I chew on my bottom lip, thinking it over. "What if I visit my mother in the morning, and then I join you for lunch at your parents' house?" I offer, hoping it'll be a good compromise.

Andrew shrugs. "That works,"

He leans back in his chair, looking at me with an intensity that makes me feel like he's trying to understand something about me. "I could come with you to see your mother, if you want," he offers unexpectedly.

I shake my head quickly, a little too quickly. "No, that's okay. It's just a quiet thing I do with her: A girls' day in."

## Chapter 13: Andrew

My stomach clenches as I pull into my parents' driveway. Sunday lunch has always been a family tradition, and after my altercation with Daniel, it feels more like walking into a potential disaster zone.

I park the car and glance around the lot. Relief washes over me when I see that Daniel's car isn't here. Good.

Stepping out of the car, I make my way around the side of the house to the backyard. My parents like to have Sunday lunch outside when the weather's good.

The smell of fresh-cut grass fills the air, mingling with the faint scent of lavender from my mother's garden, and reminds me of Emily's perfume.

"The cleaning crew has done a good job," I say, glancing around the backyard as I approach.

The space is immaculate, with no sign of yesterday's chaos. It's hard to believe that just twenty-four hours ago, this backyard hosted a wedding and that scene with Daniel.

My mother looks up from her iced tea, a pleased smile spreading across her face. "Of course. I had them here first thing this morning."

I give her a quick kiss on the cheek. "Morning, Mom."

She pats my arm, looking behind me. "Where's Emily? I was expecting her with you."

"She's with her mother," I say, settling into one of the cushioned chairs. "She'll join us for lunch."

My father, sitting with his newspaper folded in his lap, looks up. "Good to see you, Andrew." He smiles, something he rarely does. "I imagine you're all set to begin work on the Riviera Group."

"I can't wait," I say as I sit down.

"With your management, we can breathe new life into those properties," Dad says favoring me with a pointed stare.

I know what that pointed look means. *Don't fuck this up.*

"What are your plans?"

"The Army Base Riviera is the largest with a capacity of two hundred. I'll sit down with Emily and decide between that and the Lakeside Riviera. The location is fantastic but it's outdated and it needs a complete overhaul," I say.

"Well, prioritize based on what will give us the best return in the shortest amount of time. The Army Base Riviera has the potential, but the Lakeside could attract a higher-end clientele with the right updates." I can't keep my excitement from showing.

This is a chance to prove to my father that my time on tour did not mess up my head.

My father nods, his expression thoughtful as he folds his newspaper, resting it on the side table. "That's the smart play. The Lakeside's location could really draw in the upscale crowd if you modernize it."

I can tell he's pleased with my approach, which is something. Dad has always been tough to please.

"Make sure Emily's onboard with everything. This is a joint venture, after all."

"I will," I say. "She's got a sharp eye for the business. We're aligned on the main goals, and I know she's eager to see changes happen as much as I am."

"Good," he says, tapping his fingers lightly on the arm of his chair. "But keep the pressure on. We want them to start showing a profit as soon as possible."

I'm well aware of the stakes and the reminder makes my stomach churn. I glance at my watch. *What is taking Emily so long?*

Before I can respond, let's out a sigh. "Do we have to talk about business now? It's Sunday for goodness's sake." She says this, every Sunday.

"And where's Emily," she continues in an irritated tone. Mother is a stickler for time, just like I am.

"Let me call her and see how far away she is," I say, fishing out my phone. Emily is quickly becoming one of the most frequent people I call.

There's no answer. "She's probably driving," I say, setting my phone on the table. "Have you spoken to Daniel?" I direct the question to my mother, as she's the one most likely to speak to him.

My father deals with Daniel's antics by ignoring them and him. He picks up his newspaper and continues reading.

Her face tightens. "No and I would prefer it that way. He caused us a lot of embarrassment yesterday, thank God it was just family. But let's not talk about that, it'll sour my mood, which is the last thing I want for my first lunch date with my new daughter-in-law."

I hide a smile. I've never seen a hint of my mother needing an addition to the family, but she's taking to the idea of a daughter-in-law with surprising enthusiasm, even if it's all part of a business arrangement. I can tell she's excited to play the role of the welcoming, doting mother.

Thirty minutes later, though, Emily still hasn't shown up, and the tension at the table is starting to rise. My mother, glancing at her watch for the third time, lets out an exasperated sigh.

"I'll go inside and let the butler know we're ready for lunch," she says, standing and smoothing her dress before heading toward the house.

I check my phone again. Nothing. No text, no missed call. I'm trying to stay calm, but my frustration is building. Emily knew this was important. I told her as much this morning.

When my mother returns, lunch is served. Plates are placed in front of us, but all I can think about is Emily and where the hell she is.

"She must be caught up with something," I say, trying to sound casual, though inside, I'm boiling. "She'll be here soon."

My mother raises an eyebrow but doesn't comment. My father simply digs into his food, clearly uninterested in the drama of it all.

We continue eating, but I'm barely tasting the food. Every few minutes, I glance at my phone, hoping for some sort of explanation. Nothing.

By the end of lunch, my frustration has turned into full-blown anger. Sure, things come up—people get held up. But for fuck's sake, she could've called or texted. She knows how important this lunch was, and yet she's left me to sit here making excuses on her behalf.

It shows how little respect she has for our arrangement.

After the plates are cleared and coffee is served, my mother gives me a sympathetic smile. "Maybe something came up," she says. "Emily's a wonderful girl. I'm sure she has a good reason."

I nod, but internally, I'm seething. A wonderful girl? What do we know about her, really? Her actions today have shown she's self-centered, inconsiderate, and clearly has no regard for what we agreed upon.

As I get up to leave, my mother pats my arm, her smile warm but tinged with concern. "Don't worry too much, Andrew. I'm sure she wanted to be here with us."

I give her a tight-lipped smile in return. But in my mind, all I can think is, she wanted to be here with us? I doubt it. This is the first real test of our partnership, and she's failed it miserably.

I had hoped we could at least be cordial—maybe even become friends. But I won't be foolish enough to entertain that thought again.

When I get home, only Bear and Bruno greet me. Emily's not here. I grit my teeth, realizing she's setting boundaries—letting me know that she has no intention of acting like my wife. I need to work out this anger. Changing quickly, I head to the house gym.

An hour of lifting weights brings me some relief. My muscles burn, but my head feels clearer, more grounded, focused.

Later, when I'm sitting in the kitchen with a drink, reading market news on my iPad, I hear the front door creak open. Emily finally walks in.

Her eyes darting around the room before they land on me. "Hey."

*Hey? After being a no-show for lunch.* I set my iPad down and wait for an explanation. Not that there's a good enough reason for not communicating.

She tucks a strand of hair behind her ear, her gaze shifting from the floor to the dogs, anywhere but directly at me. "Sorry about earlier. Something came up with my mom."

My chest tightens. It was just as I thought. A complete lack of respect.

"Look, I'm really sorry but we can reschedu—"

"Is my office ready?" I say, cutting her short.

Her eyes widen for a second, then she recovers. "Yes, it was ready a week ago."

"Good." I keep my voice cool, not giving away the hurt I feel inside. Hurt that I shouldn't be feeling. I brought this on myself. "The sooner we start, the sooner we achieve the reason for this marriage."

I turn back to my iPad, my tone signaling the end of the conversation. She stands in the same position then she turns and leaves the kitchen.

## Chapter 14: Emily

I sit at my desk, phone pressed to my ear, my eyes darting to the clock every few seconds. My mother's voice is on the other end and she sounds exhausted. Guilt floods me. I slept soundly last night, while I'm sure she barely got any rest.

"How is he?" I ask, my fingers tapping restlessly on the surface of the desk.

"The doctor is with him now," my mother says, sounding worn out. "They're running more tests this morning."

I let out a slow breath, nodding even though she can't see me. "What kind of tests?"

"They're checking for any signs of infection. The fever's worrying them," she says, her voice cracking slightly.

I picture her sitting beside my father's bed, hands wringing together, eyes watching every breath he takes. I hate that I wasn't there last night.

The day had been just as grueling with Dad's fever spiking and then coming back down. We had come close to rushing him to the ER. He'd been sweating buckets and so pale.

"Did the doctor say anything else?" I ask, trying to keep my voice steady.

"Not much. Just that the test results would determine the next steps."

My stomach knots. It's difficult to keep up this secrecy if my father is admitted to hospital. My father's wishes to keep everything quiet are really pushing us into a corner. Every flare-up feels like the edge of a cliff, and every time, we hope he pulls back just enough to keep going.

"Okay," I say softly. "Let me know what the results say."

"I will," my mother says but there's a strain in her voice which wasn't there. She's trying to hold it together, trying to be the rock, but the cracks are starting to show.

"How are you holding up, Mom?"

There's a pause. "I'm alright. Just tired."

I want to be there day and night but I have to be here, running the business and keeping my Dad's a secret from Andrew means I can't disappear any time I want to.

"Why don't you try to get some rest?" I suggest, even though I know the answer. It's impossible to rest when Dad is in this state.

"I'll rest when he's better," she says. "But don't worry about us. You focus on work today, okay? I'll keep you posted."

I sigh, nodding again. "Okay. But call me the moment you know anything."

I hang up and stare at my phone for a moment, trying to push down the guilt that's clawing at my chest. It's getting hard to juggle everything and this is just the beginning.

I glance at the clock again, knowing I have to pull myself together before Andrew walks in. As if on cue, the intercom buzzes, jolting me out of my thoughts.

"Emily?" Catherine's voice comes through, calm and efficient. "Mr. Bennett is here."

I take a fortifying breath. "Please show him in."

The door opens a moment later, and Andrew walks in, all businesslike, with Catherine trailing behind him. I smile, rising from my desk.

"Andrew," I say, motioning toward Catherine. "This is Catherine, my PA. She'll be assisting you as well while you're working here at Riviera."

Andrew nods curtly. "Good to meet you, Catherine."

Catherine flashes him a polite smile before turning back to me. "Anything else you need?"

"No, thank you. That'll be all for now," I say, and she leaves us alone, the door clicking shut behind her.

I glance at Andrew. He's still distant, his posture stiff. The coolness between us isn't lost on me, and I know why. I feel terrible about skipping lunch with his family yesterday, but it had flown right out the window the second I walked into my parents' house and saw my father in such a bad state. I can't explain it to him, though, and that gnaws at me even more.

"Let me show you to your office," I say, gesturing toward the door. "I've also organized a meeting with the team."

Andrew follows me as I lead him next door. "Good," he says, his voice clipped but businesslike. "But I want to tour the hotels as soon as possible. I need to see firsthand what we're working with."

I nod. "Of course. We can schedule that after the meeting."

I open the door to his new office, stepping aside so he can enter first. As he walks by, I catch a whiff of his cologne. It's a citrus scent that make me want to move close to him and inhale deeper.

Pushing away those thoughts, I follow him in. The space is modern, and spacious, with large windows overlooking the city. I hold my breath, waiting for Andrew's verdict.

Andrew scans the room briefly before giving a slight nod of approval.

I hate his coldness and wish I could explain everything to him.

But I can't. "Let me know if you need anything before the meeting."

Andrew barely glances my way. Instead he sits down and clicks on the monitor in front of him. We're loaded it with all the information he needs to see how The Riviera group is run.

"I'll let you know," he says.

I step out of the office, closing the door quietly behind me, my heart sinking as I walk back to my own desk. I knew he would be upset but I hoped my apology last night would suffice.

*Clearly not.*

An hour later, I'm still at my desk responding to emails when Catherine's voice comes through the intercom again. "The team are in the conference room."

"Thanks. Have you let Mr. Bennett know?" I ask.

"Yes, he's on his way there," Catherine says.

I leave my office and head to the conference room. Everyone is already seated and I walk in as Andrew is introducing himself. I take a seat next to him.

"Thank you all for coming," I begin, my voice steady as I glance around the room. "As you know, we're here to give Andrew a comprehensive briefing on the current state of the Riviera Group. Amy, would you like to start?"

Amy, the Director of Operations, leans forward, her expression serious. "As Director of Operations, I've been closely monitoring all our properties, and frankly, we're facing significant challenges.

"Every one of our properties is underperforming. Outdated facilities are taking a toll on guest satisfaction, which in turn is impacting our bookings."

Matthew, the CFO, nods, adding weight to Amy's words. "Financially, we've been running in the red for the past two quarters. The Army Base Riviera is a major concern—it's bleeding money due to its lack of modernization."

The rest of the team chime in. The situation is bleak, but none of this is news to Andrew. He's already familiar with the financial, legal, and operational reports that were sent to Bennett Developers before they acquired a 50% stake in the Riviera Group.

Andrew listens intently, absorbing every detail without interrupting.

When everyone is done with their briefing, he says, "So, we're dealing with two major issues here—outdated facilities and a lack of competitive marketing. Both of which need immediate attention if we're going to turn this around."

This is music to my ears and I nod, as does everyone else.

The meeting continues for another hour, with discussions around logistics, timelines, and strategies. Andrew takes control, laying out the steps we need to take, and the team responds with a renewed sense of purpose.

The energy in the room shifts as everyone sees a renewed future for the Riviera group.

As the meeting wraps up, everyone gathers their things and heads for the door, leaving just Andrew and me alone in the room.

"I would love a tour of this hotel," he says.

"Sure." I was expecting that and I'm excited to show him what makes the Riviera hotels so special.

We step out through the private entrance used by management, which offers a discreet way for me and my team to enter and exit without crossing through the main hotel.

It's a quiet corner of the building, separate from the hotel's hustle and bustle, and as we walk through, the atmosphere between us starts to thaw.

"I've always liked this location," Andrew says, glancing out of the windows that line the hallway, offering a glimpse of the busy Back Bay streets. "Your father had an eye for great spots."

I smile, feeling a small sense of pride. "He did. He always said location is everything."

As we continue, I give him a rundown of the rooms. "The standard rooms are cozy, perfect for guests who want something intimate but still luxurious. Each one has a reading nook with views of either the tree-lined streets or the skyline."

Andrew nods, his gaze moving around, absorbing every detail. "It's smart. It gives the guests something personal without overdoing it."

We take the elevator up to the fourth floor, where I show him the deluxe rooms. "These are a bit larger, with premium views of the Charles River or the skyline. We've incorporated a lot of rich fabrics and mahogany touches to give the rooms a more elegant, timeless feel."

He steps into one of the rooms and glances around. "This has potential. The size and design cater to an upscale crowd, but you can see where things need refreshing. The fabrics are a bit dated, and some of the amenities could use an upgrade."

"Café Riviera is on the first floor," I say as we descend in the elevator.

"It's well thought out," Andrew says, taking in the atmosphere of the cafe. "Your father definitely knew how to strike a balance between elegance and modern appeal. But there's still a lot we can work with."

His approval makes my chest tighten with unexpected warmth.

We head back out toward the private entrance, the tour winding down. The more we talk, the easier it becomes.

As we step out into the cool afternoon air, I glance at him. "You know, my father didn't start off in hotels."

Andrew's brow furrows with interest. "Oh?"

"He actually started with one small bar in Back Bay. It was a tiny place, practically a hole in the wall, but he turned it into a popular spot. From there, he bought a small bed-and-breakfast and grew it, expanding his reach bit by bit."

"Sounds like my father," Andrew says.

I nod and continue. "He worked hard for everything he had. The Riviera Group wasn't built overnight. It's one of the reasons I'm so committed to keeping it afloat."

I need Andrew to understand that this is not just business for me. It's about ensuring that my father's hard work was not in vain.

## Chapter 15: Andrew

"So, what did you think of Lakeside and Army Base?" Emily asks, her voice cutting through the silence. "I'm thinking that we should start the renovations with Army Base, as it has the largest capacity."

I stare out the window of the car as it glides through the city streets, trying to shake the lingering tension in my chest.

The Army Base Riviera was right next to a military base. One look at the rows of barracks, the hum of soldiers training, and it felt like I was back in Afghanistan.

"I think..." I trail off, my throat tightening as I fight to focus. "Army Base has potential, but it's going to need more work than Lakeside."

Emily is sitting next to me, watching me carefully, but I keep my gaze fixed outside.

My mind is a minefield right now, littered with images I don't want to revisit. The distant sound of boots hitting the ground, the grainy feeling of sand and dust clinging to my skin.

The memories rush at me, uninvited, like they always do when I'm caught off guard. I'm pissed off at myself for my lack of preparation.

The Army Base Riviera is named that because it's next to a military base. I should have known that would be a trigger.

"Andrew?" Emily's voice pulls me back slightly. She sounds concerned. I can feel her eyes on me, and I know I'm not doing a great job of hiding how rattled I am.

I clear my throat, forcing my voice to stay steady. "We'll figure it out. We'll sit down and go over the numbers later."

Silence stretches between us for a moment. I can tell she wants to ask more, maybe push, but thankfully, she doesn't.

I can't handle that right now. All I can think about is getting home, getting out of this suit, and pounding out the memories on the treadmill until they disappear.

The car pulls into the driveway, and I'm out the door before the driver can even fully stop. Emily follows, but I don't give her a chance to say anything.

"I'm going to the gym," I say abruptly, not meeting her eyes. I can feel her confusion, her hesitation, but I don't wait for her to respond. I just need to get away, need space to clear my head.

I make a beeline for my room, stripping off my suit and changing into workout gear like a man on a mission. Adrenaline pumps though me, the need to push myself to the limit, to drown out the chaos in my head.

The gym is a sanctuary. I hit the treadmill hard, the sound of my feet slamming against the belt matching the frantic rhythm of my heartbeat.

Every step is an attempt to shake the memories loose, to leave them behind where they belong.

*Focus, Andrew. Don't let this get to you. Not again.*

I increase the speed, forcing my body to keep up. The burn in my muscles, the pounding in my chest—it helps. It's the only thing that ever helps.

I can't afford to fall apart. Everyone's watching me. The Riviera project, my family, this ridiculous marriage to Emily—it's all riding on me keeping it together.

PTSD isn't going to ruin my life. I won't let it.

After what feels like an eternity, the tension finally starts to ease. The memories fade to the background, replaced by the satisfying ache of overworked muscles.

By the time I step off the treadmill, drenched in sweat, my mind is clearer.

I grab a towel and head upstairs to take a shower, letting the hot water wash away the lingering tension. By the time I'm out and dressed, I'm feeling more like myself again.

The house is quiet. Emily isn't here, and I find a note on the kitchen counter.

*Popped out for a bit. Be back later.*

It's tempting to ask her where she's gone, but I remind myself that she's not my real wife. I have no right to care, no right to ask. This arrangement is just business, nothing more.

I head out to the backyard to play with Bear and Bruno.

Emily still hasn't returned by dinner time, and a part of me is relieved. I'm still feeling off, and the last thing I need is to deal with awkward conversation.

I eat alone, the quiet of the house settling around me like a blanket, and by the time I finish, I'm more exhausted than I'd like to admit.

I head to bed, but sleep is elusive. My mind keeps pulling me back to the Army Base Riviera, to the military base next door. To the life I thought I'd left behind.

Every time I close my eyes, I'm back there. The smell of gunpowder, the heat, the constant threat. I toss and turn, trying to will the memories away, but they cling to me, seeping into my dreams.

At some point, I fall asleep, but it's disturbed—jolting awake with the sound of explosions ringing in my ears. I squeeze my eyes shut, trying to force my mind to calm down.

The next time I wake up, there's a warmth pressed against me. My mind is still groggy, caught somewhere between the vivid dreams and the present, and it takes me a moment to realize there's a soft body in my arms.

*Emily.*

My breath hitches, and I freeze, unsure of how or why she's here, but I don't let go. I can't.

The familiar weight of the nightmares lingers in the back of my mind, and without thinking, I tighten my grip, needing something—anything—to ground me.

She's here, warm and real, and for the first time in hours, the tension starts to ebb.

I press my face into her hair, inhaling deeply. She smells like lavender, the same scent that's been haunting me since we first met.

She shifts slightly, turning to face me, and her soft breath fans across my skin. It sends a jolt through me, something primal, something urgent.

"Andrew—"

I cut her off by sealing my mouth to hers. Her lips part under mine, yielding to the hungry desperation that simmers just below the surface.

She doesn't respond at first and I'm about to pull back when her hands move to my shoulders her nails digging into my skin with a fierce need that mirrors my own.

The memories of war and trauma fade into the background, replaced by the raw, unbridled need coursing through me.

I push her back against the pillows, trailing kisses along her jawline, down her neck. Emily moans and arches her back as I move down her chest. I reach down and pull up her nightdress, until her breasts are bared to my eyes.

*She's so fucking beautiful.*

I cup her breasts, feeling their weight and softness in my hands, the nipples hardening under my touch. I suck on one of them, feeling her shiver beneath me as I blow on it.

I then move down her body, kissing every part of her exposed skin. Her heart is beating so fast, I can feel it through her skin. My dick is so hard that it's painful. I want to be inside her, to feel that connection, that closeness. I need this, more than anything else right now.

I move lower, kissing her stomach, then trail kisses down to her hip.

I run my hands up and down her thighs, feeling the muscles tense and relax under my touch. She moans softly as I kiss my way down her inner thigh, slowly getting closer to my goal.

When I finally reach her pussy, I can feel the heat radiating from it. I press a soft kiss to her mound before slowly parting her folds with my fingers.

“Andrew,” she says in a pleading voice.

Hearing her say my name like that does something to me.

It makes me want to take her right there and then. Instead, I slip a finger inside her, feeling how wet she is for me. She moans loudly as I tease her with my fingers.

“Please,” she whispers again, and I groan at the sound.

Pulling my finger out, I spread her legs and arrange myself between then, then lower my head to her pussy.

The scent of her arousal wafts up my nostrils and I inhale deeply before plunging my tongue into her core. A gasp rips out of her mouth and her hands grip my head.

I lap at her folds, savoring her every taste and texture.

Emily's hands tangle in my hair as she gasps in pleasure, her hips bucking against my face.

I slide another finger inside her as I suckle on her clit, feeling her muscles flutter around me. Her moans grow louder and more desperate as she nears the edge.

“Andrew,” she cries out, her nails digging into my scalp. “I'm going to...I'm going to come!”

Her release floods against my tongue, her sweet nectar coating my lips and tongue. I feel her shudder beneath me, her body wracked with pleasure as she cries out my name.

As her orgasm subsides, I kiss her inner thighs softly, trailing my fingers through the remnants of her release. I guide myself to her entrance and slowly thrust inside her, feeling her muscles constrict around me.

I want to go slowly but the demons inside me won’t let me.

I take her hard and fast, Emily’s nails digging into my back letting me know that we’re together.

“Andrew,” she moans, her name a hoarse whisper that sends a jolt through me. “I need more.”

I drive into, burying myself to the hilt. I pull out and ram into her again. Emily wraps her legs around my waist, pulling me even deeper.

My mind is empty, save for the pleasure coursing through me and Emily’s tight pussy milking my dick.

Emily whimpers as my release builds up.

Her whimpers grow more desperate, her hands clawing at my back, urging me on.

“Andrew,” she gasps, her voice barely audible above the sound of our bodies slamming against each other. “I'm close.”

Her words set off a spark inside me, and I thrust harder, faster, feeling the pressure build until I can't hold back any longer.

“I'm going to come,” I grunt, my voice rough with need.

Emily's breath hitches as she cries out my name, her hands clutching at me tighter. “Andrew!” she says again, the urgency in her voice matching my own.

And then it happens. Her body flutters around me, pushing me over the edge. My release floods her, her muscles clamping down against me in response.

I feel as if I’ve run a three-thousand-mile race. Spent, I collapse besides Emily and pull her close. My eyes are heavy with sleep. There’s a thought nagging at me but I’m too exhausted to chase it. I give in to sleep.

## Chapter 16: Emily

I wake up, disoriented, my cheek pressed against something warm and solid. It takes a moment for my eyes to adjust, and when they do, I realize I'm nestled against Andrew's chest, his strong arms wrapped around me.

His chest rises and falls as he breathes steadily, the faint scent of his cologne mixed with something purely him—masculine, familiar, intoxicating.

*Oh God.* My heart pounds as the events of last night come rushing back, and I want to scream. What the hell was I thinking?

I replay everything in my mind, the way I crept down the hall, tiptoeing to Andrew's room after hearing him cry out in his sleep.

I remember standing by his bed, his face twisted in anguish, the sound of his ragged breathing. I'd shaken him gently, whispering his name, trying to wake him from whatever nightmare had its grip on him.

And then he'd pulled me into his bed, his arms tight around me, like he was drowning and I was the only thing keeping him afloat. I should have stopped it, should have stepped back, but instead, we kissed.

And once his lips were on mine, all rational thought evaporated.

I was so aroused, so desperate for him, that nothing—absolutely nothing—could have made me leave. The way he held me, the heat of his mouth, the urgency in his touch. I didn't think, I just felt.

But now, in the cold light of morning, my heart thuds for a different reason. The reality of what we did crashes over me, and I can't breathe.

He was obviously reacting to his nightmare, needing something, someone, to hold onto. But what was my excuse? Why did I let that happen?

*Oh my God.* Shame surges through me, burning hot. I can't bear the thought of facing him when he wakes up. What will he think of me? That I took advantage of a vulnerable moment?

Slowly, carefully, I pry myself out of his hold, moving inch by inch, trying not to wake him. His arm tightens around me for a moment, and I freeze, my breath catching.

But then he shifts, and I manage to slip free, tiptoeing out of his room like a thief in the night.

Back in my own room, I practically dive into the shower, letting the hot water cascade over me, hoping it will wash away the embarrassment, the confusion.

I scrub at my skin, trying to forget last night. I dress quickly, my heart still racing, and grab my bag. I need to get out of here, need to put as much distance as possible between me and Andrew.

By the time I arrive at the office, my mind is still a chaotic mess. I pull out my phone and, without thinking, dial Lisa's number. She picks up on the third ring, her voice groggy.

"You better have a good reason for calling me so early," she says with a yawn.

"I did something stupid," I blurt out, my voice loud and laced with panic.

"Uh-oh, spill," Lisa says, suddenly sounding more awake.

I take a deep breath and recount the whole thing to her—how I'd gone to check on Andrew, how he'd pulled me into bed, how we'd kissed and... everything that followed.

By the time I finish, my hands are shaking. I brace myself, expecting her to scold me, to tell me how reckless and irresponsible I'd been.

But instead, she bursts out laughing. "Way to go, girl! It was about time you removed those cobwebs."

"Lisa, I'm serious!" I say, exasperated. "This is a business marriage. We're not supposed to be having sex."

"I don't see why not," she says, completely nonchalant. "He's your husband, isn't he? That's just part of the territory."

I shouldn't have expected any different from the woman who treats one-night stands as casually as changing her underwear. "Lisa, this is different. This isn't a real marriage. We have rules, boundaries—"

"Stop overthinking it," she interrupts, a teasing edge in her voice. "Andrew is hot as hell, and if I were in your shoes, I'd be enjoying that hot body every night. You've got a golden ticket, Em. Enjoy the ride."

She's not getting it. "It's not just the physical aspect I'm worried about," I admit, my voice quieter now. "What if I fall for him?"

Lisa goes silent for a moment, and when she speaks again, her tone is serious. "You won't. You can't. That's the fastest route to getting hurt, and you know it. Keep your emotions out of this, Em."

"Easier said than done," I mutter, knowing she's right but also knowing how hard it will be to follow that advice.

There's a pause, then she says cheerfully, "Don't forget yoga today! You could use the zen after your wild night." She laughs, and before I can respond, she hangs up.

Maybe Lisa is right. Maybe I'm overthinking this. But there's a sinking feeling in my gut that tells me last night wasn't just a one-off moment of weakness.

My mind drifts back to Andrew, his arms around me, the way he held me like I was the only thing keeping him steady. The way his hands worked my body as if he was familiar with every nook.

I've never been that turned on. Never wanted someone as badly as I wanted Andrew. An ache forms between my legs from the memories. It was the hottest sex I've ever had.

I push away the memories but my body obviously has a mind of its own because it won't let me forget. I'm so shameless and so wet right now. My breasts are heavy and I ache in my core.

Then, with a jolt of panic, I remember—I haven't called my mother. Guilt floods me as I realize I've been so caught up in my own drama that I haven't checked on my dad.

I find my mother's number, my heart in my throat, and it feels like an eternity before she picks up.

"Emily," she answers, her voice softer than usual, but there's no immediate panic in her tone, and that gives me a sliver of hope.

"Morning Mom," I say, trying to keep my voice steady. "How did Dad sleep last night?"

"He's stable," she says, and I release a breath I didn't realize I was holding. "The doctor was here earlier this morning. He explained that a coma brings down a person's immunity, so he's bound to catch a few infections. But they're keeping a close eye on him, and the fever seems to be under control for now."

Relief washes over me, but it's quickly replaced by the familiar weight of worry. "That's good to hear. That fever is worrying."

"I know, sweetheart," she says gently. "But the doctor thinks it's manageable. We're doing everything we can to keep him comfortable."

I close my eyes, letting her words sink in. "Thank you, Mom. For everything. Please let me know if there's any change, okay?"

"I will," she promises, and then there's a pause, like she's considering saying something more. "Is everything okay with you?"

"I'm fine," I lie, forcing a smile even though she can't see it. "Just a lot on my plate right now."

"I know," she says softly, and I can hear the concern in her voice. "But don't forget to take care of yourself, too."

"I won't," I say, even though it feels like I've been doing anything but that. "I'll check in later, okay?"

"Okay. Take care, Emily."

I hang up, my heart still heavy but a little more settled knowing my father is stable. For now, at least. I lean back in my chair, staring up at the ceiling, and tries to gather my thoughts.

There's a knock on my office door, and I jump, my heart skipping a beat.

For a moment, I panic, thinking it might be Andrew, but then Catherine pokes her head in. "Hey, just a reminder that you have a meeting with the marketing team in thirty minutes."

“Thanks, Catherine,” I say, forcing a smile. “I’ll be ready.”

She nods and closes the door, and I take a moment to compose myself. I don’t have time to dwell on last night or the mess I’ve gotten myself into.

I have a business to run, a father to worry about, and a marriage that needs to stay strictly professional, no matter how complicated it’s gotten.

I power through the meeting with the marketing team, nodding and making notes, but my mind keeps drifting. I’m operating on autopilot, responding to their ideas, offering feedback, but barely processing a word they’re saying.

I just need to get through this day without falling apart.

As soon as the meeting wraps up, I return to my office, grateful for the brief moment of solitude. I’ve barely settled back at my desk, scanning through the revised marketing plan, when the intercom buzzes.

“Emily?” Catherine’s voice is calm, as usual. “Mr. Bennett is here to see you.”

I freeze, my heart lurching. Of course, Andrew would show up now, when my nerves are already frayed. “Please show him in,” I manage to say.

The door opens, and Andrew walks in, his expression unreadable. He’s dressed sharply, as always, but there’s a tension around his mouth that wasn’t there before.

As he strides across the room, I can’t help but notice the little details I probably shouldn’t—like how his dark brown hair curls slightly at the nape of his neck, or the way his shirt stretches over his broad shoulders.

Or how it felt to rake my fingers over his muscular chest.

*God, get it together, Emily.*

“Andrew,” I say, standing up and trying to act natural. “Have a seat.”

He sits down across from me, his eyes briefly meeting mine before flicking away. "I wanted to discuss the Riviera Lakeside renovations," he says, diving straight into business, his tone clipped.

I swallow, trying to push away the nervous energy twisting in my stomach. "Sure. What are your thoughts?"

"We need to revamp it completely," he says, leaning back slightly. "The Lakeside is a prime location, but the facilities are outdated. If we're going to attract high-end clients, we need to go big—modernize the rooms, upgrade the amenities, overhaul the design."

I tense. Lakeside was my father's first hotel. The one closest to my heart, just it was close to his. I'm not ready to have it touched. Not yet.

"I understand where you're coming from, but I think our priority should be the Army Base Riviera. It has the largest capacity, and updating it would give us the quickest boost in revenue," I say trying to keep my tone neutral.

Andrew's eyes narrow slightly, and the muscles in his jaw tighten. "I disagree. The Lakeside has more potential to draw in a higher-end clientele. We need to make a statement with our first renovation, and Lakeside is the place to do it."

I can feel my own temper flaring up, but I try to keep my tone calm. "But the Army Base Riviera is bleeding money. If we don't address it first, we're going to keep losing revenue. We need to stabilize it before we take on a full revamp of the Lakeside."

We go back and forth for a few minutes, our voices getting louder, each of us refusing to back down. I know he has a point, but so do I, and I can't let him bulldoze me just because he's used to taking charge.

Finally, Andrew lets out a sigh, his shoulders dropping slightly. "Fine. We'll start with the Army Base Riviera. But I want the plans for Lakeside drawn up simultaneously. Once we start seeing a return, we move straight to that project."

"Deal," I say, a little surprised that he's conceding so easily.

But before I can breathe a sigh of relief, Andrew leans forward, his eyes locking onto mine. “There’s one more thing we need to discuss.”

I know immediately what he’s talking about, and my heart skips a beat.

“We should talk about last night,” he says.

“It was mistake,” I say quickly. “It shouldn’t have happened, and it won’t happen again.”

“Emily,” Andrew starts to say.

I glance down at my watch, desperately trying to end the confusion. “I have a meeting with the finance team in ten minutes,” I say, my voice a little too bright. It’s a hint, and we both know it.

Andrew stands up, smoothing down his jacket. “Of course,” he says, his voice flat. “We’ll talk later.”

I watch him walk out, the door clicking shut behind him, and my shoulders slump with relief. Talking about it will humiliate me further. Best to forget about it.

# Chapter 17: Andrew

It's been three weeks since Emily and I decided to start renovations at the Army Base Riviera, and it's been nonstop ever since. I've made it a point to be at the site almost every day, overseeing the work, making sure things are on schedule.

The first thing we tackled was the exterior. The building's facade was a mess—faded gray, cracks running along the walls, and weeds creeping through the cracks in the pavement.

It looked more like a rundown barracks than a hotel, which, given its proximity to the actual military base, probably wasn't helping. We're giving it a complete facelift—new paint, fresh landscaping, modern signage. I want it to catch people's attention the moment they drive by.

But every time I see that damn base in the distance, my stomach twists.

It's like a shadow, hovering on the edge of my vision, a constant reminder of things I'd rather forget. I thought I'd be able to handle it—just keep my head down, focus on the work.

But some days, all it takes is the sound of heavy equipment or the sight of a uniformed guard patrolling nearby, and I'm right back there, in the thick of it.

My heart starts pounding, my skin prickles, and I have to force myself to breathe, to remember where I am.

So far, I've managed to keep it under control. But it's exhausting, always being on edge, always fighting to keep the memories from dragging me under.

I check my watch, realizing it's almost evening, and there's still so much to be done. I find Stephen, the lead contractor, near the lobby, going over a blueprint with his team. He's a burly guy, probably in his late forties, with a no-nonsense attitude that I appreciate.

"Stephen," I call out, striding over. "How's everything going with the interior updates?"

He looks up. "We're making progress, but there've been a few hiccups. The plumbing in the guest bathrooms on the third floor is worse than we thought. We'll need to replace most of the pipes, which is gonna push us back a few days."

I bite back a curse, glancing at the floor plan. "How many rooms are affected?"

"About half of them," he says, his tone apologetic. "We've already started tearing out the old pipes, but it's slow work."

I nod, trying to keep my frustration in check. "Alright. Prioritize those rooms, and let's see if we can speed up the process without cutting corners. We need to have at least two floors fully operational by the end of the month."

Stephen nods. "We'll do our best, but I'm not making any promises. This place is a maze, and every time we open up a wall, it's like we're finding new surprises."

I knew the Army needed a lot of work, but the magnitude of it was shocking. "I get it. Just keep me updated. If we need to bring in more manpower, then do it. We can't afford any major delays."

Stephen nods, making a note on his clipboard, and I can tell he's already thinking of ways to get around the issue. I appreciate that. He's been reliable, and in a project like this, that's worth its weight in gold.

"We're also waiting on the materials for the new flooring," Stephen adds. "They were supposed to arrive this afternoon, but there's been a delay. Should have them first thing tomorrow, though."

I glance at the worn, scuffed tiles beneath our feet, already imagining the sleek, modern flooring that will replace them. "Make sure they're installed as soon as they arrive. The lobby is the first thing guests see when they walk in. It needs to make a statement."

Stephen nods, and I'm about to head back to the makeshift office we've set up when I catch sight of someone walking towards us from the entrance. Emily.

My breath hitches. I've barely seen her in the last three weeks. We've both been going out of our way to avoid each other.

The sight of her has my heart doing this weird, unsteady thing. She's dressed in a fitted navy dress, her hair loose around her shoulders, and even in the middle of a construction site, she looks effortlessly composed.

"Hey," she says, a bit breathless as she approaches. "I wanted to check in before heading home."

I nod, trying to act casual. "Good timing. We were just discussing the plumbing issues and the delay with the flooring."

She raises an eyebrow, glancing at Stephen. "Anything I should be worried about?"

Stephen gives her a reassuring smile. "Nothing we can't handle, ma'am. Just a few hiccups. We'll keep pushing through."

Emily turns back to me, her eyes searching mine for a moment. "Are you okay? You look tired."

I stiffen slightly, not wanting to get into it. "I'm fine. Just a long day."

She hesitates, and for a second, I think she's going to press, but then she just nods. "Alright. Well, if you need anything, let me know. I'll be around."

Stephen clears his throat, glancing between us. "I'll leave you two to it. Got some more things to check on before I wrap up."

"Thanks, Stephen," I say, watching as he heads back to his team.

Now it's just me and Emily, standing in the middle of this half-renovated lobby, with the sounds of drills and hammering echoing around us.

"Is it really bad?" she asks quietly, gesturing to the construction chaos around us.

"It's not great," I admit. "But we'll get there. It's just going to take more time and more money than we originally planned."

She nods, biting her lower lip in that way she does when she's deep in thought. I have to look away because seeing it makes me want to kiss her, and I can't afford to go down that road again.

“Well, if anyone can turn this place around, it’s you,” she says, her voice soft, and I can tell she means it. “You’ve already made so much progress. It’s starting to look hopeful.”

Something in her tone makes me glance up, and I see her watching me with this quiet, unguarded expression that makes my chest tighten. For a moment, I forget where we are, forget about the work, the noise, the stress. It’s just us.

“Thanks,” I say, my voice rougher than I intended. “That means a lot.”

She smiles, and it’s like a breath of fresh air. For a second, I think about reaching out, slipping my arms around her waist. Inhaling that maddeningly intoxicating lavender scent.

“How about dinner?” I say without thinking and immediately regret my words. The last thing I should be doing is getting close to Emily.

Her face creases with a smile and my regret dissipates. “I’d like that.”

We walk around the site discussing the renovations, then we leave in different cars, with her following me.

I took her to a small, cozy bistro not far from the hotel. It’s one of those hidden gems tucked away on a quiet street, with ivy crawling up the brick exterior and warm, golden lights glowing through the windows.

I’ve been here a few times before, and I like the atmosphere—intimate, unpretentious, and not overly crowded. I need that tonight.

The hostess smiles and takes us to a table near the back, away from the handful of other diners. The place is warm, the air filled with the faint aroma of herbs and freshly baked bread.

There’s a low murmur of conversation, the kind that blends into the background without intruding. It’s perfect.

We settle into our seats, and I pick up the menu, though I’ve already memorized most of it. I’m not even sure what I’m in the mood for.

Mostly, I'm just trying to keep my mind off the way Emily looks right now—hair loose around her shoulders, that navy dress hugging her curves. She's beautiful, but that's not new.

What's new is how damn hard it is to keep my distance when she's sitting across from me, looking so damn at ease, even after the past few weeks of us barely speaking.

A waitress appears, and we order drinks. Emily glances around the bistro, her eyes taking in the flickering candles, the rustic wooden tables, the low-hanging lights.

"It's cute," she says, her gaze finally landing back on me. "Not what I expected."

"What did you expect?" I ask, raising an eyebrow.

She shrugs, a playful smile tugging at her lips. "Something fancier. Like a business dinner."

I can't help but grin at that. "No, this isn't about business. Not tonight."

Her expression shifts, a guarded look passing over her face. "Then what is it about?"

## Chapter 18: Andrew

Before I can answer, Emily's phone rings.

She glances down at the screen, and I can see the name "Owen's agent" flash across it.

"I'm sorry, I have to take this. It'll just be a minute." She gives me an apologetic look before swiping to answer the call.

I try not to listen, but it's impossible not to catch snippets of her conversation. "That's the figure? Are you sure, Owen? It just seems low." She pauses, her brow furrowing, and then she listens for a moment. "Alright. Send over the details, but I'm not convinced. Thanks."

When she hangs up, frustration is drawn all over her face. "Everything okay?" I ask.

"It's about my apartment," she says, running a hand through her hair. "Owen thinks it's not worth as much as I expected. But I'm sure he's undervaluing it."

"Oh, you're ready to put in on the market?" I ask.

Emily nods. "If Owen's right, I might not get much out of it."

I lean forward, resting my elbows on the table. "Do you have Owen's contact information? If you don't mind, I'd like to take a look at the listing. Maybe there's something he's missing."

She hesitates for a moment, and I can see the gears turning in her head, like she's deciding whether to let me get involved in this part of her life. But then she reaches for her phone. "Sure. I could use a second opinion."

A moment later, my phone buzzes, and I see a text with Owen's details.

"Thanks," I say, giving her a small, reassuring smile. "I'll check it out."

Before we can delve further into her property woes, the waitress arrives with our meals, setting the plates down in front of us.

Emily has a plate of grilled salmon, the skin crispy and glistening, laid over a bed of herbed quinoa and sautéed vegetables. It smells fantastic, the aroma of garlic and rosemary mingling in the air.

I opted for the steak—a perfectly seared ribeye, with a side of roasted potatoes and a drizzle of rich, peppercorn sauce. The meat is tender, practically melting in my mouth as I take a bite.

I watch Emily cut into her salmon, the flaky pink flesh separating easily under her fork. She takes a small bite, her lips curving into a smile as she tastes it.

"Good?" I ask, trying to ignore how much I like watching her enjoy her meal.

"Delicious," she says, nodding. "How's yours?"

"Perfect," I say, slicing off another piece of the steak. "They always do a great job here."

But I can't let this dinner pass without addressing the elephant in the room.in when I realize this is as good a moment as any to address the elephant in the room.

"I think we should talk about what happened *that* night," I say. I'm not big on revisiting things that have happened but this is my wife. We live in the same house. We work together.

She tenses, her fork poised over her plate. "I'm well aware of what happened that night, Andrew," she says, her cheeks coloring. "You didn't know who I was."

What the hell does she mean? I stare at her, baffled. "I knew who you were all along. My wife."

"In name only," she shoots back, her tone sharp.

I swallow, choosing my next word carefully. "I had a great night, Emily," I admit. "After that, I slept so deeply I didn't even hear my alarm."

Her lips part slightly, surprise flickering across her face. "I had a great night too," she says in a softer tone.

I can't help the grin that tugs at my lips. "Just for the record, I'm usually a more attentive lover," I say.

Emily cocks her head, a playful glint in her eye. "I thought you were pretty awesome," she says, and her voice is flirtatious, the tension between us easing.

I laugh, but it's a little strained because the truth is, I don't know how to handle this. I want her—God, do I want her—but I also know how dangerous it is to want her. It blurs the lines, makes things messy, and I've spent my entire life keeping things neat and compartmentalized.

"So where do we go from here?" she asks, her tone casual, but I can see the way she's watching me, the way her eyes search my face for some kind of answer.

My mind races. I should say we forget it happened, keep things professional, stick to the plan. That would be the smart thing, the safe thing. But when I try to force those words out, they don't come.

Every night, all I can think about is how Emily felt in my arms, the taste of her lips, the way she whispered my name. I want her, and I'm done pretending that I don't.

Aloud, I say, "I want to believe that we're two adults who need a physical outlet. You're a beautiful woman, Emily, and I'd be lying if I said I wasn't crazily attracted to you."

Her eyes widen, and for a second, I think she's going to laugh it off, make a joke. But she doesn't.

Instead, she leans back, taking a slow sip of her wine, her gaze never leaving mine. "So, you're saying this is just about satisfying a need?" she asks.

"Maybe," I reply, my voice lower, more serious. "Or maybe it's more than that. I'm still figuring it out. But I know I don't want to stop. Not unless you want to."

She considers this for a moment, her eyes searching mine, and I can practically see the gears turning in her head.

Finally, she sets down her glass, a slow, careful smile spreading across her lips. "I don't want to stop either," she says, and it feels like a weight has been lifted off my chest.

Suddenly, I lose my appetite and all I want is to take Emily home.

The air between us shifts, electricity crackling between us. My pulse quickens, and I can see that she's feeling it too.

I lean forward, lowering my voice, "We could leave now. Head back to the house."

Her cheeks flush, and she bites her lower lip, glancing down at her plate before looking back up at me. "What about dinner?" she asks, but there's a teasing lilt to her voice.

I can't help but grin. "I'm suddenly not very hungry for steak."

She laughs softly, and the sound is warm, unguarded. "Alright," she says, her tone light but her eyes dark with intent. "Let's go."

I wave the waitress over, asking for the check, and she raises an eyebrow but doesn't comment, simply bringing the bill over and thanking us for dining. I barely glance at it before throwing down my card, impatiently waiting for the transaction to go through.

Emily finishes her wine, watching me the entire time, a small smile playing at the corner of her lips. When the waitress returns with my card, I grab it and slide it back into my wallet, ready to get out of here.

As we step outside, the cool evening air hits us, a welcome relief after the warmth of the bistro. Emily is quiet, but her eyes are bright, and there's a slight tremor in her hands as she adjusts the strap of her purse.

I reach for her, fingers brushing against hers, and she doesn't pull away. I inhale sharply. I've never done this with any woman. Never felt a need to hold her hand or keep her close to me.

My thumb grazes the back of her hand, and she responds by lacing her fingers with mine, a small, simple gesture that sends a jolt straight to my chest.

The drive home is charged, electric. Every time I glance at Emily, she meets my gaze, her eyes dark and inviting. She doesn't look away, doesn't flinch. The silence between us is heavy, but not uncomfortable.

It's like we're both caught in this current, unable to break free, and I'm not sure I want to.

We're both quiet but it's not the awkward, tense silence of the past few weeks. It's charged, electric, and every time I glance over at her, I can see the same anticipation mirrored in her expression.

I park the car in the driveway, turning off the engine, but neither of us moves to get out right away. I can feel her gaze on me, and when I look over, her lips are slightly parted, her breath shallow.

I turn to her, and for a moment, I forget everything else—why this shouldn't happen, why I should be keeping my distance. I forget the complications, the rules we set. There's just her, looking at me like she wants this just as much as I do.

It's impossible to resist.

Without a word, I lean in, closing the distance between us, and press my lips to hers. The kiss is soft at first, almost tentative, but the second she responds, everything else fades away.

I deepen the kiss, my hand sliding to the back of her neck and pulling her closer. She makes a soft sound, somewhere between a sigh and a moan, and it's like a match to dry tinder.

I'm lost, completely lost in the feel of her, the taste of her, and I can't get enough.

I break the kiss, just for a moment, to catch my breath. "Let's go inside," I say, my voice rough and barely steady.

Emily nods, her lips slightly swollen, her eyes wide and dark. "Okay."

We get out of the car, and I walk around to her side, taking her hand again. She lets me, and it feels like the most natural thing in the world.

The moment we step inside, I pull her into my arms, my mouth crashing down on hers. She melts against me, her hands gripping my shoulders as she kisses me back with a desperation that matches my own.

Her fingers thread through my hair, tugging slightly, and I groan against her lips.

"Upstairs?" she whispers breathlessly, breaking the kiss for just a moment.

"Yeah," I murmur, kissing her again, harder this time, because I've been thinking about this for days, weeks, and I'm done waiting. "Upstairs."

We barely make it up the stairs, tripping over each other, hands roaming, mouths seeking. By the time we stumble into the bedroom, clothes are already half-off.

I push her down onto the bed, following her, and she pulls me closer, her breath coming in ragged gasps, eyes dark with want. I don't know what this means for us, where we go from here, but right now, all I care about is the way she feels beneath me, the way she sighs my name.

"It's front clasping," Emily says breathlessly as I fumble with the clasp of her bra.

I shift my hands to the front of her bra, unclasp it and let her bra slide off her shoulders, admiring the sight of her gorgeous breasts. They are just as full and beautiful as I remember.

I reach out and lightly run my fingers over her nipples, feeling them harden beneath my touch. I can't hold back a groan of pleasure as I feel her hands on me, pulling my pants down.

Moving away from her, I push down my pants along with my boxers, tossing them aside.

I kiss her again, our bodies pressed so close together that I can feel her hardened nipples against my chest.

Her fingers trail down my chest, tracing the lines of my abs before she reaches my dick. She wraps her fingers around my hard length and I moan into her mouth.

My hips buck against her hands as she strokes me. The feeling is incredible, and I know I won't last long with this kind of attention.

## Chapter 19: Emily

I whimper as Andrew drags his finger up and down my sensitive slit.

"Feel good, baby?" he asks, his voice low and husky.

*Baby?* The endearment makes my heart swell with warmth. It's a word I never thought I'd hear from Andrew, but it sends a thrill through me nonetheless.

"Yeah," I manage to breathe out, arching my back slightly as his fingers slide inside me. He hits that sweet spot that makes me moan loudly.

My breaths come out in short gasps, each one more ragged than the last. Just when I'm about to explode, Andrew's fingers slide out leaving me feeling needy.

"Andrew..." I start to say but before I can voice my protests, his tongue replaces his fingers, doing things that make me feel as if I'm literally losing my mind.

His tongue swirling around my clit is nothing short of explosive. I've never felt this way before, and it feels like I'm on a different planet.

I moan loudly, my body arching of its own accord as his tongue dances over my most sensitive spots. My hips thrust forward, desperate for more contact as his tongue continues to explore me.

His hand wraps around my thighs, pulling me closer to him as his tongue flicks over my clit again and again. Each touch sends lightning bolts through my body, igniting an uncontrollable fire.

"Andrew!" I cry out as he continues his tortuously sweet assault.

My orgasm builds and builds until I finally explode with a shriek, the intensity of it overwhelming me. Wave after wave of pure ecstasy crash over me until I finally lay back onto the bed, panting raggedly.

As I come down from my high, Andrew's hand leaves my leg and he gently turns me over.

"I want you on all fours," he says in a serious, sexy voice that has me positioning myself in the way he wants me.

"That's it, baby," he murmurs, his breath warm on my ear. His hands gently trail down my back, sending shivers up and down my spine. "You're so beautiful right now," he adds, his voice thick with desire.

Andrew in bed is quite different from who he is out of it. I love this uninhibited, sensual side of him.

"So wet and ready for me," he says softly, his breath caressing my ear again. "I'm going to make you feel so good."

My heart races with anticipation as I wait for him to enter me from behind, the thought of his large cock filling me up making me shiver in anticipation.

He slowly guides himself into me, his breath hitching as he does so. "You feel amazing," he whispers, his voice shaking slightly with emotion.

I moan in response, my body adjusting to him. He begins to thrust slowly at first, but the pace rapidly increases until we're both panting and groaning with pleasure.

His hands grip my hips, his fingers digging slightly into my skin with each thrust. The sensation is intense, pushing me closer and closer to a second orgasm.

"That's it," I cry out, arching my back to meet each thrust. "God, yes!"

Andrew groans in response, his breath coming in short gasps. His hips thrust harder, deeper, and I feel him hit a spot that sends electricity zinging through me.

"I'm going to come," I gasp, my body tensing. The feeling is overwhelming, the pleasure building up within me until it's almost too much to bear.

"That's it," Andrew growls, his voice low and filled with lust. "Come for me, Emily."

His words send me over the edge, my orgasm crashing over me like a tidal wave. White-hot flames seem to race through my veins as I scream out in ecstasy. Stars burst behind my eyelids as I'm swept away in the rapture of my orgasm.

I feel Andrew's body stiffen and then he thrusts deeper into me one last time before he cries out his own release.

He falls back onto the bed, his chest heaving.

"Fuck," Andrew says after a moment. "Are you safe?"

His words bring me back to the present. Shit. We didn't use protection. Again. "I'm on the pill." I've never slept with a man without protection.

"Good." He turns to face me. "I'm clean. I get checked every couple of months."

"Me too," I say. Not important for him to know that the last time I had sex was more than a year ago and I used protection.

The soft glow from the lights outside spills into Andrew's room, casting shadows on the walls. It's smaller, and cozier than mine, and I can't help but notice the difference. My room feels massive in comparison, with its high ceilings and spacious layout.

"Why did you choose the smaller bedroom?" I ask, glancing around, curious.

Andrew hesitates for a moment, then shrugs casually. "I figured you'd want the master. It's bigger, and, well, women tend to have more stuff," he says, a small, almost shy smile tugging at the corner of his lips. "It just made sense."

Warmth spreads through me. It's such a simple gesture, but it's also thoughtful. Considerate. I don't know why it touches me so much, but it does.

"You didn't have to do that," I say, my heart tightening. "But thank you."

He shrugs again. "It wasn't a big deal."

For a moment, I'm caught between wanting to keep things light, and wanting to let him know how much it meant. Instead, I just give him a small smile, hoping it conveys at least a little of what I'm feeling.

A loud scratching sound breaks the silence, and I realize it's coming from the door.

I can't help but smile. "Sounds like Bear and Bruno want in."

Andrew groans, tilting his head back against the pillow. "Tonight they're just going to have to wait for attention."

I laugh. "I love how attached they are to you."

I shift closer, propping my head on my hand, wanting to keep the conversation going. "So, did you always want dogs?"

"Not always," Andrew says. "I mean, I liked them well enough growing up, but I never thought about having one until I was in the military. We had these K-9 units, and the way those dogs worked, the bond they had with their handlers was incredible."

I listen, fascinated.

"Bear was my first, and he's been with me through a lot. Bruno came along later. Figured Bear could use a friend."

I smile, reaching out to trace patterns on the sheets between us. "It sounds like they've been good for you."

"They have," he agrees, then adds quietly, "More than they'll ever know."

His words make me curious, and I can't help but press a little further. "Why did you join the military?"

Andrew falls silent, his gaze drifting past me, as if he's looking at something far away.

For a moment, I think he's not going to answer, and I almost regret asking. "You don't have to talk about it if you don't want to," I say, hoping to give him an out.

But he shakes his head, his expression thoughtful. "No, it's okay. I guess I was at a crossroads," he begins, his voice low. "I needed to do something that was mine. Working for my father felt like I was just going through the motions. He made all the decisions, and I was just expected to fall in line. It wasn't enough for me."

I nod, understanding more than he probably realizes. "So, joining the military was a way to break free?"

"Yeah," he says, a small, almost wistful smile tugging at his lips. "It was my chance to step out of his shadow, to prove I could make my own choices, handle my own battles—literally and figuratively."

"And now?" I ask gently. "Do you think he's still the same?"

Andrew sighs, his eyes meeting mine, and there's a flicker of something vulnerability in his gaze. "No, he's different now. He's older, and I think he's starting to realize he's not going to be around forever. He's letting go, bit by bit, but it's hard for him. He's been in control for so long."

I squeeze his hand. "I'm glad you're getting the chance to prove yourself."

"Yeah, me too," he says. "I don't want to be at odds with him anymore. I want to build something—something that's ours, not just his or mine."

He's easy to talk to, and I find myself drawn to his quiet strength, the way he opens up bit by bit. When I finally drift off to sleep, I'm feeling more connected to him than ever, like we're slowly chipping away at the walls we've both built.

I wake up in the middle of the night to the sound of ragged breathing, the bed shifting beside me. My heart stutters, and I turn to see Andrew sitting bolt upright, his chest heaving, his eyes wide but unfocused, like he's seeing something far away.

"Andrew?" I whisper, my voice soft, trying not to startle him.

He doesn't respond, his gaze fixed on some invisible point in the room, his whole body tense, coiled like a spring.

I reach out, gently touching his arm. "Hey, it's okay. You're safe."

It takes a moment, but he blinks, his eyes slowly coming back into focus. He looks down at me, and for a second, there's a flicker of confusion, like he's not sure where he is.

Then he exhales, his shoulders slumping back onto the bed. “Sorry,” he mutters, rubbing a hand over his face. “I didn’t mean to wake you.”

“It’s okay,” I say, scooting closer and wrapping my arms around him.

He’s warm, but he’s trembling, like whatever he was dreaming about still has a hold on him. “Do you want to talk about it?”

“No,” he says quickly, almost too quickly. “It’s fine. Just a bad dream.”

His muscles are still taut and his heart is pounding beneath my cheek. It’s not fine, but I don’t push him.

Instead, I just hold him, running my hand up and down his back, trying to soothe him the way I’d comfort a scared child. Slowly, he starts to relax, his breathing evening out.

As his breathing steadies, I start to drift off again, but my mind is whirring, piecing together things I’ve noticed about Andrew.

The way he tenses at certain sounds, the way he always seems so tightly wound, like he’s ready to spring into action at a moment’s notice is concerning.

I’ve heard about PTSD, read a few articles here and there, and I can’t help but wonder if that’s what this situation is.

My heart aches for him. He’s been trying to hide it, but it’s clear that whatever happened to him during his time in the military still haunts him.

## Chapter 20: Andrew

"I never pegged you as the type to sneak out before your lover wakes up," I tease Emily, a smirk playing on my lips as I watch her stir her coffee.

We're having breakfast together in the kitchen, the first real breakfast we've shared in weeks. The smell of fresh-brewed coffee mingles with the aroma of eggs and toast.

Emily laughs. "Well, I'm full of surprises," she says, arching an eyebrow at me. "But seriously, I didn't want to wake you. You looked like you needed the sleep."

She grows solemn and I tense, knowing she's about to bring up what happened last night.

"Andrew, I think you need help. This is more than normal nightmares," she says.

I've heard that before, from my mother specifically but coming from Emily, it knocks the air out of my lungs.

I set my coffee cup down, my jaw tightening. "I'm handling it," I say, my voice flat, not meeting her eyes. "I don't need help, Emily."

She doesn't back down, though. "You might think you are, but last night—"

I cut her off, not wanting to hear what she has to say. "I said I'm handling it," I repeat, more forcefully this time. "I don't need you trying to fix me. This is my business, and I'd prefer if you didn't interfere."

The words come out harsher than I intended, but I don't regret saying them. I see the flicker of surprise and hurt cross her face, but she quickly masks it, sipping her coffee to hide her reaction.

The lightness that was there a moment ago is gone, replaced by a tense silence.

"Fine," Emily says quietly, setting her cup down. "I won't interfere."

A pang of guilt grips me, but I push it aside. This isn't something I'm willing to discuss, not now, not with her.

"The cleaning company is coming later this morning," I say, changing the subject. "They'll be taking care of the whole house, so if you need them to focus on anything in particular, let me know."

She nods, her eyes guarded. "Okay. But don't forget we're meeting with the interior decorators for the hotel this afternoon. We need to finalize the design elements for the lobby and guest rooms."

"Right," I say, feeling relieved to be talking about work. "I'll be there."

"I'll see you at the office," she says, her voice polite.

"See you," I reply, watching her walk out of the kitchen, her shoulders stiff.

I know I've pushed her away, but it's better this way. If she gets too close, she'll see everything I've been trying to hide, and I'm not ready for that. Maybe I never will be.

A moment later, I hear Emily murmuring to Bear and Bruno, her voice soft and affectionate as she says goodbye to them. I can't help but smile a little.

The dogs have taken to her, and I think they'd follow her anywhere if she let them.

I hear the front door close, and then the house is silent, just me and my thoughts.

I pull out my phone and scroll through my contacts until I find Owen's name. I hit call, and after a few rings, Owen answers.

"Hey, it's Andrew Bennett, Emily's husband" I say. "I'm calling about the apartment. I'd like to swing by and take a look at it myself if you're available."

"Of course, Mr. Bennett. I can meet you there in an hour," Owen says.

"Perfect. I'll see you then," I say, before ending the call.

I get up from the table and head to the back door. Bear and Bruno are already sitting there, their tails wagging in anticipation.

"Alright, guys," I say, opening the door. "Out you go." They bolt into the backyard, chasing each other around, and for a moment, I envy their carefree energy.

Once they're outside, I grab my keys and head out. The drive to Emily's apartment is quick.

When I pull up to the building, a man I assume to be Owen is already there, leaning against his car. He straightens up when he sees me and offers a polite smile.

"Morning, Mr. Bennett," he says as I step out.

"Morning," I reply, shaking his hand. "Let's take a look."

We head inside, and as I walk through the apartment, I try to see it through Emily's eyes. It's well-kept, but dated. The layout is a little cramped, the fixtures could use an upgrade, and it's clear that the place hasn't had a proper renovation in years.

Still, there's a charm to it.

"So, what's your take on the value?" I ask Owen as we finish the tour.

He runs a hand over his jaw, clearly thinking. "It's a tough market, and the area's competitive. The apartment's in good condition, but without some updates, it's going to be hard to get the price Emily's hoping for."

I nod, absorbing his assessment. "And if it were renovated?"

Owen raises an eyebrow, a spark of interest in his eyes. "If it were renovated, we'd definitely be looking at a much higher price.

"Modernize the kitchen, upgrade the bathroom fixtures, maybe even open up the living area a bit more, and you'd have something far more appealing to potential buyers. It could stand out, even in a competitive market."

I think it over, already seeing the possibilities. It's the same way I look at properties when we're working on a project—seeing beyond the flaws, picturing what it could be.

"Alright," I say finally. "Let's move forward with the renovations. I want this done right, so I'll oversee everything myself."

Owen's eyes widen slightly, but he nods. "Of course, Mr. Bennett. I'll make sure to keep you updated."

I need him to understand that he's not to bother Emily from now on. "From now on, you'll deal with me directly. I'll handle all the details, and if there's anything you need, you come to me."

"Understood. I'll start lining up the necessary contractors and suppliers. We'll get the ball rolling as soon as possible," Owen says.

"Good," I say, extending my hand. "Let's make this work."

He takes my hand, his grip firm. "We will, Mr. Bennett. I'll be in touch soon with the initial plans and cost estimates."

It feels good to know that in some way, I'm making Emily's life easier. I need to go through the budget before the meeting with the interior decorators.

As I drive to the Riviera offices, I make a mental note of what I need to do before the meeting with the decorators.

I need to go through the budget and make sure we're still on track with the timeline. There's a lot riding on this project, and now that my father has handed off my other responsibilities to someone else, I can finally give it my full attention.

I wasn't thrilled when he first pulled me from my usual projects, giving them to someone else to oversee.

It felt like he was sidelining me, like he didn't trust me to handle multiple things at once. But now, I'm glad he did. The Riviera Group needs someone dedicated, and right now, that's me.

When I step into the office building, I take a moment to collect myself before heading up to the floor where Emily's office is.

We're getting ready for a big meeting, and I need to be focused, not thinking about things I have no business thinking about.

As I walk through the halls, the familiar rhythm of the office noise greets me—phones ringing, muffled conversations, the hum of printers churning out pages.

Catherine lets Emily know that I'm here and shows me in. I want to give her an update on what we discussed with Stephen. The first thing that hits me is the smell. It's strong and overpowering, like I've just stepped into a florist's shop.

Emily's apartment and the plans I want to discuss with her fly out of my mind when I'm confronted by a room filled with flowers—bouquets everywhere.

Roses, lilies, peonies, some in vases, others still wrapped in cellophane. They're on her desk, the windowsill, even the small table by the corner.

I stop in my tracks, staring at the mess of petals and colors, and then I look at Emily, who's sitting at her desk with a sort of resigned expression. "What the hell?" I say, unable to hide my confusion. "Where did all this come from?"

She looks up, and there's a flicker of something—embarrassment, maybe—before she schools her expression. "Daniel," she says simply, her tone flat.

## Chapter 21: Emily

As soon as I tell Andrew that the flowers are from Daniel, he doesn't say a word. He just nods, his jaw clenched tight, and stalks out of my office without looking back.

Daniel's antics are starting to wear me down too. *What does he want now?* First, he calls off our wedding, then picks a fight with Andrew at my new one, and now this—flowers, like some twisted form of an apology. It's exhausting.

I turn back to my desk, trying to focus on the design samples I need to review, but my phone buzzes, lighting up with a new message. I glance at the screen and my stomach flips when I see Daniel's name.

**Morning, beautiful. I'm in town and thought you'd like to have dinner with me.**

I stare at the text, my mind reeling. What the hell? He broke off our wedding, for crying out loud. And now he wants to have dinner? I'm married to his brother, for goodness' sake. What is he playing at?

I pick up my phone and, without thinking, call Catherine. She answers almost immediately, her voice cheerful as always. "Hey, Emily. Need something?"

"Get rid of all the flowers," I say. "Every single one."

There's a pause on the other end. "All of them? What do you want me to do with them?"

I pinch the bridge of my nose, feeling a headache coming on. "I don't know or care. Give them away. Take them to a hospital, drop them at a charity—just get them out of here."

"Got it," Catherine says in a professional tone. "I'll take care of it."

"Thank you," I say, and hang up, breathing a little easier knowing that soon my office will be free of the sickening scent of the flowers.

I glance back at Daniel's text, my thumb hovering over the screen. I should just tell him off, send him a curt reply telling him to back off. But no matter how much I try to craft the perfect message, it doesn't feel right. This isn't a conversation I want to have over text.

If he's going to keep pushing, then fine. We'll have it out face to face. I quickly type a response: **Sure. Let's have dinner.** I hit send before I can change my mind.

Barely a minute later, my phone rings. I see Mom flashing on the screen and take a deep breath before answering. "Hi, Mom."

"Emily," she says, sounding more excited than she has in weeks. "Your father is looking so much better today. His color is back, and he was moving a little this morning. Emily, I think he might be coming around. The doctor said so, too."

Excited courses through me. My father might be waking up. Oh God. Emotions come over me. *Please let it be true.* I've missed him so much. Missed his leadership. Missed our conversations.

"I really hope so," I say, my voice breaking a little.

"Will you come by this evening?" she asks.

I feel bad that I have to say no but I have to deal with Daniel as swiftly as I can. "I can't tonight, Mom. I have a dinner invitation."

"Oh, that's wonderful," she says. "You and Andrew should go out and have some fun. I'm so pleased that things are working out between you two."

My stomach twists at her words, but I don't correct her. Telling her the truth—that I'm having dinner with Daniel, not Andrew—would lead to a barrage of questions and explanations that I don't have the energy for.

"Yeah," I say instead, forcing a smile she can't see. "I'll come by tomorrow, okay?"

"Of course, darling. Have a lovely evening," she says, her voice warm and full of hope. "And don't worry about your father. I think we're finally turning a corner."

I hang up the phone, feeling a mix of hope and anxiety twisting in my chest. My father might be waking up. It's the best news I've had in weeks, and yet I can't shake the nerves.

I push those thoughts aside and turn my attention back to the design samples scattered across my desk.

I scan through the color palettes, fabric swatches, and layout sketches, trying to visualize the final look. I don't want to make drastic changes; just a refresh that will bring the place up to date without losing the character that keeps guests coming back.

Warm tones, clean lines, a touch of modernity—it's not groundbreaking, but it doesn't need to be.

As I'm lost in thought, I hear the soft murmur of Catherine's voice outside my office. She knocks on the door and enters, followed my two men from the maintenance.

In no time at all, the flowers are out and hopefully, soon that nauseating smell will be too.

I check the time, realizing an hour has passed. It's time to head over to the Army Base Riviera and meet with the design team. I need to see how the samples will look in the actual space, make sure everything feels cohesive.

Gathering my things, I step out of my office and nearly bump into Andrew as he exits his. He's got that same focused expression he always wears, but there's a tightness around his eyes.

"Ready to head out?" he asks, glancing at me briefly before looking away.

"Yeah, let's go," I say, trying to sound upbeat even though I'm well aware that Daniel's flowers pissed him off. That makes two of us.

"We can take my car," he says, already moving toward the elevator.

I follow him, my heart beating a little faster. We don't talk on the way down or as we get into his car.

The silence feels heavy, and I know it's my fault. I shouldn't have pushed him to see a therapist. I was only trying to help, but maybe I overstepped.

His curt dismissal this morning hurt more than I'd like to admit, but there's no point in dwelling on it now.

We pull out of the parking garage, and I stare out the window, watching the city blur past. I want to say something, break the ice, but the words don't come.

Instead, I force myself to focus on what matters—work.

If the doctor is right, and my father is close to coming out of his coma, I want him to wake up to find everything in order, the company thriving.

I want him to see that I've been taking care of things, that I'm capable, even if everything feels like it's balancing on a knife's edge.

But then there's the matter of my marriage. What will he think when he learns I married Andrew? The thought fills me with apprehension, and I clench my hands in my lap, trying to suppress the anxiety.

One thing I'm sure of is that he'll like Andrew. They're so alike in many ways—serious, driven, but with a playfulness beneath the surface.

My dad always had a soft spot for people who could surprise him, who could match his wit and push back when needed.

*God, I miss him.* I miss our conversations, his advice, the way he'd make everything seem manageable no matter how overwhelming it was.

I need him so much right now.

As we pull up to the Army Base Riviera, the driver slows to a stop, and Andrew and I step out into the crisp afternoon air.

The design team is already gathered near the entrance, a mix of familiar faces and a few new ones.

Andrew and I exchange quick, polite nods with the team before we head inside, making our way to the boardroom. It's a stark contrast from the bustling noise of the construction going on outside.

The room is quiet, spacious, with large windows that offer a view of the base in the distance. I catch Andrew's eyes flicker toward it, and his jaw tightens slightly.

The head designer, Mila, is already setting up her materials—color swatches, fabric samples, and floor plans spread out across the long table. "Good afternoon, everyone," she says, her tone bright and professional. "We have a lot to get through, so let's jump right in."

I sit down, trying to focus, but as soon as the discussion starts, Andrew and I are already clashing.

He leans forward, his expression serious. "I still think we should lean into a more modern, minimalist design for the guest rooms. Something sleek and clean."

I shake my head, my frustration bubbling up. "I disagree. The guests at this location are mostly here for long-term stays, visiting family at the base. They want comfort, warmth, something that feels like home—not a sterile, modern space."

Andrew's eyes narrow slightly. "Emily, we can't just do the same thing over and over because it's safe. We need to set a new standard. We're trying to elevate the brand."

"And we can elevate the brand without alienating the people who actually stay here," I argue, refusing to back down. "The design needs to reflect that. We're not just building showrooms, we're creating spaces where people will live, sometimes for weeks or even months."

The room goes silent for a moment. I don't want to fight with Andrew, but I'm not going to let him bulldoze over what I know works for our guests.

Mila clears her throat, stepping in smoothly to defuse the tension. "I think you both bring up excellent points. There's a way to merge these ideas, to create a design that's both modern and inviting. We don't need to choose one over the other."

For the next hour, she takes us through her plan and explains to use contemporary furniture but to soften it with warm tones and textured fabrics.

Andrew listens carefully. I can tell he's weighing her words, and I appreciate that he's at least open to considering a compromise. "That could work," he says finally, his tone a bit more relaxed. "We could experiment with a few rooms first, see how they come together."

I nod, relieved that the conversation is moving in a more positive direction. "I like that idea. We can have a few mock-ups prepared and get feedback before we roll it out across the entire hotel."

Mila smiles, clearly pleased that she managed to bridge the gap between us. "Great. I'll have the team prepare a few design boards based on that concept, and we can review them at the next meeting."

The rest of the meeting flows much smoother after that. The team discusses fabric choices, furniture arrangements, and possible color schemes.

Andrew offers his insights, and I add mine too, and we manage to find a balance, with Mila expertly guiding us through the process.

By the time the meeting wraps up, Andrew seems more at ease.

We step outside, and Andrew grins at me, a rare lightness in his expression. "We survived that without killing each other," he says, his tone teasing.

I laugh, relief washing over me. For a moment, it feels like we've found a middle ground, and maybe things can start to feel less strained between us.

But just as I'm about to respond, a loud, sharp noise cuts through the air, reverberating from the direction of the military base.

It sounds like an explosion—a controlled one, maybe part of a drill, but the noise is sudden and jarring.

Before I can even process what's happening, Andrew suddenly flinches. His whole body stiffens, and in an instant, he's in a defensive stance, his eyes wide and alert, scanning the area.

His hands curl into fists, his breathing sharp and ragged, like he's bracing for an attack.

My heart clenches as I watch him, realization dawning on me. It's not just a reflex; this is something deeper, something raw.

I've never seen him react like this, but the way he's coiled up, ready to fight or flee, it's as if he's been transported somewhere else entirely.

"Andrew," I say softly, stepping closer, trying to bring him back. "It's okay. It was just a drill."

He doesn't respond right away. His eyes are distant, unfocused, and I can see the struggle, like he's trying to claw his way out of whatever dark place his mind has taken him.

I reach out, gently touching his arm. "Andrew," I say again, a little firmer this time. "Look at me."

His head snaps around, and when he meets my eyes, it's like a switch flips. The tension in his shoulders eases slightly, and he blinks, as if waking up from a bad dream.

"Sorry," he mutters, shaking his head, his voice rough. "I wasn't expecting that."

I don't know what to say. My chest tightens with a mix of concern and sadness, but I don't want to push him, not after this morning. "You don't have to apologize," I say softly, my hand still on his arm.

The driver brings the car around and we get in. We're both quiet on the drive back to the office, until Andrew speaks.

"Do you want to grab dinner tonight?"

For a moment, I'm tempted to say yes. I want to spend more time with him, to see if we can get back to the easy camaraderie we had earlier today. But then I agreed to dinner with Daniel.

"I can't," I say. "I have a prior engagement."

Andrew's face falls slightly, the light in his eyes dimming. "Oh." He tries to hide his disappointment. "No problem," he says with a shrug, trying to sound casual. "Another time, then."

"Yeah, another time," I echo.

## Chapter 22: Emily

"Why didn't you tell him the truth, that you were going to have dinner with Daniel and explain your reasons for that?" Lisa asks me in between yoga poses.

I'm sweaty and struggling to hold the downward dog, my mind swirling as I try to find the right words to explain my decision to Lisa.

"Because I knew how he'd react," I say. "He would have gotten mad with Daniel and I don't want to make things worse between them and us."

Lisa straightens up, shifting into a warrior pose effortlessly. "Maybe, but keeping it a secret doesn't exactly help either. You're just adding more tension."

I know she's right, but admitting that makes me feel even more tangled up. "I'm not trying to hide things," I say, switching to a different pose, my muscles protesting. "I just I don't know how to bring it up without making everything a hundred times more awkward. Andrew already has enough on his plate."

"And yet, you're still going to see Daniel," Lisa points out, her tone light but sharp. "Don't you think Andrew deserves to know why?"

I push myself up to stand, grabbing a towel to wipe the sweat off my face. "It's not like I want to have dinner with Daniel. But I need him to back off."

"Or you need closure," Lisa says, her eyes sharp, like she's seeing right through me. "Maybe that's why you're doing this. Because part of you needs to close that chapter, once and for all."

"Maybe," I admit softly. "But it doesn't change the fact that I'm married to Andrew now, and I need to handle this without causing more drama."

Lisa moves into a seated position, crossing her legs and looking at me intently. "Emily, you're overthinking this. If you're meeting Daniel to clear things up, then just be honest about it. You're not doing anything wrong."

I nod. "The plan is to make it clear to Daniel that I'm not interested." Class is almost over.

"Tell Andrew, because he needs to know. If you don't, it's just going to look worse when he finds out."

I sigh, rolling up my mat, trying to absorb her advice. "I'll think about it," I say, even though I already know she's right.

As we walk out of the studio, the late evening sun feels warm against my skin, but it does little to ease the cold knot of anxiety in my chest.

Andrew is not home and relief surges through me. I'd rather tell him about the dinner with Daniel after, not before.

The dogs rush up to me, their tails wagging, and I can't help but smile as I give them a quick pat before nudging them toward the backyard.

"Out you go," I say, watching them scramble through the door. I wait until they're outside, chasing each other around, before I head upstairs to get ready.

I take a quick shower, dry off while glancing at the clock. After rifling through my closet, I settle on a sleek, dark blue dress.

It's fitted, with clean lines and a modest neckline—elegant but not too flashy, the kind of dress you'd wear to a business meeting. Perfect. I need Daniel to see that this isn't a date, that I'm here to set boundaries, not rekindle anything.

I slip on a pair of black heels, brush out my hair, and add a touch of makeup, just enough to feel polished. A quick glance in the mirror tells me I look the part—calm, composed, completely in control. Even if I don't feel it inside.

Grabbing my purse, I head out the door, the cool evening air brushing against my skin as I make my way to the car.

The drive to the restaurant is quick, but my thoughts keep looping back to Andrew. Part of me wishes it was him I was meeting tonight, that we could sit down and have a real conversation, without the awkwardness and distance that's been hanging between us lately.

When I arrive at the restaurant, one of the trendiest spots in town, the valet takes my keys, and I make my way inside. The ambiance is elegant with low lighting and soft music that fills the space.

The hostess greets me with a smile and leads me through the dimly lit room, past tables of well-dressed couples and groups, to where Daniel is already waiting.

He stands when he sees me, a smile spreading across his face, but there's something off about him. His tie is slightly askew, and there's a faint redness around his eyes. I've seen that look before—Daniel's been drinking.

"Emily," he says warmly, stepping forward like he's going to hug me. I keep my distance, nodding politely instead.

"Hey," I say, taking the seat across from him.

He signals to the waiter, who appears almost instantly. "A bottle of your finest red, please."

"I'm fine with water," I say quickly, catching the waiter's eye. Daniel glances at me, and his smile falters just a bit.

As the waiter walks away, Daniel leans back, studying me with a lazy grin. "You look beautiful tonight."

I ignore the compliment, folding my hands in my lap. "Daniel, we need to talk."

He reaches for his glass, taking a slow sip before setting it down. "Can't we just enjoy dinner first?"

"No," I say, trying to keep my voice steady. "This isn't a social call. I'm married to Andrew. You need to stop sending flowers, stop texting, and respect that."

His eyes narrow slightly. "Married," he repeats, almost mocking. "To Andrew. And you're telling me this like it's the most natural thing in the world. You know that arrangement is just as much a business deal as ours was supposed to be."

"Maybe it started that way," I admit, "but that doesn't change the fact that I am his wife now, and you have to respect that."

He leans in, his eyes gleaming, and I catch the faint smell of alcohol on his breath. "You picked the wrong brother, Emily," he says, his voice dropping to a low murmur. "You know it, and I know it. You just got scared."

I feel my stomach twist, but I hold his gaze. "I didn't pick the wrong brother, Daniel. You called off our wedding. You made that decision, not me."

"And I made a mistake," he says, almost pleading now. "I shouldn't have let you go. I realize that now. I was scared of committing to something I didn't understand. But I know better now."

I shake my head. "Daniel, this isn't about being scared. We were never right for each other, and you know that. Our engagement was a business arrangement, just like my marriage to Andrew. But it's different now. I'm with him, and I need you to let this go."

He leans back, laughing softly, but there's no humor in it. "You think it's different? That you and Andrew have something real?" He shakes his head, his eyes darkening.

"You're fooling yourself, Emily. He doesn't care about you. All Andrew cares about is business."

His words cut through me, sharp and deep, like a knife. I feel a pang in my chest, and it takes everything in me to keep my expression neutral, to not let him see how much that hurts. Because a part of me is terrified he might be right.

I want to believe that what Andrew and I have is different, that it's more than just a business arrangement. But Daniel's words worm their way into my head, stirring up doubts.

"Maybe so, but he's my husband," I say with a nonchalance that I don't feel. The truth is that Andrew treats me with more kindness and consideration than Daniel ever did in the short time we were engaged.

Daniel's face hardens, and he leans forward, his hands clenched on the table. "I'm not giving up on you. I don't care if you're married to Andrew. By the time your arrangement is over, I'll have shown you that we could have something real, something better than this farce you're living in."

I want to laugh but it will infuriate him further. Daniel has rewritten history. He has put it into his head that we were a love match made in heaven.

The waiter arrives with the wine, pouring it into Daniel's glass, and I take a sip of my water. Alcohol must be twisting the reality in Daniel's. I need to be careful. I don't want to be the reason he goes over the edge.

He's Andrew's brother after all. He's family.

***

I walk through the front door, my mind still spinning from everything Daniel said. The house is quiet, and I head upstairs, slipping out of my dress and into a pair of comfortable leggings and a soft sweater.

I brush my hair out of my face, then wander over to the window, glancing outside. That's when I see him.

Andrew's in the backyard with Bear and Bruno, tossing a ball for them to chase. The dogs are all over the place, tails wagging furiously, tongues hanging out, pure joy radiating from them. My heart lifts at the sight.

Andrew's broad shoulders are relaxed, a rare sight lately, and there's a smile on his lips as he watches the dogs bound around him.

I head downstairs, drawn to the sound of their laughter. The moment I step outside, Andrew glances up, and our eyes lock.

My heart skips a beat. He looks so handsome in shorts and a light sweater.

"Hey," I say, stepping closer, feeling the cool evening breeze on my cheeks. "Mind if I join you?"

"Not at all," he replies, tossing the ball again.

Bear leaps after it, Bruno hot on his heels. I stand beside Andrew, watching the dogs race across the yard. For a few minutes, we just stand there in comfortable silence.

I know I need to tell him about dinner, and my stomach twists at the thought, but I don't want to keep anything from him.

"I had dinner with Daniel," I say finally, my voice steady, even though my heart is hammering. "He asked me to meet him."

Andrew doesn't say anything but his body posture stiffens. He takes the ball from Bruno's snout and tosses it again. "What did he want?"

"He thinks he can salvage what happened between us," I say to Andrew's back as he's facing away from me. I hate that I can't see his face.

"My purpose for going was to tell him directly that he needs to back off. No more flowers or text messages," I say, feeling as if I'm rambling. The speech I had rehearsed has flown out of my mind.

"He was texting you?" Andrew asks in a terse voice.

"Just today." I take a breath and continue. "I wanted to make it clear that whatever we had is over. I'm your wife now, and he needs to accept that."

Andrew is silent for a moment, then he turns to face me, stepping closer, his presence suddenly commanding. "Did you make that clear enough, or does he need to see our wedding certificate?" His tone has an edge to it, a possessiveness that sends a thrill down my spine.

He moves closer, until there's barely any space between us, his eyes dark and intense.

"I did," I say, my breath hitching as he closes the distance, his body heat mingling with the cool night air. "I made it very clear."

The air between us is charged, electric, and I can barely breathe. Andrew's gaze drops to my lips. He lifts his hand, cupping my jaw, and his thumb brushing gently over my cheek.

"Good," he murmurs, his voice low. His thumb softly traces my bottom lip, sending a wave of desire washing over me.

Thoughts of Daniel leave my mind. All I can think of is how badly I want Andrew's lips on mine.

Andrew's eyes are filled with a raw intensity. "You're mine, Emily," he says fiercely.

He slants his mouth over mine in a searing kiss, his tongue sliding into my mouth, tasting me with a hunger that matches my own. His hand pulls me closer, our bodies now pressed intimately together.

I wrap my arms around him, feeling his heart pound through his chest as we kiss.

Finally, we pull away, both panting slightly and our eyes locked in a passionate gaze.

"Let's go in," Andrew says taking my hand.

We make it as far as the kitchen. Easily lifting me up, Andrew perches me on the counter top. His hands rake over my thighs, pushing my dress higher and higher until my black lacy panties are visible.

Andrew's breath hitches as he hungrily takes in the sight before him.

"You're so beautiful," he murmurs, his voice deep and gruff with want. His fingers trace the curve of my hip, then slowly slide under the elastic of my panties, his touch sending a shockwave of desire coursing through me.

"Andrew," I groan, my body arching towards his touch.

"I need you, Emily," he growls, his eyes burning with lust.

He lifts me onto the counter, spreading my legs apart and pulling my panties aside. His fingers find their mark, and I gasp at the sensation of his touch on my most sensitive place.

He looks up at me, his eyes dark and intense. "Are you ready for me?"

I nod, unable to speak past the lust and pleasure gripping me.

Andrew wastes no time, undoing his pants and positioning himself between my thighs. With one swift movement, he pushes inside me.

I gasp at the sensation of his hardness filling me, stretching me in the most exquisite way. He moves slowly at first and I wrap my legs around him, pulling him closer, my hips rising to meet each thrust.

Our bodies move together, pleasure building up inside me until it is almost unbearable.

Andrew's thrusts become more fervent, his movements faster and deeper. I moan his name, my fingers gripping his shoulders as I draw him closer.

“That's it, Emily,” Andrew growls, his breath hot on my cheek. “Take me.”

My release builds up, the pleasure intensifying with each thrusts. I cry out as the climax crashes over me, my body shuddering with the force of it.

Andrew's face contorts with pleasure, his eyes squeezed shut as he pushes even deeper inside me. With a final thrust, he cries out my name, his release filling me completely.

We collapse against each other, panting and sweating.

## Chapter 23: Andrew

The bar is buzzing with the low hum of conversation, clinking glasses, and the occasional burst of laughter. The smell of grilled steak and freshly fried fries mingles with the faint scent of beer.

Jack and I are sitting in a corner booth, plates in front of us loaded with thick, juicy steaks and cold beers within reach.

Jack cuts into his steak, his knife gliding smoothly through the meat. "So, I've been thinking," he starts, his tone casual but his eyes serious. "About starting my own personal protection outfit."

I look up, surprised but interested. "Yeah? You thinking of leaving the company?"

"Not right away," he says, taking a bite and chewing thoughtfully. "But a lot of the guys we knew from the military are struggling to find stable work. I've got a few who've reached out, looking for gigs. I was thinking I could make a go of it—start something small, just a handful of guys, and see how it goes."

I take a sip of my beer, nodding. "Sounds solid. You've got the skills, and you know what to look for in a good team. It could work."

Jack leans back in his chair, looking relieved. "I needed to hear that. I wasn't sure if it was a crazy idea or not."

"It's not," I say, cutting into my own steak. "And if you need contacts, I've got a few I can introduce you to. Might be able to help you get off the ground."

"Man, I appreciate that," Jack says, raising his beer in a toast. "I owe you one."

We eat in comfortable silence for a few moments, the sounds of the bar filling the space around us. Jack studies me for a moment, then grins. "You know, I've never seen you look this relaxed."

I chuckle, shaking my head. "Yeah, apart from those dreaded episodes."

Jack's expression changes, his brow furrowing. "Still getting them?"

"Yeah," I admit, setting down my fork. "Emily suggested I go for therapy. I've been considering it."

Jack nods slowly. "You should. I did it myself, after I left. It helped a lot more than I thought it would. I can refer you to someone if you want."

I hadn't realized Jack had gone through that. "Yeah, I'd appreciate that. I'll give it a shot."

He leans forward, pointing his knife at me with a grin. "Emily's good for you, man. You seem different. In a good way."

I think about it for a second, then nod. "Yeah, she is. I've never felt this in tune and comfortable with a woman before. Except I don't feel like we really know each other. Not really."

Jack shrugs, like it's the simplest thing in the world. "Then get to know her. Take her out for dinner. Go on dates. And maybe stay off her bed while you do so," he adds with a wink.

I laugh, but the idea sticks. He's right. I want to know Emily, beyond just what we've shared so far. I pull out my phone and, almost without thinking, shoot her a text: **Dinner tomorrow night?**

The reply comes almost immediately, a laughing emoji followed by, **You could have asked me at home, but yes, I'd love to.**

I smile at my screen. Jack was right. I want to get to know Emily without the complication of sleeping together. Maybe this could be the start of something more, something real.

"So," Jack says, "How's it been, working with Emily?"

I can't help but grin. "Exasperating. She drives me nuts half the time, but she's brilliant at what she does."

Jack chuckles, raising an eyebrow. "Sounds like she's got you on your toes."

"She does," I admit, taking a sip of my beer. "But it's good. Keeps things interesting."

"Speaking of brilliant," Jack says, a twinkle in his eyes, "Sarah and I are expecting."

I blink, caught off guard. "Wait, what?"

"Sarah's pregnant. Seven months along," he says, his grin widening. "I'm going to be a dad."

I reach over to clap him on the shoulder. "Jack, that's amazing, congratulations, man."

"Thanks," he says, beaming. "We're both over the moon about it. She keeps asking when you're going to come over for lunch or something. I've told her you're a busy man, but she doesn't let up."

A pang of guilt comes over me. It's been a while since I've made time to see Jack and Sarah outside of work or these bar nights. "I'll come by soon. I promise."

"You better," he says, his tone mock-stern. "Because you're going to be the godfather, and I suggest you start acting like one."

For a moment, I'm at a loss for words. "Me? The godfather?"

Jack nods. "Yeah. I can't think of anyone else I'd want. You've been like a brother to me for years, and I want our kid to have someone solid to look up to."

I'm touched, more than I can put into words. I reach out, and we do a quick, firm handshake that says more than any words could. "I'm honored, Jack. Really."

"Good," he says, picking up his beer and lifting it in a toast. "To godfathers, babies, and brilliant, exasperating women."

I laugh, clinking my glass against his. "To all of that. And to you, Dad."

We stay in the bar for a couple of hours, then I head home.

I unlock the door and step into the apartment, the scent of home washing over me. Since Emily moved in, it feels more like home and her feminine scent are everywhere.

Emily's in the kitchen, leaning against the counter, sipping a cup of tea. She's wearing one of those casual tank tops and shorts that make my dick stir. For a moment, I just stand there, taking her in, before she notices me.

"Hey," she says, smiling as she puts down her cup. "You're back. How was dinner with Jack?"

I walk over and drop my keys on the counter, then lean against it, facing her. "It was good. Steak, beer, and a lot of catching up. He had some exciting news, actually."

"Oh?" Her eyes light up with curiosity. "What's that?"

"Jack and Sarah are expecting. Seven months along." I can't help but smile as I say it. "He's going to be a dad."

She smiles. "That's amazing. I'm so happy for them."

"Yeah, and he asked me to be the godfather," I add, trying to sound casual, but I can't hide the pride that sneaks into my voice.

Emily steps closer. "I can't think of anyone better for the job."

Her words make me feel ten feet tall. There's something about the way she looks at me, like she truly believes in me, that makes me want to pull her in and kiss her senseless.

I want to take her to bed and forget the world for a few hours, just us, tangled up in each other. But I remember the promise I made to myself earlier tonight. I need to do this right. I want to know her, truly know her, without rushing things.

"Thanks," I say, my voice.

"I'd love to meet them," Emily says.

I blink, a little surprised. "Really?"

"Yeah, they sound wonderful, and they mean a lot to you," she says, giving me that smile that makes my heart skip a beat. "I'd love to see that part of your life."

"Okay," I say, grinning. "I'll make it happen. Sarah will be pleased, trust me."

I step closer, my hand reaching out to brush a stray hair behind her ear. God, she's so beautiful, and it's taking every ounce of willpower not to just pull her into my arms.

I lean in and kiss her on the cheek, a slow, deliberate kiss, close to the corner of her mouth.

"Good night, Em," I murmur against her skin before pulling back.

Her eyes search mine, a flicker of confusion in them. "Good night, Andrew."

I step back, forcing myself to turn away from her. Every part of me wants to stay, to cross that line, but I have to do this the right way. I head towards the bedroom, my fists clenching and unclenching as I fight the urge to change my mind.

God, if only she knew how much it's taking me to walk away, to go to bed alone. But I want this to last, and for that, I need to slow down, no matter how much it drives me crazy.

## Chapter 24: Emily

I glance at the clock on the wall, trying to keep my focus on Anita's presentation. It's almost five, and my mind is already half out the door, eager to get home and prepare for my date with Andrew.

Anita, the head of marketing, is in full swing, going over the revamped social media strategy for the Army Base Riviera launch.

She's animated, her hands moving as she talks about engagement rates, targeted ads, and influencer partnerships. It's exciting to see how everything's coming together.

The renovations are almost complete, and the project feels like it's finally falling into place.

"The new social media layout has been a hit," Anita says, flipping to the next slide on the screen."

"We've seen a 30% increase in engagement, and the influencers we've partnered with are pushing the brand exactly how we hoped. We're all set for the pre-launch campaign next week."

I nod, trying to hide my impatience. "That's great, Anita. Let's make sure we have everything locked down by Monday so we can focus on the final touches for the launch. We're almost there."

Anita beams, clearly proud of her team's efforts. "Absolutely, Emily. I'll send you a detailed update by the end of the day."

"Perfect." I stand, gathering the papers on the conference table. "Thanks for all the hard work. I'll see you on Monday."

Anita gathers her things, and as she heads out the door, she pauses and gives me a knowing smile. "Have a great evening, Emily."

My face heats up. Am I that obvious? "Thanks."

The door shuts behind her and I quickly organize my desk so I can head out. My phone buzzes, and I see Andrew's mom's name flash on the screen. My stomach tightens a bit, and I almost consider letting it go to voicemail.

Taking a breath, I swipe to answer. "Hello, Mrs. Bennett," I say, trying to sound as cheerful as possible.

"Hello Emily, I'm so glad I caught you. How are you, dear?" she says, her voice bubbling with enthusiasm.

"I'm good, thank you. How are you?" I reply.

"I'm doing well, thank you. Listen, I was thinking it's been ages since we've had a proper chat. I'd love it if we could do a girls' lunch next week. Just the two of us. How does that sound?"

I hesitate, unsure of what to say. As much as I appreciate Barbara's friendliness, it worries me. What will happen when you and Andrew part ways.

*What if this thing with Andrew develops into something more? Something permanent.*

The thought brings on a wave of dizziness. I can't think like that now. I can't afford to fall for him.

*You already have.*

I push away that frightening thought.

"Emily?" Barbara asks in a soft voice, bringing me back to the present.

I inhale deeply and smile, then realize that she can't see my face. "That sounds lovely," I say. "When were you thinking?"

"How about next Wednesday? I'll pick a nice place. It'll be my treat," Barbara says.

"Okay, Wednesday works. I'll see you then."

"Oh, wonderful! I'm so excited, Emily. Have a great weekend, dear."

"You too, Barbara. Bye."

I really need to get going if I'm to have enough time to get ready for the date with my husband. It feels nice saying that. My husband.

***

I stand in front of my mirror applying the last touches of mascara. It's been a while since I felt this way—nervous, excited, and eager all at once.

Tonight feels different. Andrew and I have been spending time together, sure, but this is a real date. I want to look perfect.

I take a step back and assess my reflection. My dress is a deep shade of blue, hugging my body in all the right places. It's elegant but understated, something I hope he'll like.

I've spent way more time on my makeup than usual—soft smoky eyes, a touch of blush, and a nude lip. My hair is styled in loose waves, cascading over my shoulders.

I smooth down the front of my dress, my heart beating a little faster as a knock comes on my bedroom door.

"You look beautiful," Andrew says the moment I open the door, his eyes taking me in with an appreciative gleam.

A rush of pleasure swamps me, warming my cheeks. "Thank you," I manage to say, my voice a little breathless. "You don't look too bad yourself."

He's wearing a dark suit, tailored perfectly to his lean, muscular frame. The white shirt underneath is crisp, and there's a hint of cologne that fills the space between us.

For a moment, I forget to breathe. He looks incredible. The suit jacket molds to his broad shoulders, and the dark fabric makes his blue eyes stand out even more.

He smiles, that slow, easy smile that always makes my heart skip. "Ready?"

I nod, grabbing my clutch. "Let's go."

We talk about our day as we drive to the restaurant.

"No more work talk," Andrew says when he parks the car.

"I agree," I say intrigued at what his plans are for the evening.

The restaurant is beautiful, all soft lighting, plush chairs, and elegant décor. The host leads us to a table by the window, and

Andrew pulls out my chair for me, a gesture that's both gentlemanly and a little old-fashioned. I love it.

Once we've ordered a bottle of wine, the conversation flows easily. Over time, it grows more personal.

"So, how were you in school?" Andrew asks, swirling his wine glass, his eyes fixed on mine. "Were you the popular girl, or the bookworm?"

I laugh, thinking back. "A little of both, actually. I was friendly, but I didn't like being the center of attention. What about you?"

"I was studious," Andrew says with a cute grin. "Daniel was the one who got all the attention. But I liked it that way. It gave me space."

There's a moment of silence, a comfortable one before I ask. "Did you and Daniel get along?" They are so different. It's hard to believe that they come from the same set of parents.

"For the most part. He's the typical younger brother—annoying at times but sweet when it matters." I tilt my head. "What about you? Growing up as an only child, did you ever wish you had a sibling?" Andrew asks me.

I take a moment to think about how honest I want to be. The wine and the atmosphere has loosened my inhibitions and I decide to be honest.

"I wanted a sibling so badly when I was younger. I remember asking my mom, and she finally told me the truth. She was unable to have more kids after me." I shrug. "I moved on after that, as kids do."

"I guess it's never enough," Andrew says with a laugh. "I wanted a sister and I guess my mother longed for a daughter judging by the way she's taken to you."

"Speaking of which, she called me before I left the office and we agreed to have lunch next week."

Andrew's face lights up, then a frown follows in quick succession. "I hope it's not a bother. She can come on too strong sometimes."

Guilt bubbles up inside my chest when I remember how hesitant I had been. "It's no trouble at all."

Relief etches itself on his features. "Just let me know when she's too much. I'll tell her to back off."

I laugh and wave a dismissal hand in the air. "I'll be okay. She's a wonderful woman and I look forward to getting to know her better."

He smiles as if I've just offered him the world.

"Do you want a family in the future?" I ask after a moment.

The question slips out before I can stop myself, and I quickly add, "I don't mean with me, but when you actually get married for real."

"Honestly?" Andrew says. "I never thought I did. I was always focused on my career, on getting things done, and kids just didn't seem to fit into that plan. But now I think I might want to. Someday."

My heart flutters at his words, and I try to keep my tone casual. "I think you'd make a great dad."

He raises an eyebrow. "Yeah?"

"Yeah," I say, smiling. "Judging by how you treat Bruno and Bear. You're patient."

"Well, I'm working on that patience part," he says with a laugh.

An image forms in my mind. "I can just picture you teaching your kids how to ride a bike or helping them with their homework."

Andrew chuckles. "Well, that's a nice thought. What about you? Do you see yourself with a family in the future?"

"I'd like to," I say, nodding. "I've always wanted a family of my own. But it has to be with the right person. Someone who really gets me."

Andrew's gaze is intense when he says, "Yeah. I get that."

The server arrives at our table, breaking the moment, and she places two plates in front of us.

The aromas of our meals fill the air. Andrew's seared salmon with a light, lemony sauce and roasted vegetables, and my perfectly cooked filet mignon.

"Bon appétit," the server says, smiling at us before stepping away.

We dig into our meals, and for a few minutes, the conversation quiets as we savor the food. I didn't realize how hungry I was until I take the first bite, and everything melts in my mouth.

"So," Andrew says after a while. "Thanks to you, I've made an appointment with a therapist that Jack recommended."

I blink in surprise. "Really?" I grin, unable to believe that the Andrew who was so adamant that he was fine has finally accepted that he has a problem. "That's great."

"We'll see how it goes," he says.

As we eat, the conversation flows easily, moving from lighter topics to more personal ones. Andrew makes me laugh with stories of the antics that Daniel got up to when they were kids.

I'm struck by how carefree he looks, how relaxed. It's a side of him I don't see often, and it makes me wish for more moments like these.

On the way home, I can't stop replaying snippets of our dinner conversation, the way Andrew's eyes softened when he talked about his family, the way he laughed at my silly stories. It felt so natural, so right.

Inside, I kick off my heels, feeling the plush carpet under my feet. I turn to Andrew, a smile on my lips, but before I can say a word, he steps closer, catching me off guard.

He cups my face gently in his hands and leans down, kissing me.

My heart races, and I kiss him back, letting myself get lost in the moment. But just when I think he's about to deepen the kiss, he pulls away, his eyes searching mine.

"Good night, Emily," he says, his voice low. Then he turns and heads upstairs, leaving me standing there, bewildered.

I'm still for a moment, trying to process what just happened. *Good night?* That's it? After the night we've had, after that kiss?

I head upstairs, trying to shake off the disappointment.

Maybe he was just tired. Maybe I'm reading too much into everything.

I crawl into bed, pulling the covers up to my chin, and stare at the ceiling, replaying the night over and over. I thought we were moving toward something more, but now I don't know what to think.

## Chapter 25: Andrew

It's a Saturday afternoon, and Emily and I are just leaving the Army Base Riviera. I'm behind the wheel, and as we pull out of the parking lot, I catch a glimpse of the hotel in the rearview mirror.

It's slowly coming together, room by room.

We're headed to Jack and Susan's place. They've got a house out in the suburbs, with a backyard big enough for cookouts.

I haven't been there in a while, and I'm actually looking forward to it. Jack's one of the few people who doesn't treat me like I'm about to explode, and Susan is family, even if she isn't mine by blood.

As we hit the main road, Emily's voice breaks through my thoughts. "Can we make a quick stop?" she asks, glancing at me from the passenger seat. "I want to pick up something for Jack and Susan. A little gift."

I'm a bit surprised. "You don't have to do that," I say, glancing over at her. "They're just happy to have us over."

"I know," she says, her lips curving into a small smile. "But I want to. It's just polite."

It's a simple gesture, but it catches me off guard, makes me feel, something. She doesn't have to do it, but she wants to.

I try to focus on driving, but my mind drifts back to last night. It had been rough, one of the worst since we'd moved into the same house.

All I could think about was Emily in the next room, and how much I wanted to be close to her. I'd even gotten out of bed, made it all the way to her door, but then I'd stopped.

Stood there like an idiot, staring at the doorknob, giving myself a pep talk. I'd reminded myself that we needed to figure out who we were to each other, without just jumping back into bed.

We needed to get to know each other without intimacy clouding everything. So, I'd turned around and forced myself back to bed, but sleep had been elusive.

"Alright," I say, changing lanes so I can pull off at the next exit. "Let's make a quick stop."

We find a small, local shop just off the main road. It's the kind of place that sells everything from fresh flowers to gourmet jams, and as soon as we step inside, I'm hit by the warm, rich scent of freshly brewed coffee.

The place is well stocked and Emily's eyes light up as she looks around.

I trail behind her as she selects handmade soap, a small bouquet of wildflowers, and a box of artisanal chocolates.

"Those are perfect," I say, and I mean it. "You've got a good eye."

She looks over at me and smiles. "Thanks. I just thought it'd be nice to bring something."

We pay for the items and head back to the car.

As we get back on the road, I can't keep my gaze from Emily. She's watching the scenery pass by, her fingers playing absentmindedly with the ribbon on the flower bouquet. I'd give anything to know what is on her mind.

We get to Jack and Susan's neighborhood. The houses are spaced out, each with a decent yard, the kind of place where you can actually breathe. We pull up to their place, and Jack's already out on the porch, waving as we park.

"Good to see you two," he calls out, grinning as we step out of the car. "It's been too long."

"Yeah, it has," I say, walking over to shake his hand. "Hope we're not too late."

"Not at all," Jack says, clapping me on the shoulder. "Susan's just got the salads ready."

Emily holds out the little gift bag. "We brought a few things," she says, her voice warm, and Jack's smile widens.

"Well, aren't you two sweet?" Jack says, taking the bag. "Susan's gonna love this. Come on in, make yourselves at home."

We follow Jack through the house, passing through the kitchen and out to the backyard, where Sarah is busy setting out a spread of salads, bread rolls, and other accompaniments on a long wooden table.

The scent of freshly cut herbs and grilled meat wafts through the air, making my stomach rumble. It feels like home, and it hits me how much I've missed this—just relaxing, no meetings, no renovations, just being with friends.

Sarah looks up as we step outside, and her face lights up.

"Andrew." She wipes her hands on a dish towel before walking over to give me a hug. She pulls back, holding my arms, and looks me over with a smile. "It's been too long. You look good."

I smile back, giving her a quick squeeze. "You too, Sarah." I glance at Emily, who's standing just behind me. "This is Emily," I say, putting a hand on her back, gently guiding her forward. "My wife."

Sarah smiles at Emily. "It's so nice to finally meet you."

Emily smiles warmly, extending her hand. "It's great to meet you too, Sarah. I've heard a lot about you."

"Oh, I hope all good things." Sarah laughs, shaking Emily's hand before pulling her into a quick, friendly hug. "Come on, sit down, make yourselves comfortable."

As we settle into the backyard, Jack heads over to the grill, checking on the steaks. I turn to Sarah. "Jack told me the news," I say. "Congratulations."

Sarah's cheeks flush slightly, but she's grinning. "Thank you," she says, glancing over at Jack, who catches her eye and grins back. "We weren't exactly planning on it, but we're expecting."

"That's amazing," Emily says, her face lighting up. "Congratulations! Do you know if it's a boy or a girl?"

"Not yet," Sarah replies, her hand going to her stomach. "We'll find out at the next appointment, but honestly, we're just excited either way. It's still early, but we couldn't keep it to ourselves any longer."

Jack chimes in from the grill, his tone light. "We're already debating names, which has been an interesting exercise." He winks at Sarah, who laughs and shakes her head.

"We are not naming the baby after your favorite hockey player," she says, rolling her eyes.

We all laugh. I can't help but envy what Jack and Susan have. The kind of effortless, easy love that comes from truly knowing someone, from being completely comfortable together.

I glance over at Emily, who's laughing at something Sarah just said. The sound of it, the way her eyes crinkle at the corners, does something to me.

I wonder if she could be that special person for me, the way Sarah is for Jack. It's a thought I've been pushing away, but it keeps coming back, stronger each time.

Before I can delve any deeper into my own thoughts, Jack calls out, "Alright, everyone, food's ready. Let's eat."

It's a nice afternoon and evening and by the time it's over, Emily looks relaxed and so do I.

The evening ends with hugs and warm goodbyes, Emily and Sarah exchanging numbers and promising to stay in touch.

I watch them, a bit amazed at how easily they've connected, like they've known each other for years instead of just for a few hours.

Emily settles into the passenger seat, her face still glowing from the laughter and conversation of the evening.

As I drive, she turns to me, a smile tugging at her lips. "That was such a great evening, don't you think?"

I nod, glancing over at her briefly. "Yeah, it was," I say, my voice quieter than usual. "Sarah and Jack are good people."

She nods, gazing out the window, her fingers absentmindedly tracing patterns on her lap.

We lapse into a comfortable silence for the rest of the drive, but as we pull into the driveway and I turn off the engine, I don't get out.

Instead, I sit there, gripping the steering wheel, trying to figure out how to say what's on my mind.

Emily turns to me, her expression curious. "Andrew?"

I take a breath, my heart pounding a little harder than it should. "Seeing Jack and Sarah tonight, how they are together, it made me think about us. About our marriage."

Her eyes widen slightly, and I can see her brace herself, as if she's not sure where this conversation will lead. "What do you mean?" she asks.

"They're so comfortable with each other. So natural," I say, feeling as if I'm fumbling for the right words. "And it made me realize that with time, I want the same thing for us."

I can't look at her as I say it because it feels too raw, too vulnerable, like I'm setting myself up to be hurt. But I force myself to continue. "I guess what I'm trying to say is, I want us to get to know each other. Really know each other."

There's a pause, and I can feel her eyes on me, studying me, trying to read between the lines. "Why haven't you wanted to, you know, get intimate with me?" she asks, her voice hesitant.

I turn to look at her. She's so damn beautiful. "It's not that I don't want to. Sometimes I can't sleep for wanting you. Knowing you're in the next room drives me crazy."

Her eyes widen with surprise and her lips part slightly.

"But I don't want to rush this. I don't want us to fall into something just because it's easy or because it's expected. I want to get to know you, really know you, without the distraction."

She's silent for a moment, and I'm half-expecting her to tell me I'm overthinking it, or that I'm making things more complicated than they need to be.

But instead, she nods. "You're right. I think sleeping together would be a distraction right now. I want this to work too, Andrew. I want us to figure out what this could be."

## Chapter 26: Emily

"I'll miss you," Andrew whispers into my ear, then trails kisses down my jawline. I giggle, trying to pull back but not really wanting to.

"It's just lunch," I say, but my words come out breathless. His lips are warm and soft, and his hands on my waist make it hard to think straight.

"Lunch without you," he murmurs, nipping at my earlobe. "That's like torture."

I laugh and finally manage to push him away, just enough to see his face. He's got that playful grin, the one that always makes my heart skip a beat. "You're ridiculous."

"Yeah, for my wife," he says, and the way he says it, so casually and confidently, makes my cheeks flush. He's been saying things like that more often, and every time, it sends a thrill through me.

"Well, try not to starve while I'm gone," I tease, patting his chest. "I'll be back before you know it."

"Not soon enough," he says, but he finally lets me go, his hands lingering on my waist for a moment longer.

I step back, smoothing down my dress and trying to compose myself. It's getting harder to leave him lately. The more time we spend together, the more I don't want to be apart.

"Alright, I'm really going now," I say, grabbing my purse from his desk. "I don't want to keep your mom waiting."

I find myself sashaying as I walk to the door and when I look over my shoulder, I'm rewarded by Andrew's heated gaze on me.

The last few days have been like a honeymoon. A belated honeymoon. We've been all over each other at work and at home. I'm falling in love with Andrew.

I leave the office and head to my car in the basement with a smile.

I slide into the driver's seat, already planning my afternoon. Before I turn on the ignition, I call Owen. He picks up on the second ring.

"Hey, Emily," he says, his voice bright. "I was just about to call you. I've got some news."

"Good news, I hope?" I ask, crossing my fingers. If he's finally found a buyer willing to meet my asking price, it would be one less thing to worry about.

"We'll talk when we meet later," he replies, a hint of mystery in his tone. "Can you swing by the apartment this afternoon?"

"Of course," I say, a smile spreading across my face. "I'll be there after lunch."

"Great. See you then."

I hang up, my spirits lifted. Maybe things are finally falling into place. I turn the key in the ignition and head out, making my way to the restaurant where I'm meeting Barbara.

When I walk into the restaurant, Barbara is already there, seated at a table by the window. She waves at me, a warm smile lighting up her face, and I make my way over.

"Emily, darling," she says, standing up to give me a hug. "It's so good to see you."

"You too, Barbara," I say, returning the hug. "Thank you for inviting me."

I sit down and the server comes over to talk my order for a drink. I glance at Barbara's water and order the same.

"I'm so excited that we're doing this," she says, leaning across the table.

"Me too," I echo, her joy infectious.

"How are your parents?" she asks. "Have you heard from your father?"

The server brings my water and I take a large sip before answering. This is one of the reasons I have preferred to stay away from Barbara.

"They're okay," I say hoping it's the end of the questions. I hate that I'm lying to this woman who only wants to get to know her son's wife.

"Your father must be enjoying his travels," she continues.

"He is," I say. Resentment comes over me. My father should not have made a promise that would turn into a lie. A lie that could destroy what me and Andrew and I are trying to build.

The only saving grace will be him waking up from that coma. Each day, Dad's doctor assures us that it will happen any time. But time is running out. I'm digging myself more into a hole every day that he doesn't wake up.

The server hands us each a menu and I peruse it, glad to have something else to focus upon.

"So, you and Andrew," Barbara says after we've given our order. She reaches across the table and takes my hand. "I've never seen him so happy."

Her words warm me. It feels good to know that other people are seeing it. I'm happy too. Happier than I've ever been.

Barbara squeezes my hand and pulls away, her face taking on a faraway expression. "It reminds me of how he was as a little boy. Always so serious, even as a toddler. But when he smiled, it could light up a room."

I smile, picturing Andrew as a little boy. "I can definitely see that. He still has that serious look, but when he smiles..."

Barbara nods enthusiastically. "He's always been that way. But after he came back from his tour, he was different. Lost. We were all so worried about him."

A pang comes over me. "He's been through a lot."

Barbara takes a sip of her drink, then looks at me with an intensity that makes me sit up straighter. "But lately, he seems happier. Like he's found himself again. And I know you have a lot to do with it."

I'm caught off guard, not sure what to say. "Actually, he's started going to therapy," I say, deciding to be honest. "It was something he chose to do recently."

Barbara's eyes widen in surprise, and then they soften. "Therapy? Really?"

"Yes," I say, nodding. "He's taking it seriously."

She reaches across the table and takes my hand, her eyes glistening. "Thank you, Emily."

"For what?" I ask, genuinely confused.

"For helping my son," she says, her voice choked with emotion. "I know Andrew. He wouldn't have agreed to this unless you encouraged him."

I shake my head, trying to deflect the credit. "I didn't do anything, really. He made the decision on his own."

Barbara squeezes my hand, her grip firm. "You're good for him. I'm hoping that this marriage can be something more, and now I'm confident that it will."

Warmth spreads through me, and for once, I don't try to push it away. "Me too," I admit, the words slipping out before I can stop them.

She beams at me. "I'm so glad to hear that. And I hope to see you at the family dinner on Sunday."

"I'd love to be there," I say, my heart lighter than it's been in a while.

We finish our lunch, talking and laughing, and for once, I feel like I truly belong in this family.

As I leave the restaurant and head towards my old apartment, I can't help but think that Andrew and I do have a future together. Not just the one year stated in the contract.

I pull into the parking lot of my apartment building and spot Owen, leaning against the entrance.

"Hey, Emily," he calls, waving me over. "I was wondering when you'd get here."

"Sorry, I'm a little late," I say. "I had a lunch date with my mother-in-law." The words still sound strange coming out of my mouth, but they feel good.

Owen grins. "Hope you had fun."

"I did," I say, meaning it. "So, what's this news you've got for me?"

"Come inside. You'll want to see it for yourself," he says, pushing off the wall and leading the way into the building.

I follow him, my curiosity piqued. When we reach my apartment, he unlocks the door and gestures for me to go in first. The moment I step inside, I freeze.

The apartment is completely transformed. The tired old carpet has been replaced with sleek hardwood floors, the dingy walls are now painted a soft, inviting cream, and the kitchen is unrecognizable.

It looks like something straight out of a design magazine, with gleaming countertops, modern cabinets, and stainless steel appliances.

"What happened here?" I ask, my voice barely above a whisper as I take it all in. It's like walking into a completely new space.

Owen's grin widens. "I've been working with your husband. Mr. Bennett gave me firm instructions not to bother you and to deal with him. This is what we've done so far.

"Emily, we already have people asking when it will be ready. I predict a bidding war," he says with a chuckle. "Come on, I'll show you around."

For a moment, I just stand there, stunned. Andrew did this? With his money? Without consulting me? How dare he make such huge decisions without consulting me?

My shock quickly gives way to a simmering anger, but I force a smile for Owen's sake as he starts showing me around, explaining all the improvements.

"We had the bathroom redone, too," he says, leading me down the hallway. "New tiles, new fixtures. It's practically spa-like now."

I nod absently, hardly hearing him. My mind is spinning, trying to process how Andrew could make such a big decision behind my back. This is my apartment, my investment.

How could he not think that I'd want to be involved?

Owen continues his tour, showing me the upgraded bedrooms and the new lighting fixtures, but I barely pay attention. All I can think about is getting out of here so I can have it out with Andrew.

By the time Owen wraps up, I've managed to keep my cool, but just barely. "Thank you for showing me everything, Owen. I appreciate it," I say, my voice tight.

"No problem, Emily. Honestly, I think this place is going to sell in no time. Your husband really did a great job organizing everything."

I nod, forcing another smile. "I'll be in touch."

As soon as I get back into my car, I grip the steering wheel so hard my knuckles turn white. How could Andrew do this? Did he think I wasn't capable of handling it myself?

My phone rings jerking me out of my thoughts. Lisa's name pops up on the screen, and I answer, putting her on speaker.

"Hey, what's up?" she asks.

"I'm too angry to talk right now," I snap, my voice sharp.

"Whoa, what happened?" she asks.

I take a deep breath, trying to rein in my frustration. "Andrew had the apartment renovated without telling me. Apparently, he's been working with Owen this whole time, making all these decisions without even consulting me."

"That's a big deal," Lisa says carefully. "But I'm guessing his heart was in the right place."

"I don't care where his heart was," I say, my voice rising. "He had no right to do that. It's my apartment, my decision. How could he just take over like that?"

"I get why you're upset," Lisa says gently. "But maybe give him a chance to explain. It sounds like he was trying to help."

"I don't want his help," I mutter, but even I can hear how childish it sounds. "I can handle my own life."

"Em, just talk to him. It's not worth starting a war over."

"Fine," I say, but I don't mean it. I'm too angry to be rational right now, and all I want to do is confront Andrew. I end the call with Lisa, my head pounding as I drive home.

When I finally walk through the door of the house, Andrew is there, sitting on the couch with a casual smile on his face. The sight of him only makes me angrier.

"Hey, you're back early," he says, looking up at me. "How was lunch with my mom?"

I ignore his question. "You went behind my back," I say, my voice shaking with barely contained fury.

Andrew's smile fades, replaced by a look of confusion. "What are you talking about?"

"The apartment," I snap. "You had it renovated without even telling me. Do you have any idea how disrespectful that is?"

He gets up, his brow furrowing. "Emily, I was just trying to help—"

"I didn't ask for your help," I interrupt, my voice rising. "That's my property, my investment, and you had no right to make decisions without me."

"Hey, calm down. I actually thought you would be happy that someone had taken it off your plate," he says, his tone defensive. "I know you've been stressed about selling it, and I wanted to make it easier for you."

"I didn't ask you to," I say between gritted teeth. "You can't just take over someone's life under the pretext of helping. Just because we're married doesn't mean you get to control me."

His eyes widen. "Control? Is that how you see it?" He doesn't wait for me to answer and instead, turns and stalks out.

Bear and Bruno stare at me for a while and then follow Andrew up the stairs.

## Chapter 27: Andrew

"It's a good location," I say, glancing around the space. It's spacious, with high ceilings and lots of natural light streaming through the large windows. I can see why Jack is interested.

"And the rent is good," Jack says.

I look over at him, and the idea that's been sitting in the back of my mind all week pushes forward. "I've been giving it some thought, and if you need an influx of capital, I'd be happy to come in as an investor."

Jack blinks, clearly caught off guard. "Really?"

"Yeah," I say, shrugging. "You've got a solid plan here, and I believe in you. Besides, it's a smart investment."

Jack's face softens, and for a moment, he looks like he's struggling to find the right words. "Thanks, man. That means a lot. I'll take you up on that offer. Actually, Sarah told me I should ask you, but I didn't want to overstep or put you in a spot."

"We're friends," I say, clapping him on the back. "You could have asked."

"Thanks, Andrew," Jack says, and I can see he's genuinely moved.

I take a breath, deciding this is as good a time as any. "Listen, I need to run something by you."

"Sure, what's up?" Jack says, giving me his full attention.

"It's about Emily," I begin, and just saying her name out loud makes my chest tighten. "I did something that I thought was the right thing, but it backfired on me."

Jack's eyebrows raise slightly, but he waits for me to continue.

"I had her apartment renovated," I say. "She's trying to sell it and it wasn't moving, so I figured sprucing it up would help. I worked with her realtor and made sure everything was handled properly. I thought she'd be happy, but she was pissed."

I've never seen Emily so angry. But then I was angry too. I'd been expecting hugs and gratitude, instead, I got an angry tiger.

Jack winces, like he's feeling the sting for me. "Yeah, I can see how that might not go over well."

"I don't get it," I say, frustration creeping into my voice. "I was trying to make things easier for her, and instead, she accused me of going behind her back. Apparently I disrespected her by not consulting her."

Jack rubs the back of his neck. "I can understand why you thought it was a good idea. You were just trying to help, right? But I can also see why she would be upset. It's her property. Even if your intentions were good, she probably feels like you took over."

"That's exactly what she said," I admit. "And now, things are weird between us. I hate this."

Jack studies me for a moment. "Have you talked to her since?"

"No, not really," I reply. "We had a blowout, and I walked away. I don't know how to fix it."

"Well," Jack says, leaning against the wall, "You could start by apologizing. Not for helping, but for not including her in the process. Make it clear that you didn't mean to undermine her, but you see now how it might have come across that way."

I sigh. "Yeah, I guess I could have handled it better. But I just wanted to take something off her plate, you know? She's been under so much pressure, and I thought I was doing the right thing."

"I get it, man," Jack says. "But Emily's independent. She's used to handling things on her own, and she's proud of that. You have to respect that, even if you're trying to lighten her load."

I nod, letting Jack's words sink in. "I didn't think about it that way."

"Look," Jack says, "The fact that you care enough to want to help her shows a lot. But sometimes, helping means stepping back and letting her handle things her way."

"You sound like a damn therapist," I say, half-smiling.

Jack laughs. "Hey, you're not the only one with problems. I had to learn that with Sarah. She doesn't want me swooping in and fixing everything. She wants a partner."

We step of out the office into the quiet street.

"What are you up to? Sarah's going to visit her parents and I'm at loose ends," Jack says.

"Sorry, can't help. Emily and I going for lunch at my parents'," I say, glancing at my watch.

As I drive back home, I can't help but replay Emily's response from earlier. I texted her to let he know that I was meeting with Jack and would pick her up in time for lunch at my parents' house.

Her response – okay.

No smiley face, no extra words, just a flat, one-word reply. It's been eating at me ever since I got it.

I pull into the driveway and cut the engine, taking a moment before heading inside. I haven't seen her all morning, and I'm not sure what to expect. Has she been busy? Upset?

When I walk through the front door, I find her in the living room, adjusting the strap of her handbag. She looks beautiful, like always, but there's a slight tension in her shoulders, and she doesn't meet my eyes right away.

"Hey," I say, walking over to her. "Ready to go?"

"Yeah," she says, giving me a small smile, but it doesn't quite reach her eyes. "All set."

Outside, I open the passenger door for her and she slides in, a whiff of her lavender scent teases my nostrils, making me want to reach for her.

I can't stand this distance between us.

"Hey, I'm sorry," I say when I enter the driver's seat.

She turns to look at me.

Taking a deep breath, I continue. "I shouldn't have made those decisions about your apartment without talking to you first," I say.

"I thought I was helping, but I can see now that I overstepped. I'm sorry, Emily."

She blinks, surprised. "You really should have asked me. Those were huge decisions and I would have wanted be part of it. I don't like being kept in the dark. We're a team."

"I know," I say, fighting the urge to go into defensive mode. "I was wrong, and I'm sorry. I just wanted to make things easier for you."

Emily sighs. "I know and I'm sorry I got so mad. We should have sat down and had a rational discussion."

Relief surges through me.

She grins at me. "Friends?"

I lean forward and do what I've been aching to do. I kiss her softly, reveling in her soft lips and the heat in her mouth. God, she tastes good.

"How about we skip that lunch, go back into the house and turn off our phones," I tease.

"Yeah, right," Emily says. "Your mother will kill me."

I take her hand and keep it in mine the whole way to my parents' house. Every so often, I steal glances at Emily, catching the way her lips curve into a soft smile or how she absentmindedly brushes her hair back.

Every little thing about her fascinates me. I've never felt this way about a woman before.

When we finally pull up to my parents' house, I park the car and turn to her. "I know I messed up with the apartment, but I want to make it right. I want to be better at this, at us. So, no more secrets, no more decisions without talking to each other first."

Emily's eyes search mine, and there's a flicker of an emotion I can't identify, then she nods.

I lift her hand to my lips and kiss her knuckles, not caring who might see us from the windows. "Deal?"

She smiles. "Deal."

As usual, Sunday lunch is set up in the backyard. The sun filters through the leaves, casting dappled light over the long table covered in crisp white linen.

The staff move around efficiently, setting down platters of food and ensuring everything is perfect. Mom is arranging the final touches, while Dad leans back in his chair, sipping a drink, looking relaxed.

My eyes narrow when I spot another figure lounging at the table, casually sipping from a glass. *Daniel.* What the hell is he doing here?

I tense up, my hold on Emily's hand tightening. She glances up at me, sensing the shift in my mood, but I force a smile to reassure her. I don't want her to know just how much seeing Daniel throws me off.

We walk up to the table, and my mom turns around, her face lighting up when she sees us. "Andrew, Emily. So glad you made it."

"Hi, Barbara," Emily says warmly, letting go of my hand to give my mom a hug.

"Hi, sweetheart," my mom says to her.

Daniel looks up from his drink, a slow grin spreading across his face. "Hey, big brother," he says, leaning back in his chair as if he owns the place. "Long time no see."

"Daniel," I say, my tone clipped. "Didn't know you'd be here."

He shrugs, a lazy smile on his face. "Decided to surprise everyone. Mom seemed happy enough."

I glance at my mom, and she's avoiding my gaze, busying herself with arranging the napkins. I exchange a handshake with my father.

I grit my teeth, but before I can say anything, Emily steps forward and offers Daniel a friendly smile. "Hi, Daniel."

"Emily," he says, his eyes flicking to our joined hands. "You look radiant." The way he says it, with that slight smirk, sends a wave of irritation through me.

I pull Emily closer, slipping an arm around her waist. "She's always radiant," I say, my voice hardening slightly. "Shall we sit?"

We settle down at the table, and I keep Emily close. Daniel's presence hangs over the meal like a dark cloud, and I can feel his eyes on us, observing, assessing.

It sets me on edge, but I do my best to ignore him, focusing on Emily and the warmth of her presence beside me.

"So, Emily," Daniel says after a while, his voice casual. "How's married life treating you? Andrew being the perfect husband?"

Emily tenses and I know she's trying to navigate this without making things worse. "He's been wonderful," she says smoothly, squeezing my hand under the table. "I couldn't ask for more."

"Well, that's nice to hear," Daniel says, and there's a mocking glint in his eyes. "I always wondered if Andrew had it in him to be domesticated."

A flash of anger runs through me, but Emily's hand in mine keeps me grounded.

Lunch continues, and the conversation shifts. Dad turns to us, a rare smile on his face. "Andrew, Emily, I wanted to say how impressed I am with the work at the Riviera Army Base. When are you planning the launch?"

I allow Emily to answer.

"We're aiming for next month," she says. "Everything's coming together, and the marketing team is doing a great job of building up anticipation."

"That's wonderful," Dad says, nodding approvingly.

Emily smiles, clearly pleased by the acknowledgment. "We've had a great team helping us."

"Emily, would you mind if we had a word?" Daniel says, cutting into the conversation.

My body goes rigid. What the hell does he want to talk to her about? I glance at Emily, ready to intervene, if she looks the slightest bit uncomfortable.

"Of course, Daniel," she says.

They step a few paces away, still within view, and I watch as Daniel leans in, standing too close for my liking.

My fists clench under the table, and I have to resist the urge to go over there and pull her back to me. I've seen Daniel work his charm, and I don't trust him, not for a second.

But then Emily flashes me a quick, loving look and smile that instantly puts me at ease. It's a silent reassurance and it calms the storm brewing inside me.

# Chapter 28: Emily

"You really do love him?" Daniel asks, wonder in his voice.

I nod, surprising myself by admitting aloud the one thing I've been too frightened to give much thought to. "I love Andrew."

Daniel sighs. "No one to blame but myself. I shouldn't have—"

"Don't," I say cutting him off. "You and I would never have worked. We're too different. Andrew and I understand each other and well...we're good for each other."

Daniel throws a glance at his brother before swinging his gaze back to me. "Lucky bastard. Let me know if he ever hurts you. I'll make sure he regrets it," he says in a fierce tone that makes me laugh.

"Andrew wouldn't hurt a fly." I'm the one who's likely to hurt him.

His words in the car play back in my mind. *No more secrets.*

My stomach churns and I feel like I'm going to be sick. I can't keep lying to Andrew and to his family about my father.

He watches me for a beat longer, like he's trying to see past the mask I'm wearing, but then he nods. "Alright. But if you need anything, you know where to find me."

I offer him another smile, and we start walking back, but inside, I'm a mess. I can't keep pretending everything is fine, not with Andrew's words still lingering in my mind.

With that, we head back to the table. Andrew looks up, his eyes flicking between us, and I can tell he's been watching, waiting, trying to read the situation.

I offer him a reassuring smile, and the tension in his shoulders eases slightly.

"Everything okay?" he asks, his hand finding mine under the table.

"Perfect," I say, squeezing his hand. "Let's finish this lunch so we can go home."

Lunch wraps up with the usual light chatter, and I find myself playing the part of the attentive daughter-in-law, answering Barbara's questions and laughing at Daniel's jokes.

But all I can think about is getting out of here, back to the quiet and privacy of our own space.

Finally, after what feels like an eternity, we say our goodbyes. Barbara hugs me tightly, and Andrew shakes hands with his dad, but I can feel the impatience radiating off him. He wants to leave just as much as I do.

The car ride home is quiet, but it's a comfortable silence. Andrew rests one hand on the steering wheel and the other on my knee, occasionally giving it a gentle squeeze.

Every touch sends a warm, tingling sensation through me, and I find myself leaning closer, letting my head rest against his shoulder. Being with Andrew allows me to forget my worries. I'll deal with it soon.

I'll tell him everything soon, and when my father wakes up, he'll just have to understand why I need to tell Andrew. He's my husband. There should be no secrets between two people who are married.

As soon as we pull into the driveway, Andrew turns off the engine and looks at me, his blue eyes dark with something intense. "I don't want to talk," he says, his voice low and rough. "I just want to be with you."

I nod, my heart pounding. "Me too."

We barely make it through the front door before Andrew pulls me into his arms, his mouth finding mine in a desperate, heated kiss.

I respond just as eagerly, my fingers threading through his hair as I press myself against him. *God, I've missed this*. His arms are around me, his lips are on me, his scent is surrounding me.

"Upstairs," I murmur against his lips, and he nods, lifting me off my feet. I gasp, wrapping my arms around his neck as he carries me up the stairs, his steps quick and purposeful.

When we reach the bedroom, he sets me down gently and steps back, his eyes raking over me. "I love you," he says, and there's no hesitation, no doubt, just pure, raw emotion. “I don’t know when it happened, but I do. I love you, Emily.”

Tears sting my eyes, but I blink them back, smiling. “I love you too, Andrew. So much.”

He closes the distance between us, kissing me again, and this time there’s no rush, just a slow, tender exploration that leaves me breathless.

I’m not sure how long we stand there, wrapped up in each other, but it feels like hours, like days, like forever.

His hands are gentle yet firm as they roam over my skin, leaving a trail of fire in their wake. Every touch, every caress is a silent declaration of his affection for me, a reassurance that this is real, that we are real.

His lips leave mine and travel down my neck, planting soft kisses along the way. I close my eyes and let out a contented sigh, reveling in the sensation of his warm breath against my skin.

As he undresses me with a tenderness that takes my breath away, I feel a deep connection forming between us, one that transcends mere physical desire.

I return the favor, unbuttoning his shirt slowly, savoring the sight of his chiseled chest. His eyes never leave mine, filled with so much love and longing that it steals the air from my lungs.

I arch into Andrew’s arms as he teases my nipples while trailing my fingers along the lines of his muscular back.

His mouth follows a path of fire down my abdomen, leaving a trail of open-mouthed kisses that leave me breathless and wanting. Our intimacy feels different tonight, like a new beginning.

Andrew's hands are sure as he navigates my body, as if he knows every curve, every dip, every hollow.

I shiver with arousal as his tongue traces the sensitive skin of my inner thigh.

I cry out his name, my fingers gripping the sheets tightly as he takes me into his mouth, sucking gently on my clit.

I arch my back, moaning desperately as waves of pleasure crash over me. His skillful hands and mouth bring me to the edge, and then push me over with a single, deft motion.

Andrew looks up at me, his face flushed and his eyes dark with emotion. “I've missed you,” he whispers, his voice rough with desire.

I nod, unable to speak as I ride out the aftershocks of my orgasm. When I finally regain my composure, I pull him up to kiss him, tasting myself on his lips.

He kisses me back hungrily, his body—now hard and ready—pressed against mine. Feeling the evidence of his arousal, I kiss him harder, needing to feel closer to him.

It's been too long since we've been this intimate and my body aches with a need to be filled.

I reach down, grasping his erection firmly in my hand. Andrew moans softly into my mouth as I stroke him, relishing the feel of him against my palm.

I guide him to me, positioning the head of his cock at the entrance of my core. As he pushes inside me, I gasp, my body stretching to accommodate him.

Slowly, he begins to move, each thrust sending waves of pleasure through me, building up an arousal that threatens to swallow me whole.

“Andrew,” I cry out, wrapping my legs tightly around him.

“Yes baby,” he murmurs, his voice low and gruff. “I’m right here, I’ve got you.”

As we move faster and harder, the room fills with the sound of our bodies slapping together, our ragged breathing, and our desperate moans.

My nails dig into his back, urging him on as the intensity builds within me.

“I’m close,” I gasp, writhing beneath him.

Andrew groans, his pace becoming more frantic as my body tightens around him. "Me too," he says, his voice ragged with desire. "I need to you to come with me."

The words send me over the edge, and I cry out as pleasure washes over me.

"Fuck!" Andrew roars, his body tensing above me.

We collapse together after we've finished, our bodies still intertwined. I rest my head on Andrew's chest, listening to the rhythm of his heart as it slows.

He strokes my hair gently, his fingers massaging my scalp. The room is filled with a contented silence as we catch our breath.

Finally, Andrew pulls back slightly to look into my eyes.

"I don't think I've ever felt this way before. It feels like I've found a missing part of myself in you."

I swallow hard at the emotions in his voice. I want to say the same thing back. I feel it. But I'm holding back. There are things that he doesn't know about me. I can't keep it from him any longer, but this is not the time. Our love is still too fragile.

I feel like a fraud except my feelings for him are real. More real than anything I've ever experienced before.

"I know what you mean," I say, cupping his face in my hands. "Being with you feels like coming home after a long journey. Like finding the missing piece of a puzzle that I didn't even realize was missing."

He smiles, gently brushing my hair away from my face. "That's a beautiful way to put it."

## Chapter 29: Andrew

"How is it that a beautiful, perfect woman like you is single?" I ask Emily as we lie on my bed staring up at the ceiling.

There's nowhere else I'd rather be at this moment than lying here, naked, with my wife. Gratitude overcomes me, that she's mine. That I found her before someone else did.

She laughs in response. "Relationships have not been a priority for a while."

"When was the last time you were in a relationship?" I ask her, a weird burning sensation settling in my chest.

"About a year and a half ago," Emily says. "His name was Jaime."

"Did you love him?" I ask. A possessive surge runs through me as I picture some other guy in Emily's life. I know it's the past, but the thought of Emily with someone else just doesn't sit right.

"Did you love him?" I ask, my chest tightening in anticipation of her answer.

Emily sighs, staring up at the ceiling. "Honestly? I thought I did. But looking back, I realize we were just two people trying to fit into a life that didn't really suit either of us."

"What do you mean?" I prop myself up on one elbow, studying her face.

"He wanted a very traditional setup," she says. "A wife who'd stay home, cook, manage the house, and be there for him and the kids. He thought I'd fit into that mold eventually."

I raise an eyebrow, unable to picture Emily in any sort of "meek" role. "Clearly, he didn't know you well. I can't imagine you staying home all day, waiting for someone else to make things happen."

She laughs. "Right? The thought alone gave me nightmares. I couldn't picture myself giving up the work I love, the independence." She shrugs. "I mean, it works for some people, but I knew it wasn't for me. We broke up after that; He just couldn't see things my way."

I nod, feeling oddly relieved. "Sounds like it was for the best."

"What about you?" she asks, turning to me. "Any serious relationships before us?"

I let out a breath. "Nothing all that serious. There was Chloe. We were seeing each other just before I went on tour, but I broke it off."

"Why?"

I consider my words carefully. "I didn't know exactly what I wanted, but I knew it wasn't her. She was nice. Supportive. But there was no fire, no drive. Chloe didn't have any real goals of her own. She was content staying in her world, happy with whatever I did or decided."

Emily rolls her eyes playfully. "Well, maybe we should introduce Jaime and Chloe to each other."

I laugh. "They'd probably be a match made in heaven, right?"

"Picture it: weekly brunches, matching outfits, and a picket fence."

"Top it off with Sunday brunches and garden parties, and they're golden," I add, grinning.

We both burst out laughing, and it feels good.

"Speaking of work, we should sleep, we have a long day tomorrow," I say.

She grins. "I'm so excited. Two weeks until the grand opening."

"I know," I say, the thrill of it vibrating through me.

We're so close to the finish line.

We drift off, and I wake up to the early sunlight streaming through the blinds. After a quick breakfast, Emily and I make our way to the Army Base Riviera.

Every corner of the property is alive with activity. Workers move around in choreographed efficiency, carrying supplies, setting up equipment, adjusting and polishing surfaces until everything gleams.

Inside, the transformation is stunning. The lobby, once dull and neglected, is now a bright, inviting space with polished marble floors that reflect the soft, natural light filtering through large windows.

I make my way to the new reception area, where the sleek, modern desk stands ready.

The branding materials blend in perfectly with the modern, understated elegance of the lobby, each sign adding a touch of sophistication without overpowering the room.

I take a step back, crossing my arms as I survey the space, satisfaction swelling in my chest. This is everything Emily and I had envisioned.

"I can't wait to get started with the Lakeside Riviera," Emily says, standing next to me.

I hold my tongue. I'm not exactly jumping with joy at the disagreements that will come between us. We have vastly different ideas for the Lakeside Riviera. But this is not the time to think about that.

Emily and I go back outside.

Landscapers are carefully placing the last few potted plants by the entrance, adjusting the greenery and smoothing out the freshly laid stone paths.

The newly added outdoor seating area is coming to life with modern benches interspersed with native plants that give a natural, organic feel.

"This is so beautiful," Emily says with a sigh. "Makes me want to book a room for a week and leave the world behind."

I laugh. "That was the idea wasn't it? Make our guests never want to leave."

"Yes," Emily says, then turns to me. "We did it Andrew."

I nod. "We did."

She grows solemn. "Your father hasn't come by to see what we did."

"I'm not surprised," I say. "And to be perfectly honest, I like it. You wouldn't appreciate the other version of my father. He would have been on our faces all day, every day. This is his way of showing that he trusts us. He'll be at the launch."

Relief draws itself on Emily's features. "I'm glad."

"Speaking of which, will your father try and make it?" I ask Emily. I've noticed that she never talks about him, yet I'm pretty sure that he does communicate with his family.

Emily's face shifts, just slightly, a flash of something unreadable crossing her expression before it disappears.

"Oh, I doubt it," she says, her tone light, but there's a stiffness to it.

"Still travelling?" I ask, trying to keep it casual, though part of me is curious why her father hasn't been more involved.

"Yes, he is." She pauses, glancing away as if studying the hotel entrance.

There's a flicker in her eyes, almost like a shadow. I can tell she's holding back, guarding something, and it makes me wonder. Why wouldn't she share more about her father if they're close?

"Well," I say, hoping to ease the tension, "I suppose he's just enjoying his life. If he's anything like you, he's probably trying to see everything, do everything."

Her gaze softens, a little less guarded. "Yes, that sounds like him. He has this way of throwing himself fully into whatever he does. It's admirable, really."

But as she says it, I notice the way her shoulders tense and her voice sounds too cheerful.

"Maybe he'll surprise you and drop in for the launch," I offer, but she only gives me a small nod, her gaze dropping to the ground.

Before either of us can say anything further, a loud explosion echoes from the nearby military base, the sound ripping through the air.

My instinct is immediate; my body tenses, hands clenching, heart racing.

I force myself to inhale slowly, counting to four, then exhale just as slowly, focusing on each breath, one by one.

Another deep breath, then another. I can feel my heartbeat gradually slowing, the panic receding like a tide.

Emily's hand rests gently on my arm, her face filled with concern. "Are you okay?"

I nod. "Yeah. I breathed through it." I exhale deeply, forcing my shoulders to relax. "The therapist showed me how to handle these moments. It's helping."

There's a flicker of pride in her eyes. "I'm glad. I know how hard you're working on it."

My chest swells with the love I feel for her. This wife of mine has seen me at my best and at my worst, and somehow, she's still here. I've opened myself to her like I've never done with any other woman.

I trust her more than anyone else in this world. Emily is my world, my anchor, the love of my life.

"Thank you." The words aren't enough, like nothing could convey how much her presence means to me. "For sticking with me. For understanding."

A beautiful smile curves her lips. "That's what I'm here for, Andrew. You're not alone in this."

I reach for her hand, intertwining our fingers, and warmth spreads through me that goes beyond relief. It's love. Real, undeniable love.

## Chapter 30: Emily

I wake up to the sound of the shower running and excitement coursing through me before it hits me what day it is. Launch day.

A thrill shivers through me as I sit up, stretching out the sleepiness and letting reality sink in. Today's the day. Today, the Army Base Riviera finally reopens its doors.

Andrew comes out of the bathroom in a cloud of steam, towel around his waist, hair damp, and an easy grin on his face.

Heat uncurls in my abdomen. This man will be the death of me. All I can think about when we're together is having those muscular arms on me. I can't get enough of him.

"Morning, sleepyhead," he says, and I smile back.

He comes to the bed and plants a kiss on my lips.

"Good morning," I say back and swing my legs to the edge of the bed.

Andrew and I have taken to sleeping naked figuring there's no point in wearing our night clothes when we make love at least twice every night.

"Did you sleep well," he asks, staring down at me.

"Sort," I say, threading my hair through my unruly hair. "All I could think about was today. I'm so excited, I feel like I'm going to be sick."

Andrew laughs. "No you won't. You'll be fabulous and beautiful and in charge. I love you Emily Bennett."

"I love you too," I say, wondering how he can be so cool today, the biggest day of our lives.

He takes my hand and pulls me to my feet, then gently propels me towards the bathroom. "Shower time." He swats my behind as I pad towards the bathroom.

I laugh, glancing over my shoulder at him, feeling the warmth of his touch linger. "So bossy this morning," I tease, shutting the door behind me.

The hot water soothes the nerves in my stomach, the excitement of the day coming alive with every passing second.

I wear the dress Lisa and I shopped for today. It's a deep emerald green, off shoulder dress, that matches the color scheme of the Army Base Riviera.

I style my hair to fall in soft waves around my shoulders, then I finish off with my makeup.

The trouble I took is worth it judging by Andrew's reaction. His eyes widen and rake over me appreciatively, then he whistles.

"You are beautiful," he says.

"Thank you," I say, pleasure spreading through me. "Not too bad yourself."

He's dressed in a perfectly fitting tailored suit that makes him look every inch the successful businessman that I've fallen in love with.

He laughs, holding out his arm as we leave for the hotel, fingers intertwined as we settle into the car.

The drive is quiet, both of us lost in the excitement buzzing between us. When we pull up to the Army Base Riviera, the energy outside the hotel is electric.

Banners line the walkway, and floral arrangements in rich greens and whites adorn the entrance.

I clasp my hands together. "It looks perfect." I can't help but wish that my father was awake to see this. His beloved Army Base Riviera returned to its former glory.

"Not as perfect as you are," Andrew says.

A twinge of guilt goes through me. "No one's perfect Andrew," I say. "We all have our faults."

Before he can say anything, the driver opens my door gathering my dress, I step out to flashes of cameras.

The press moves in around us, cameras flashing as they take pictures of Andrew and me together, the crowd shifting as questions come our way.

We field each one, sharing stories about the renovation process, the history of the Riviera, and what inspired the modern, understated elegance we chose.

Andrew keeps his hand on my back, and every so often, he runs his fingers along my spine.

Finally, we're able to get away and make our way into the lobby.

Andrew's family is among the first to greet us. His father, who's usually reserved, extends a hand and shakes mine firmly, his face breaking into a rare smile. "You both did a fantastic job," he says.

Barbara beams, pulling me into a hug. "You should be so proud," she whispers, a hint of emotion in her voice.

Waiters glide between groups with trays of champagne and hors d'oeuvres, pausing now and then as guests reach for glasses and tiny plates.

I spot Lisa and wave her over; she's dressed in a sleek red dress, her usual spark lighting up her face as she pulls me aside.

"This place is stunning, Emily," she says, surveying the bustling lobby. "You and Andrew really brought it to life."

"Thank you," I say, smiling. "It's surreal seeing everyone here."

As we talk, I feel a tug at my heart, the words I've been holding onto for weeks rising to the surface. "I've been thinking about telling Andrew the truth about my dad," I say, lowering my voice.

"But it scares me, Lisa."

Lisa nods, her gaze softening. "He loves you, Emily. He'll understand. And you'll feel lighter once it's out there."

I inhale deeply. Now that the renovations are out of the way, there's nothing holding me back from telling Andrew. It doesn't feel right between us with this huge thing hanging over my head.

"You're right. I'll tell him. I just hope it doesn't change things between us."

Before I can say more, my mother approaches, smiling brightly, her face glowing with pride. She pulls me into a hug, and for a moment, it feels like nothing else matters.

"Your father would be so proud of you," she whispers. "I know it."

"Thanks, Mom," I say, my voice thick with emotion. I regret that I haven't been able to visit as often with all the final preparations, and I apologize to her quietly.

"Don't worry, sweetheart," she reassures me. "He'd understand, and he'd be thrilled with what you've done here."

Soon after, the ceremony begins, and Andrew steps up to the podium, his voice calm as he thanks everyone who helped bring the Riviera back to life.

I join him, my voice carrying the gratitude I feel for everyone in the room.

When I'm done with my short speech, the crowd erupts into applause, and a soft chime of champagne flutes fills the air as servers pass them out, one by one.

Andrew turns to me, lifting his glass, his eyes sparkling with pride and something deeper, something that fills me with warmth.

"To the new Army Base Riviera," he says, his voice carrying over the crowd, and everyone raises their glasses with a collective cheer.

"To the Army Base Riviera," I echo, clinking my glass with his.

Once the toast is finished and the clinking of glasses fills the room, the manager of the hotel, Simon, steps forward, his warm smile signaling the start of the much-anticipated tour.

"Ladies and gentlemen, if you'd like to follow me, we'll take a look around the new and improved Army Base Riviera," Simon announces, his voice carrying a mixture of pride and excitement.

His professionalism shines through as he expertly guides the crowd, gesturing toward various design features and amenities, weaving stories about the history of the hotel along the way.

As the tour wraps up, we head back to the main ballroom, where the soft strains of jazz music begin to fill the air.

As the night goes on, laughter and music fill the room, and guests begin to dance, twirling to the soft, romantic tunes.

The ambiance is exactly what we wanted: a warm, lively gathering that showcases the essence of the Riviera, brought to life by everyone who believed in our vision.

"A dance my beautiful wife," Andrew says, bowing low.

Lisa and I giggle.

"I thought you would never ask," I say, placing my hand in his. He leads me to the dance floor and holds me so close, the world fades and it's just the two of us.

"Did I tell you that you're the most beautiful woman here tonight?" Andrew whispers in my ear.

I look up and meet his gaze. "I want to be the most beautiful woman to you." Flirting with Andrew comes naturally. It doesn't feel forced. At all.

Andrew grins, pulling me a little closer, his hand resting at the small of my back. "You already are," he says.

Just then, a gentle tap on my shoulder pulls me back to reality. I turn to find my mother standing there, trying to mask her tension behind a strained smile. My stomach drops. I know that look.

"Mom?" I ask, unable to hide the fear in my voice.

She smiles but I know instinctively that it's for Andrew's sake. "Could I have a word?"

Andrew gives me a supportive nod, loosening his hold as I follow her off the dance floor, away from the crowd's laughter and music. We step into a quiet corner of the room, where my mother's face loses its practiced composure.

She takes my hands, her fingers trembling slightly. "I just received a call from the nurse. Your father has had a stroke."

Fear lodges itself in my chest. "No," I cry out, tears already gathering in my eyes. The doctors made it clear what the risks for a second major stroke were.

"They've put him in an ambulance, and he's on his way to the hospital now," my mother continues.

I tighten my hold on her hands. "We must go immediately."

"No," Mom says in a sharp voice. She shakes her head. "You can't leave. Everyone will know that something is terribly wrong."

"I can't stay here," I say in a loud voice. "What if he..." my voice trails off and a sob rips out of me. The thought is unimaginable.

I can't lose my father!

"Emily, hold yourself together," my mother says, her tone jolting me out of the maze of fear and grief surrounding me. "You need to be here tonight. Let me go and be with him." Her voice softens, the gentleness of her tone almost undoing me. "Come when you can, sweetheart. I'll be with him, and I'll call you with any updates."

I bite my lip, fighting the tears threatening to spill. She's right, but every instinct in me pulls toward being at my father's side.

I need to be strong. I need to hold it together.

I nod. "Okay. Go to him and let me know as soon as you can how he is."

"I promise."

## Chapter 31: Andrew

Emily slips back into the ballroom, but something in her posture catches my attention. She doesn't look around or search for me.

Instead, she makes a direct line for Lisa, and within seconds, the two of them are huddled together, their heads close and expressions tense.

I cross the room toward them, weaving through the remaining guests. As I approach, my attention is drawn to Emily's posture. Her shoulders are drawn tight, her fingers clenching and unclenching as she talks to Lisa.

Worry stirs in my chest.

"Emily," I say as I get closer.

She's startled, looking up, and for a split second, there's something like fear in her eyes. But it vanishes quickly, replaced by the familiar smile I know so well.

"Andrew," she says, her tone light.

"Is everything okay?" I ask, watching her closely.

She nods quickly, brushing off my concern with a wave of her hand. "Everything's fine," she replies, her smile unwavering. But there's tension there, barely hidden.

I study her face, searching for the truth behind her words. "Is it your mother?" I press gently.

"No, no, my mother's fine," she says with a small laugh that doesn't quite reach her eyes. "She was just tired and begged to leave early. I told her it was fine."

Her hand touches mine, her fingers cool and soft, and she flashes me a flirty smile, a glimmer of the Emily I know and love. She's okay.

I let out a breath I didn't know I was holding, a wave of relief flooding through me. Maybe it's just been a long day, or maybe my mind's working overtime.

I've never loved anyone this deeply before, and it's strange, this mix of worry and devotion.

Emily tilts her head toward the dance floor. "How about we finish that dance?"

I smile, holding out my hand. "Let's do it."

We return to the center of the room, and I wrap my arms around her, feeling her warmth against me as we sway to the soft music.

But she's quiet, her mind seemingly elsewhere, and I can feel the slight distance, even as I hold her close. For the rest of the evening, that same quiet lingers.

She smiles at the guests, nods when others speak to her, but she's in another world, her focus turned inward.

While she's talking to my mother, I notice Lisa at the bar counter nursing a drink. I head towards her. Even though she's Emily's best friend, we barely know each other but hopefully, time will remedy that.

"Hey," I say and she looks up at me and smiles.

"You guys did a fantastic job. It's all over the internet," Lisa says.

"Thank you." The Army Base is not what I wanted to talk to her about. "I want to ask you something and I need you to be completely honest with me," I say.

She suddenly looks uncomfortable, fidgeting. "Sure, Andrew, what is it?"

"It's about Emily. Something is obviously bothering her and I can't get it out of her. I want to make it better for her but I really need to know what's going on?" I say.

At first, I was poking in the dark but Lisa's reaction confirms it for me. She looks like a trapped animal.

She takes a gulp of her drink and makes a show out of swallowing. I'm in no rush. I'll wait for as long as necessary. I'm patient when I choose to be.

"I have no idea what you're talking about," she says in a choked voice. "Today's been a great day but tiring as well. Maybe that's what you're sensing from Emily."

I lean on the counter and lock eyes with her. I hate that I'm putting her in this spot but she's the only one who can help me right now.

"I know when my wife is tired," I say. "This is not exhaustion bothering her. It's something else."

Lisa slides from her stool and stands up. "I really need to go to the washroom." She flees, weaving between people as if she's been chased.

I'm more puzzled than ever. Frustration grows inside me and I order a drink from the barman. As I sip on it, something dawns on me. I'd been doing exactly what Emily accused me of doing when I renovated her apartment.

I'm attempting to control the situation.

If there's something the matter, Emily will tell me herself in her own time. I drain the last of my whiskey. I'm going to trust her and believe that she can make her own decisions without me.

Eventually, the last of the guests say their goodbyes, and as the lights dim in the ballroom, Emily and I step out into the night.

The quiet of the evening feels soothing after the endless mingling, and I reach for her hand, feeling the coolness of her fingers against my own.

The drive home is peaceful, and I don't push for conversation. I can sense her exhaustion, the weight of the day on her, and maybe it's just that simple. It's been an emotional night, full of nerves and excitement.

We pull into the driveway, and as we step out of the car, Emily's phone rings, breaking the stillness of the night.

She looks up at me, apologetic. "It's my mom. I'll just talk to her, then join you inside?"

I nod, squeezing her hand. "Of course. Take your time."

She gives me a small smile, gesturing for me to go ahead as she answers the call.

Inside, I head upstairs, exhaustion settling over me. A shower will perk me up. I've been looking forward to a private celebration with Emily. I step into the bedroom, pulling off my jacket and slowly unbuttoning my shirt, hoping she'll join me soon.

I strip down, the cool air prickling my skin, but in the back of my mind, I imagine Emily here with me, close and warm.

I finish showering and wrapping myself in a towel, I step back into our bedroom. Emily hasn't come yet.

I get into bed naked and lie on my back, with the events of the day running through my mind. The launch couldn't have gone any more perfectly. My father called me aside and expressed his pride and confidence in me that Bennett Construction will be in safe hands in the future.

I didn't get a chance to tell Emily. We have so much to talk about tonight, but first, we need to take care of this. I stare down at the tented duvet cover. I've never wanted my wife as I do tonight.

The doorknob turns and the door opens.

"There you are," I say to Emily. "I was about to send out a search party."

She smiles. "No need. I'll just jump into the shower." She blows me a kiss as she disappears into the bathroom.

The sound of the shower follows minutes later. I'm impatient for her to be done and in bed with me.

I want tonight to be good, to end on a high note after everything.

The bathroom door opens, and Emily steps out, wrapped in her robe, her damp hair falling over her shoulders.

She looks so soft, so beautiful, and all I want is to hold her, to forget whatever distance has come between us today. She walks to the dresser, finds her nightgown, and slips it on before coming to bed.

When she lies down, I reach for her, pulling her close, pressing a kiss to her lips, feeling her warmth. Her lips meet mine, soft and familiar, but then she pulls back slightly, giving me a small, apologetic smile.

"Not tonight," she says gently. "I'm just so tired. Can we take a raincheck?"

I nod, swallowing down the sting of rejection. I brush it off with a smile, not wanting her to feel guilty. "Of course," I say, trying to sound casual, even though I can feel something clench tight inside me. "Long day, right?"

She nods, turning to her side and nestling into her pillow. "Yeah, it was. Just a lot. I'll be fine after some rest," she says, her voice already drifting, her eyes closed.

I lie there, staring at the ceiling, trying to tell myself she's just tired, that it's not personal. But it's hard not to feel the ache, that strange hollow feeling when someone you love seems to pull away.

I turn onto my back, trying to shake the unease. She needs sleep; that's all it is. She's right here beside me, after all.

I stare at the darkened ceiling, willing myself to ignore the thoughts gnawing at me, to let sleep take over.

Yet sleep doesn't come easily. And somewhere in the quiet, all I can think about is what she's not telling me.

## Chapter 32: Emily

I wake up with a deep ache lodged deep inside my core and hands rubbing over my nipples. A moan rips out of body as Andrew's mouth finds a nipple.

His lips are gentle at first, teasing and exploring my sensitive skin. As I gasp and writhe beneath him, he grows more insistent, sucking and biting with a hunger that matches my own.

I'm caught between sleep and wakefulness, my body responding to his touch without hesitation.

I'm overtaken by a wave of intense desire, my body trembling as Andrew continues to explore me. I moan his name, feeling the pleasure build inside me until it is almost unbearable.

I reach between us, and wrap my hands around his rock-hard cock.

"I want you," I say, the ache between my legs intensifying.

Andrew groans, his hips bucking against me. He positions himself between my thighs, his erection nudging at my entrance.

"Now?" he asks, his voice hoarse with need.

"Yes," I whisper, my body trembling with anticipation.

He pushes inside me, and I gasp at the sensation of his thick length filling me completely. Our eyes lock as we move together, our bodies syncing perfectly.

The pleasure builds rapidly, and I cry out Andrew's name as the climax crashes over me, my body shuddering with the force of it.

Andrew's face contorts in pleasure, his eyes shut tight as he thrusts deeper inside me. With a final cry, he releases, filling me completely.

As soon as he rolls off me, reality crashes into me like ice water. My father is in the hospital. Panic and fear claw their way up my throat, and I scramble for my phone.

Nothing. No missed calls, no messages. That's good news, right?

Andrew plants a warm kiss on my forehead. "That was amazing." His eyes are bright, carefree, and I manage a weak smile.

Guilt swarms over me. How could I let go like that, without a thought for my parents, for my father fighting for his life? I force a smile, though it feels like a mask stretching over my face.

Andrew picks up his phone, scrolling through his messages, and within seconds, his face lights up. "Hey, Amy emailed you and copied me in. The Army Base hotel is fully booked for the next six months. Isn't that incredible?" He grins, eyes full of pride.

"That's great," I say, struggling to push my mind back to the present. He looks so genuinely happy, and I can't let him see the storm that's brewing within me. Not now.

He runs a hand along my arm, pulling me close. "I can't wait to get started on the Lakeside Riviera. How's your day looking? Think we could head over there this afternoon and brainstorm ideas?"

I swallow, my mind racing. I need to go to the hospital first thing. "The afternoon's fine," I say as lightly as I can. "Just have a few errands in the morning."

He nuzzles my neck, pressing soft kisses along my jawline. "You sure you don't want some company for those errands, hmm?" His voice is low, teasing, and it takes every ounce of willpower to keep my tone playful in response.

"Not today, lover boy," I say, giving his chest a little push. "Some things need a woman's touch."

He chuckles, sitting up and stretching. "Alright, if you say so."

Andrew heads to the shower, and as soon as I'm alone, I grab my phone and text Catherine. **Reorganize my schedule for the morning. I won't be in until later.**

My fingers tremble as I type, and I force myself to take a deep breath. This has to be quick. In and out of the hospital, then I can switch back to work mode. I have to keep it together today.

I slip into the guest room and take a quick shower, letting the warm water clear my mind. By the time I'm dressed, I feel more composed.

Andrew is in the kitchen, stirring his coffee. The temptation to rush out gnaws at me, but if I make a break for it, he'll only get curious. So, I steady my breath and walk in slowly, masking my urgency with a casual smile.

"Ready to start the day?" he asks, his eyes meeting mine.

"As ready as I'll ever be," I say, hoping he can't see the tremor of nerves hiding beneath my smile.

Andrew pours me a cup of coffee then opening the fridge, he takes out two bowls of fruit, sliding one to my end.

I push my fork around the plate, barely noticing the colors of the fruit against the white china. Andrew is talking about the renovations at the lakeside Riviera, mapping out his plans.

I can hear him, but it's like background noise, something distant and foggy, barely reaching me.

All I can think about is my father. *Is he still alive?* The question echoes in my mind, crowding out everything else.

My mother's call last night was short and direct. "Your father's in the ICU," she said, sounding calm, stronger than I expected. Maybe that's a good sign. Maybe there's hope.

My phone buzzes beside me, jolting me back to the present. Lisa. I glance at Andrew, nodding along to his words, but he doesn't seem to notice my distraction.

"When are you leaving?" Lisa asks when I pick up.

"Twenty minutes," I say, glancing at my watch.

"Alright, I'll meet you there," she says.

I drain the last of my coffee, setting the cup down a little too hard.

Andrew looks up, his brow furrowed. "You haven't eaten anything," he says, gesturing to the untouched fruit on my plate.

"I'm not hungry," I reply, giving him a small smile. "I'll eat later." Leaning down, I press a quick kiss to his forehead, trying to ignore the worried look in his eyes.

"See you at the office," I add, slipping away before he can ask any more questions.

The drive to the hospital is a blur. The route feels foreign, like I'm moving in slow motion, everything muted and unreal.

When I reach the waiting room, Lisa is already there, standing near the elevator. She gives me a brief hug, and I'm tempted to let lose, cry and get rid of the lump that is permanently lodged in my chest.

"How are you doing?" Lisa asks, her hands on my shoulders.

I give her a weak smile. "Hanging in there."

"Come on, let's go," she says, leading the way to the elevators.

The ICU is on the fifth floor and as soon as we step out, the solemn, silent atmosphere hits me, renewed fear coming over me.

My mother is already seated in the waiting room, her face pale but composed. She stands as I approach, wrapping me in a hug, her arms warm and grounding.

"How is he?" I ask, my voice barely above a whisper.

She pulls back slightly, studying my face, her expression weary. "The same," she says.

I nod, squeezing her hand before looking to Lisa, who gives me a reassuring smile.

"I'll be right here," Lisa says, her hand on my shoulder for a brief moment.

I leave them in the waiting room and approach the nurse's station, hoping they'll let me see him.

I find a friendly nurse and she looks at me sympathetically. "You'll only have five minutes," she says, and I nod, grateful for even a moment.

I step inside the ICU, and there he is, looking as he did at home, only now he's surrounded by the constant hum and beeps of machines.

Wires snake around him, measuring his heart, his breath, every vital sign. It makes it all feel so much more real, as if each sound is a reminder that he's slipping further away.

I approach the bed, my hand trembling as I reach for his. His skin is cold, so still beneath my touch. A lump forms in my throat, and my composure cracks.

"We need you," I whisper, clutching his hand a little tighter. "Please come back to us."

The words spill out, my tears falling onto the thin blanket covering him. I don't try to hold back; it's as if the floodgates have opened, and all the fear, all the worry, is finally pouring out.

After a few minutes, I take a shuddering breath, forcing myself to straighten up.

*Be strong Emily.*

He wouldn't want me to fall apart. Wiping my tears away, I try to bring back a smile.

"You'll be so proud of the Army Base, Dad," I say, my voice thick with emotion. "The launch went beautifully, and everyone loved it. I can't wait for you to see it."

For a moment, I imagine his eyes opening, his familiar smile telling me he's proud. But he remains still, his chest rising and falling to the rhythm of the machines.

After one final squeeze of his hand, I lean down, pressing a kiss to his forehead. "Please keep fighting. We're all waiting for you."

## Chapter 33: Andrew

I'm in my father's office, seated across from him as he leans back in his chair, assessing me with that sharp gaze of his.

I've just finished giving him the rundown on the Army Base project and what we're envisioning for Lakeside.

I expect questions about the plans, the finances, maybe even staffing. But instead, he steers the conversation somewhere entirely different.

"I remember when Ace Young opened the Lakeside Riviera," he muses, tapping his pen thoughtfully. "It was the talk of the town. That place was groundbreaking back then. I don't understand why or how he's let it slide like this. It was his first project, after all."

I shrug, biting back my own questions about Ace Young.

I've wondered the same thing for weeks now. Emily's father is a mystery I can't quite unravel, and every time I consider asking her, something holds me back.

Family boundaries, maybe, or the way her expression tightens whenever the topic gets too close.

Dad narrows his gaze, piercing right through me as if he can sense my hesitation. "Does Emily hear from him?"

"I'm sure they keep in touch over the phone," I say, trying to keep my tone casual, but even I can hear the hesitation in my voice.

Truth is, I don't know. I've never seen Emily so much as mention her father in passing, let alone bring up anything close to a conversation with him.

He arches a brow, unimpressed. "Would've thought he'd make the effort to be there for his own project's re-launch. It doesn't sit right with me."

Neither is it with me, I admit internally. Emily's family is a closed book, and she guards it tightly.

She's open about so many things—her goals, her passions, even her dreams for the Riviera Group. But when it comes to her family, there's a wall.

And as much as I want to respect that, I'd be lying if I said I didn't wish she'd share more. Maybe one day she will.

Dad gives a slight shake of his head, letting out a breath as if to brush off the thought. "Oh well. What matters now is where the company is going. So, what are the plans?"

I sit up, grateful to turn the focus back to business, something I can control, something I can deliver on.

I lay out the vision for the Lakeside Riviera—a modern yet timeless transformation that captures the essence of its original design while embracing the high-end, contemporary appeal that clients today expect.

I dive into specifics—rejuvenating the waterfront views, upgrading the guest suites with state-of-the-art amenities, creating a world-class dining experience that would draw locals and travelers alike.

I leave my father's office and as I walk past an office that was empty, I catch sight of someone at the desk. I back track and stare in disbelief. It's Daniel.

He's leaning back in a chair, flipping through a file. I blink, momentarily thrown. Daniel rarely shows up at the office, let alone with anything resembling work in his hands.

Curiosity gets the better of me, so I knock and step inside.

"Hey," I say, leaning against the doorframe. "What are you doing here?"

He looks up, flashing a grin. "Taking a shot at trying to be more serious in life. Sort of like you." His tone is light, but there's something sincere in his eyes.

I raise an eyebrow, nodding. "Never too late."

"Exactly my thinking," he says, shrugging with that familiar carefree air. "Figured I could start contributing around here. See if I actually have a knack for anything."

I smile, giving him a small nod of encouragement. "That's good to hear, Daniel. Really."

He just nods back.

"Good luck," I say and withdraw.

As I make my way down the hall, I can't help but hope that he means it. If Daniel could find some direction and purpose, it'd be huge—for him, for our family.

I think about the projects we're undertaking, the endless potential. Maybe, just maybe, there's hope for my brother after all.

***

On my way to meet Emily at the Lakeside Riviera, I stop by a florist and pick up a bouquet of lilies, knowing she'll appreciate the gesture.

When I arrive at the Lakeside, I'm greeted by the receptionist in the lobby with a friendly, "Welcome to the Lakeside Riviera."

The place has an old-school charm that's impossible to miss—the kind of charm that makes you feel like you're visiting a beloved countryside retreat.

Warm wood paneling, soft rugs underfoot, and scattered vintage furniture. Emily was right; we need to keep that vibe intact while adding in fresh, modern elements.

My mind races with ideas for the interior designer, and I can hardly wait to dive in.

My phone rings and thinking it's Emily, I quickly fish it out of my pocket.

It's my mother. "Hello Mom," I say.

"Good afternoon," my mother says in her cheerful tone that makes me smile. "I've been trying to get hold of Emily since morning. She's not answering her phone or messages."

I texted her mid-morning and she didn't reply either. "I'm sure she's just busy and she'll get back to you when she can. She had errands to run this morning."

It didn't escape my notice that she didn't want to go into details over what errands she was running. I know it's nothing to do with her apartment because it's already on the market.

I just don't know where to draw the line when it comes to personal matters. How much do married people tell each other?

"Okay, I'm just glad everything is all right," Mom says. "Congratulations again on yesterday. It was wonderful. I'm so proud of both of you."

"Thank you," I say glancing around. We need the same magic to happen here.

We say good bye and I glance at the time on my phone. Emily is twenty minutes later. It's not like her at all. Like me, she's a stickler for time.

I lean against a pillar in the lobby, occasionally glancing out the door. Just as a nagging worry forms within me, Emily bursts in, her face flushed and her hair slightly windblown.

"I'm so sorry," she says, catching her breath, her cheeks slightly pink. "I lost track of time, and then I couldn't find parking..."

"No problem," I say, holding up the flowers with a small smile. "For you."

Her eyes light up, and a grin spreads across her face as she takes them. "You didn't have to, but thank you." She leans in and gives me a quick peck on the cheek.

"Ready to take a look around?" I ask, gesturing toward the lobby.

"Yes, lead the way," she says.

Whatever held her up, it seems like she's back to herself now.

As we walk through the lobby, I turn to Emily, eager to share my thoughts. "You were right. We shouldn't change too much of this place. The charm it has—the warmth, the homey feel—we need to keep that intact."

She smiles, but there's a distant look in her eyes, and instead of her usual enthusiasm, she just nods. "Yeah, absolutely."

I stop and turn to her, quirking an eyebrow. "Where's Emily, and what have you done with her?"

She looks confused for a moment, then chuckles softly. "Why?"

"Well, it's not like you to agree with everything I say," I tease, half-expecting her to playfully argue back or throw in her own ideas. Instead, she simply grins.

"I happen to agree with all your ideas today," she says, a touch of that old spark returning to her expression. I relax a little, letting go of the worry that had been tugging at me.

As we continue our walk through the space, I make a mental note of the areas that need updating, my excitement building.

"Would it be okay if I scheduled a meeting with the interior decorating team for tomorrow morning? I'd love for us to review everything together."

"Okay," she replies.

I give her hand a gentle squeeze. "And tonight, I'm taking you out for dinner. Just us. No work, no business talk."

She nods, her eyes meeting mine and she smiles. "I'd like that."

But as we step through the rooms, I can't shake the feeling that something's weighing on her. I decide to let it go for now. Tonight, I'll take her out and make sure she knows just how much she means to me.

## Chapter 34: Emily

I'm fighting to keep my eyes open over dinner with Andrew. The atmosphere is cozy too, with scented candles giving it a romantic atmosphere and soft music playing in the background.

I'd thought that a warm shower would rejuvenate me but it had the opposite effect. I'm dog-tired. Spending all morning with the doctors, desperate for answers and not getting any.

Andrew reaches across the table. "Is it my company or my restaurant choice? You look like you're fighting to keep your eyes open."

I shake my head. "Neither. You're the best company. I'm just tired." A yawn escapes my mouth.

Andrew's words catch me off guard. "You've been tired a lot lately," he says, his tone light but laced with a hint of concern. "Maybe you're... you know... pregnant?"

I freeze, my heart pounding in my chest. *Pregnant?* He thinks I'm pregnant. Hysterical laughter bubbles up my throat but I push it down.

I really have to tell him. There's no right time for this. I can't hide anymore. Keeping this huge secret from Andrew is the worst thing I've ever done in my life.

My heart pumps hard in my chest. "I'm not pregnant." I say, then meet his gaze. "But there's something I need to tell you." I inhale deeply. Oh God. I'm going to be sick.

He meets my gaze with trusting, worried eyes.

How will he react when he finds out that I've been lying to him all this time? That my father has not been traveling but has been lying in a coma at home, all this time.

"Tell me Emily," Andrew says in a soft voice. "Whatever it is, we can figure it out together. That's why I'm your husband. For better, for worse, remember?"

His words bring tears to my eyes.

I open my mouth, ready to finally confess everything, to tell him the truth I've buried for so long. But just as the words begin to form, my phone rings, shattering the moment.

I glance at the screen, and my heart drops. It's my mother.

"Emily," she says, her voice panicked and raw. "You have to come. It's your father. Please, come to the hospital."

The line goes dead. I stare at my phone, the words echoing in my mind, paralyzing me.

"Emily?" Andrew's voice pulls me back to the present. I push myself up from the table, nearly knocking over my chair in my haste.

"I have to go," I manage, my voice shaking.

Andrew stands too, his expression darkening with concern. "I'm coming with you. Wherever you're going."

"Okay," I whisper, too overwhelmed to argue or find an excuse. There's no hiding now, no more sidestepping the truth. All I can do is get to my father.

I wait for Andrew outside his car as he settles the bill. I fish out my phone from my purse and immediately call Lisa. She answers on the first ring as if she can sense my need for her.

"I just got a call to go to the hospital," I tell her, gripping the phone tightly. "I'm scared Lis."

"I'm coming too," she says and I can hear her moving around. "Everything will be okay."

I spot Andrew and say a hurried goodbye to Lisa. What am I going to tell him now? How do I explain why we're going to a hospital? I can't deal with it right now.

He unlocks the car and without waiting for him to open the door for me, I do it myself and enter, buckling my seatbelt.

As I wait for Andrew to do the same, I struggle to hold back my panic. I feel Andrew's eyes on me, searching for answers I'm not ready to give, but I can barely process anything beyond my mother's words. In a dull voice, I manage to tell him the name of the hospital.

He starts the engine without another word, his jaw clenched in concentration. Silence blankets the car as we drive through the city, the hum of the engine and the occasional soft honk of distant traffic the only sounds.

My hands are twisted together in my lap, fingers digging into my palms as I replay the call in my head.

*Is he worse?* Has there been another stroke? The doctors warned us it was possible, especially with how long he's been in this state.

Andrew reaches over, gently prying one of my hands free from its grip. He holds it tightly, grounding me, his warmth calming my racing thoughts even though he has no idea what's going on.

"It's going to be okay," he says, his voice steady and reassuring.

Luckily at this time of evening, there are a lot of parking spaces and we get one right near the entrance. I don't know what Andrew is thinking as he races after me.

The sterile lights of the hospital blur as I rush through the doors, Andrew by my side. I barely register the receptionist's quick glance in our direction as I head straight to the elevators.

My heart pounds, each beat heavy with dread. The elevator ride to the fifth floor feels excruciatingly slow, the quiet hum doing nothing to soothe my panic.

As soon as the doors open, I'm out, practically running down the hallway. I see my mother, standing in the corner, her shoulders shaking. As I close the distance between us, I see the tears streaming down her face, her usually composed expression crumbling.

The moment she sees me, she rushes forward and clings to me, her hands trembling as she grips my arms.

"He's gone, Emily," she chokes out, her voice thick with grief. "He's gone. His heart just stopped."

My heart feels like it stops, too. I pull her close, feeling her shake against me as she sobs, her pain raw and unfiltered. My mind refuses to process the words.

He can't be gone. He was supposed to wake up. He was supposed to come back to us.

Andrew stands nearby, his hand resting gently on my back. I feel his support, his quiet strength as he stays by my side, though he must be confused about what's going on.

"It happened so fast," my mother whispers through her tears. "One minute, he was stable, and the next..." Her words trail off, lost in another sob.

I don't know how long we stand there, the weight of the moment pressing down on me, suffocating and inescapable. The world around us feels distant and hazy, a harsh contrast to the searing pain in my chest.

I glance up at Andrew, and he gives me a slight nod, his expression filled with compassion and understanding.

The air feels thick, stifling, as I stand with my mother, her body trembling against mine. I don't know how to comfort her; I don't know how to comfort myself.

My father is gone. The words echo hollowly in my mind, and I'm not sure if I'll ever be able to grasp their reality.

Then I spot Lisa rushing into the waiting room. She spots us immediately, her face stricken, and she hurries over, wrapping her arms around me and my mother without a word.

The warmth of her embrace is grounding, giving me something to hold onto as my world unravels.

She doesn't need to ask. She knows without my telling her that he's gone.

After a moment, I glance up at Andrew. His face is drawn with concern, but there's patience there too—a willingness to wait until I'm ready to explain.

It hits me how little he knows, how I've kept so much from him, and the weight of it is like something sitting on my chest.

I take a deep breath, letting go of Lisa and my mother, and walk over to him. My hands shake as I reach for him, feeling like an imposter.

"I'm so sorry, Em." His voice is low, his gaze warm but laced with sympathy. He takes my hands, his thumbs brushing over my knuckles as he holds me.

He pauses, his brows knitting together. "Who died?"

## Chapter 35: Andrew

"My father," Emily whispers, her voice breaking.

Confusion scrambles through my mind. "Your father?" I repeat, needing to hear it again to make sure I didn't misinterpret her words.

She nods, her gaze cast downward. "He's been in the hospital these last few days. It was a stroke."

Shock roots me in place. "You didn't tell me?"

Emily's eyes flicker with guilt. "It's not the only thing I didn't tell you. He wasn't traveling, Andrew. He had a major stroke almost ten months ago. He's been at home ever since, in a coma. We hoped he'd wake up, but now..."

Her voice cracks, and she can't finish the sentence. Tears spill down her cheeks, and she looks small, fragile.

Before I can process it all, she starts to cry, and instinctively, I pull her into my arms. She shakes, her grief raw and deep, and I hold her but my mind is reeling.

Her father has been in a coma all this time? Not overseas? The man she mentioned in passing, always 'somewhere else,' was actually fighting for his life at home.

A surge of disbelief twists in my gut, and I struggle to keep it from showing on my face.

The woman I'm holding in my arms, the one I thought I knew, feels like a stranger in this moment. All this time, she's been carrying this, hiding it from me.

"Why didn't you tell me?" I ask her, drawing back to look at her face.

"He didn't want anyone to know. He made my mother and me promise to keep it a secret," Emily says.

Lisa taps her on the shoulder. "We need to sort out a few things."

There are practical arrangements to be made and I trail after the three women around the hospital. I'm shocked and frankly I desperately need to get out of here.

Finally, we leave. Outside, Emily says, "I have to go home with my mother."

I nod, relief surging through me. Right now, I can't bear to look at her.

I watch her go, her form disappearing down the hallway with her mother and Lisa by her side, and the relief is almost overwhelming.

The weight of what I've just learned presses down on me, suffocating and raw. I need air.

Outside, the cool night air bites against my skin, but it does little to ease the storm inside me. I lean against the car, struggling to process everything she just told me.

Her father, the man she spoke of as if he were traveling the world, was in a coma this whole time. I'd never questioned her stories, never thought to.

Every time she said she was visiting her mother, I'd assumed it was exactly that. But all along, she'd been going to see her father. It makes sense now.

The disappearances, the way Emily would sometimes look as if she was carrying the weight of the world on her shoulders.

What doesn't make sense is the lies. Why? Why would you lie to a man you were married to? A man you claimed to love. Hurt wedges itself deep in my chest.

A part of me tries to understand, to make sense of her secrecy. She said her father didn't want anyone to know, that it was his wish.

But she was my wife, wasn't she? Shouldn't that have meant something? Shouldn't she have trusted me enough to share that part of herself, of her life?

The anger simmering beneath the shock builds. This wasn't a small omission; it was a lie woven into every interaction, every moment we spent together.

And all those times I'd been there, wanting to support her, to get closer to her, she kept me at arm's length with a story that wasn't real.

I shake my head, running a hand through my hair. The realization stings. I don't know her as well as I thought I did. The truth is I don't know Emily, at all.

After a few deep breaths, I get into the car and sit there, gripping the steering wheel tightly. I'd wanted a partner who'd be open with me, someone I could trust unconditionally.

And like an idiot, I thought I'd found it with Emily. Intense pain rumbles through me.

Was it all a lie? The pretense at having feelings for me? Memories sear my heart. Us lying in bed after making love. Talking. Opening our hearts to each other.

What had Emily been thinking at the time? Had it all been a game to her? Pain ripples across my chest in waves.

Unable to face the emptiness of home, the place now haunted by every memory I've made with Emily, I find myself at the Bennett Developers offices instead.

There's a faint glow coming from Daniel's office down the hall, the only light in the building.

I push open his door, and Daniel looks up, surprised. "What are you doing here at this hour?"

I manage a shrug. "Could ask you the same thing."

He sighs, rubbing his neck. "Trying to finish some work." He pauses, then adds, "You look like hell, Andrew. What's going on?"

I step in, my resolve wavering as I take a seat. Daniel's the last person I'd ever want to open up to, but right now, I don't think I can hold this in alone. The truth tumbles out, raw and strained.

"Emily's father is dead."

Daniel's eyes widen, his brow furrowing. "Dead? But wasn't he traveling?"

"That's what I thought too," I say bitterly. "But he's been here the whole time, in a coma. Since before we even got married."

Shock flashes across Daniel's face. He shakes his head slowly. "A coma? And you didn't know?"

I let out a humorless laugh, rubbing my hands over my face. "All these months. I was there, by her side, while she told me he was overseas, off on some trip. Meanwhile, he was here. Fighting to survive." The words taste bitter. "And I didn't even know."

Daniel lets out a low whistle, taking it all in. "Wow. I don't even know what to say."

"Everything I thought I knew about her was a lie. How do I trust her now?"

Daniel leans forward, watching me carefully. "She must've had her reasons, Andrew. And you said they were following his wishes to keep it a secret. But yeah, it's a hell of a thing to find out like this." He pauses, searching my face. "You need a drink. Come on. I'll keep you company."

I nod, needing the break from my own spinning thoughts, and follow him as we head out to a nearby bar.

We find a quiet corner, away from the noise. I order a whiskey, while Daniel sticks to water.

As the amber liquid burns its way down, my mind turns back to Emily. "She should have told me, Daniel. I'm her husband. I should have been part of this."

Daniel leans back, his face thoughtful. "Maybe she didn't know how. Or maybe she thought you'd not understand."

I look up sharply. "Why wouldn't I understand?"

Daniel shrugs. "The need for secrecy. I imagine she would have had to swear you to secrecy and knowing you, I don't know if you would have agreed."

"That's not the kind of secret you keep. The man was in a coma. How can you keep that from people you consider family?"

Every time I think of the magnitude of the lie, it baffles me. I just don't get it. Daniel is right. I would never have been a party to such a lie.

I motion to the waiter for two more doubles, draining them faster than I should. The alcohol hits my veins, my body warm and numb.

"Maybe you should get some water now," Daniel says, eyeing me with concern.

I order two double whiskies and drain them in less than five minutes. I'm probably getting drunk, but I don't care. I just need something to numb the pain in my body.

"You're slurring," Daniel says at some point. "Maybe you should get some water now."

I laugh. "That's you saying that I should get some water?"

Daniel doesn't laugh. "Listen, I know how it feels like to use alcohol to cover up your pain or shame. Trust me bro, it doesn't help. It makes everything a lot worse than it is and makes you do really stupid things."

I stared at him incredulously. "I stared at him incredulously. "What am I going to do? Go to Emily when she's mourning her father and tell her what? That she's a liar? An imposter? Cold-hearted?"

A thought crosses my mind. Something I hadn't thought of before. Another laugh leaves my mouth. "My she's good. She had us all fooled. The only thing Emily is interested in is saving her father's precious company."

I grip Daniel's hand. "Which woman would agree to marry her fiancé's brother after he ditched her?" I shake my head at how deep in the sand my head had been.

"I don't think that's fair," Daniel starts to say.

"No, what's not fair is how stupid I was," I continue, then I take a generous sip of my whisky.

The pain is gone. I feel nothing.

"I'm guessing this is the wrong time to put some sense into you," Daniel says with a sigh.

I shake my head, bitterness creeping in. "I was supposed to be there for her. To support her through anything. I thought we had that kind of marriage. But I'm nothing more than a stranger to her."

Words leave my mouth without my brain filtering them. “She doesn’t even love me,” I mutter, barely coherent. “I was just convenient.”

“Alright, that’s enough, man. Come on, I’m getting you out of here.” Daniel gets up and pulls me to my feet.

I stumble, my legs shaky, the room spinning slightly, and Daniel’s grip on my arm as he leads me out.

The night air is cool against my face, and as I half-collapse into the passenger seat, Daniel chuckles dryly. “Guess I’m driving.”

I sink back into the seat, the alcohol thick in my veins, the hurt buried somewhere I can’t reach for now. I close my eyes, letting the world blur around me, glad for the silence.

## Chapter 36: Andrew

A shrill sound cuts through my pounding head, dragging me from a haze of deep sleep. My phone vibrates insistently on the nightstand, and with a groan, I reach out, squinting as the harsh light pierces my eyes.

"Damn it," I mutter, memories of last night flashing by in snippets—the whiskey, the bitter words spilling from my mouth, Daniel seeing me unravelling.

My father's voice crackles through the phone, jolting me further awake. "I heard Ace is gone?"

For a second, the words don't land, then the reality crashes down, flooding me with that sick weight in my stomach.

"Yes," I manage, voice raw. "He's gone."

A pause stretches between us. "Come by the house. We need to talk."

I rub my face. "Yeah, I'll stop by."

I toss the phone aside, groaning as I sit up, my skull feeling like it's trying to split itself open. The faint sounds of scratching at the door echo in from the hallway.

Bruno and Bear are probably hungry and eager to start the day, blissfully unaware of the mess their human has made of his life.

I force myself up, dragging my feet over to the door. They rush past me, tails wagging, bouncing around my legs. I head downstairs to the kitchen, grab their bowls, fill them with food, and open the backdoor, letting them bound out into the morning sun.

I make my way to the shower. The cold spray hits like needles, and for a second, it's torture. But slowly, it works. The fog in my mind lifts a little, though it doesn't wash away the regret coiled inside me.

Why the fuck did I drink so much last night? It solved fuck all.

I grip the sides of the shower, remembering the words I threw around last night, my anger unraveling like a thread I'd lost control over.

After dressing and grabbing my keys, I head out, steering toward my parents' house in a fog that's half hangover, half emotional numbness.

I feel like an old man as I park my car and amble to the front door. My mother greets me at the door, her face drawn and eyes rimmed with red.

She gives me a quiet hug, and together we walk into the living room where my father is waiting, seated with his hands clasped tightly in front of him.

I take a seat across from them, the silence heavy and expectant. My mother's gaze searches my face. I know they have as many questions as I did.

"So, what happened?" my father finally prompts, his voice low and serious.

I swallow, and the words spill out—how Emily's father had been in a coma all this time, how she'd kept it from me, from everyone, pretending he was simply off traveling.

I lay it all out, every lie, every moment of deception.

My father nods slowly, absorbing it all, and then he speaks with that familiar, pragmatic tone. "Well, this doesn't change anything as far as our partnership is concerned."

I nod, relief that we're talking business. I'm too drained for anything else. "I agree," I say.

My mother breaks in, her voice trembling. "But why didn't Emily tell us? Tell you, Andrew? You're her husband."

"I've been asking myself that question since yesterday," I say, the anger a dull ache now.

My father sighs, looking as if he's working through a puzzle. "Maybe she was worried about how it would impact the company's reputation. I imagine keeping it quiet seemed like the safest choice for her."

My mother's brow furrows, and she glances over at me, pain in her eyes. "Didn't you suspect something was going on? That's a huge secret to hide and you lived with her, Andrew."

There's an accusing tone in my mother's tone. I don't blame her. I've gone through everything with a tooth comb, but the truth is that Emily was very clever.

She showed no signs of keeping secrets. She seemed open with me and as for going to her parents' home so often, I chalked it up to their being close. After all, she's the only child.

I shake my head, my chest tight. "I was in the dark too. Found out yesterday when she got that call to go to the hospital."

There's a pause, and then my father speaks up. "We have to keep moving, keep building momentum from the launch.

"This could be a turning point for the company—let's take advantage of these wins while we have them. How far along are you with the Lakeside Riviera project?"

I'm about to answer when my mother interjects, horrified. "You can't be thinking about business right now. Emily just lost her father, for heaven's sake."

My heart hardens. Emily herself felt no qualms about lying to me. For months.

"No," I say firmly, ignoring the flicker of my mother's protest. "Father is right. This is business. That's all there is now." I turn to my father. "I'll go forward with the renovations, make sure Lakeside gets the same treatment as Army Base."

"Good," my father says, satisfaction in his voice.

With that, I leave the house, heading straight for the Riviera.

As I step into the building, a somber atmosphere greets me. Phones ring incessantly, and the staff's usual chatter is subdued, everyone restrained in light of the news.

Half an hour later, Catherine knocks lightly on my office door, and steps in, a file under her arm.

"The press are asking for a statement, sir," she says, her voice hesitant. "What should we tell them?"

I close the records I've been reviewing. "That's Emily's call," I say, trying to keep my tone even, though just the thought of her sends a mix of emotions surging through me.

Catherine nods but shifts uncomfortably. "The thing is, there are rumors circulating. Speculation that Mr. Young had been in a coma for months."

I let out a sigh, pressing my fingers to my temples. "I'll get hold of Emily and let you know."

I pick up my phone, scrolling to her contact, and hit call. It rings twice before her voice comes on the line. Just hearing her sounding fragile and lost, tugs at something deep in me, but I push the feeling aside.

"The press is all over this," I say after we've exchanged politely painful pleasantries. "What information do you want to give them?"

There's a pause on her end. "I don't know," she whispers. I can almost hear the struggle in her voice.

"When will I see you? Will you come over?"

Her question hits me hard. I can feel her waiting on the other end, the silence stretching between us, thick with everything left unsaid.

"I can't, Emily." The words leave me before I can second-guess them.

Another pause, then, "I understand," she says, her voice barely audible.

We disconnect the call, but I'm left with a strange ache, one I can't quite shake. She sounds so lost, so vulnerable, but then again, she's the same woman who lied to me, deceived me about something monumental.

I remind myself of that, forcing myself to remember why I need distance.

I sit back in my chair, staring at the phone in my hand, fighting the temptation to call her back. No. This is where I draw the line.

Instead, I type up a statement for the media, something neutral but respectful.

**Ace Young has been ailing for some time. At this moment, the family is asking for privacy as they cope with their loss.**

I read it over a few times, ensuring it's precise and leaves nothing more to be questioned. Once satisfied, I call Catherine.

She enters, and I hand her the draft. "Use this for the statement," I say, keeping my voice even.

Catherine glances at the words, nodding slowly. "Thank you, sir. It's such a shock for everyone in the company." She looks up, her expression one of genuine concern. "I can only imagine what it must be like for you."

If only she knew. This is just as big a shock for me as it is for everyone else, maybe more. I nod, dismissing her as she leaves with the statement.

Sitting back, confliction whirls in my mind. Emily's voice haunts me. She sounded so broken. All my instincts are screaming that I should go to her.

But in doing so, won't I also be lying? Best thing is to keep my distance. I'll attend the funeral service, but not as Emily's husband. That part of our life is over.

## Chapter 37: Emily

"Have you spoken to Andrew at all?" my mother asks gently, her hands folded in her lap.

I sit in the living room, a strange emptiness settling over me. My mother and Lisa are beside me, their concerned gazes fixed on me.

It's been two weeks since we laid my father to rest, and though the physical exhaustion is slowly fading, an ache lingers that I can't shake.

The mention of Andrew deepens the ache.

*God, I miss him.*

I miss him with every fiber of my being. I miss his steady presence. His practical nature. His loving, sweet side that I got the rare opportunity to see. I miss his gorgeous face. I miss his arms around me.

I shake myself out of my thoughts and force myself to focus on the present.

"I only saw him briefly at the funeral service," I reply quietly. "We barely spoke." The words feel hollow, a reminder of how distant he feels from me now.

Despite everything, I know Andrew has already started work on the Lakeside Riviera. Amy has been updating me. Not that I have much interest.

The one thing I was obsessed about has faded into the background. My father isn't here to see any of it. Andrew can renovate it any way he wants; none of it matters the way it once did.

"What happens now?" Lisa asks softly, her voice careful. "Will you stay married?"

A painful twist forms in my heart as I recall that last conversation with Andrew, his voice echoing in my mind when I asked him if he would come see me.

*I can't.*

I had known immediately what he meant, had felt it settle inside me. The lies had fractured something irrevocable between us.

"No," I murmur, barely able to say it aloud. "I know Andrew. He won't forgive this."

My mother's hand comes to rest on mine. "It was out of your hands, Emily. You were keeping your father's promise."

I shake my head, looking down at her hand on mine. "Andrew is my husband, Mom. I lied to him, again and again. There's no excuse for that."

Lisa lets out a quiet sigh, her eyes filled with empathy. "So you'll move out?"

"Yeah," I reply, forcing a small, empty smile. "That's the plan. Thankfully, my apartment hasn't been sold yet. I'll move back in while I figure out what comes next."

"Or you could come back home," my mother suggests, her voice filled with a quiet hope that tugs at me.

I glance around the familiar walls of my childhood home. Being here these past two weeks has reminded me how much I need space—time alone to fully process, to grieve, to heal from losing both my father and my marriage.

I squeeze my mother's hand. "I'll come often, Mom," I say. Then, drawing a deep breath, I stand. "No point in putting it off any longer."

Lisa stands with me, a hesitant look in her eyes. "I'll come with you," she offers.

I give her a grateful smile but shake my head. "Thanks, but Andrew might be home. We'll probably need to talk."

She nods, understanding. "Okay. But call me if you need me."

With a last hug for my mother and Lisa, I gather my things and head to the door. The drive back to Andrew's house—our house, I remind myself—feels longer than usual.

I pull up in front of the house, my heart a confused mess of longing and dread. I'm barely aware of shutting off the engine, of stepping out of the car and walking to the door.

This place that once felt like home, where I imagined a future with Andrew, now feels cold, unfamiliar.

As soon as I step inside, Bruno and Bear come bounding out from the kitchen, their tails wagging.

A small smile manages to find its way to my face, and I kneel, running my hands over their warm, familiar fur. “I’ve missed you guys so much,” I murmur, rubbing their ears.

But then I hear footsteps, and I look up. Andrew stands in the hallway, watching me with an expression I can’t quite read.

He looks exhausted, with shadows under his eyes, his face tight with strain.

My heart races as I take him in, every nerve in my body buzzing to life. He looks like he hasn’t slept, like he’s been carrying his own storm of emotions—and seeing him like this turns my knees to jelly, sending a shiver through my lungs.

I get to my feet, and we stare at each other, the silence stretching painfully between us. There are so many things I want to say, so many explanations on the tip of my tongue, but none of them feel right.

Instead, I gather what strength I have left and manage, ‘I’ve come to get my stuff. The rest will be collected by the movers.”

He nods, his face impassive. “I think that’s best.”

The tiny hope I had clung to—some miracle that he would want to talk, that he might give me a chance to explain—shatters.

He doesn’t say another word. He just turns and heads toward the kitchen, leaving me standing there, aching and hollow.

Blinking back tears, I steel myself and head up the stairs, the dogs following close behind me, wagging their tails.

Once in my room, I grab a suitcase from the closet and look around.

Memories flood over me with each item I touch, each familiar corner of this space we once shared. My hand shakes as I zip open the suitcase and start to pack, but the numbness wears off quickly, replaced by a fresh wave of grief.

My chest tightens as I remember how Andrew gave up the master bedroom without a second thought, just to make me feel at home.

The tears I've been holding back finally spill over, silent and hot against my skin.

I never wanted this. All my life, I've done my best to keep my promises, to honor my commitments. And keeping my father's last wish—it felt sacred, something I couldn't betray.

But what has it cost me? The man I love, the life we could have built together. And for what? A lie that grew so big it consumed everything.

I clutch my suitcase, anger rising as I think of my father, of the promise he made me swear to uphold, binding me to silence. I loved him, and I wanted to honor his wishes, but it was unfair.

This secret has cost me so much. It's broken the one thing I thought would last—the one man I thought I could rely on. The man I love more than I ever thought I could, with his steady, dependable presence, his deep, unwavering love.

And I've let him down. I've destroyed us.

Lost in my thoughts, I almost don't hear the soft knock on the door. I look up and see Andrew standing there, his hand resting on the frame.

His gaze moves to the suitcase at my feet, and he pauses, as if debating whether to say anything at all. After a moment, he speaks.

"Do you need help carrying anything out?" he asks, his voice calm, neutral.

I shake my head, trying to keep my voice steady. "No, I've got it."

For a moment, we just stand there, locked in this unbearable silence. The air between us feels charged with everything we haven't said, everything we can't take back.

I want to tell him how sorry I am, that I never meant to hurt him, that I would give anything to undo it all. But the words won't come, and I'm not even sure they'd make a difference if they did.

"I thought I knew you," Andrew says.

I freeze, his words piercing through me. His gaze is intense, filled with an ache I recognize because it mirrors my own.

"Andrew..." My voice is barely audible. "I never wanted to lie to you. I was trying to keep a promise, to honor my father. I didn't want to hurt you."

He takes a step closer, and the raw emotion in his face is almost too much to bear. "You did hurt me, Emily. Every time you looked me in the eyes and told me your father was traveling, every time you chose the lie over me, over us..."

His voice breaks slightly, and he shakes his head, struggling to keep his composure. "I was your husband. I thought you trusted me."

Tears spill over my cheeks as I nod, my heart splintering. "I did trust you. I do. But I felt trapped, and I thought I was doing the right thing, even though it feels so wrong now."

His jaw tightens, and he looks away, his shoulders tense. "How am I supposed to move past that, Emily? You had every opportunity to tell me the truth. But you chose to lie, over and over again. I can't just forget that."

I open my mouth to reply, but the words stick, swallowed by the weight of everything I've done. He's right. I had every chance to tell him, every chance to choose him, but I let my fear control me, let it dictate my choices. And now, it's too late.

Andrew takes a deep breath, his face hardening. "I think it's best if we both move on. You've got your life to live, and I've got mine."

His words are like a final blow, and their harshness leaves me breathless. I had hoped for a miracle, some way to make this right, but now, I realize it's truly over.

He's not coming back. The man I love, the man who had once looked at me with such warmth, is gone.

I nod, swallowing back tears. "I understand," I whisper, though the words feel hollow. How am I supposed to live without him?

He steps aside, and I drag my suitcase down the stairs, each step heavy, the dogs watching me as if sensing the shift.

When I reach the front door, I pause, glancing back one last time.

Andrew stands at the top of the stairs, his hands shoved into his pockets, his gaze distant.

I want to say something, anything, to make him look at me the way he used to, to bring back the man I knew. But I know he's already gone, lost in the hurt and betrayal I've caused.

"Goodbye, Andrew," I say, my heart breaking all over again.

He doesn't respond, doesn't even look at me. He's already looking past me, to a future that doesn't include us.

With a shaky breath, I step outside, the cool air hitting me like a slap. The tears finally spill over as I walk to my car, closing the door softly behind me.

The world feels empty, and I know that whatever life I have left will feel like this—cold, barren, without him.

## Chapter 38: Andrew

As I enter the maternity wing, I clutch a bouquet of soft pink roses and a box of chocolates. I know Sarah has a sweet tooth, and she deserves all the treats today.

Jack's already by her side when I step into the room, and Sarah's face lights up when she sees the flowers.

"For you," I say, handing them to her along with the chocolates.

She beams, holding the bouquet up to her nose. "Thank you, Andrew. These are beautiful."

Jack chuckles, taking the chocolates from me with a grin. "You know her too well. She'll probably go through half of these before we leave the hospital."

Sarah laughs, giving Jack a playful nudge. "And I'll enjoy every bite."

I smile, settling in as I watch them share a look that's both familiar and full of excitement. Then Sarah glances down at the little bundle in her arms and looks back at me, her expression soft.

"Do you want to hold him?" she asks gently, and my heart skips a beat. "You're his godfather. Might as well get used to it," she teases.

"I don't know, Sarah," I mumble, hesitating. "He's so small."

Jack chuckles, nudging me. "C'mon, Andrew. It's not as terrifying as it looks. You won't break him."

I take a deep breath, then nod. Sarah carefully hands the baby over, and I sit down, cradling him as I try to settle into this unexpected moment.

Liam's eyes are tightly shut, his little face peaceful. The world outside fades away as I look at him.

"He's so tiny," I whisper, almost to myself. There's an awe in my voice that I can't disguise, and Jack chuckles softly.

Sarah watches us. "Isn't he? But he's a fighter. You'll see."

A pang hits my chest, and I can't stop my mind from drifting back to Emily. We'd talked about this, about someday having a child of our own. But now...

I brush away the thought, trying to focus on the here and now, the miracle I'm holding.

Jack breaks the silence, beaming as he says, "We've named him Liam. After my grandfather."

"It's a strong name," I say, glancing up with a small smile. "Your grandfather would be proud."

Jack gives me a nod, pride filling his expression. After a few more moments, I carefully hand Liam back to Sarah, feeling an unexpected emptiness as I let him go.

When it's time to leave, Jack walks me out. He's grinning, his eyes still glowing with the excitement of fatherhood. But then his expression softens, and he glances over at me.

"How's Emily?" he asks quietly.

I shake my head. "I don't know, Jack. We haven't spoken in over six weeks."

Jack frowns, giving me a searching look. "You know, people make mistakes, Andrew. That doesn't make them bad people."

The words hit me hard, but I don't know how to respond. I swallow, looking away. "It's all in the past," I say finally, not wanting to dig into the raw ache that's still there.

Jack sighs, nodding slowly. "Alright. I won't push." He hesitates, then gives me a small, hopeful smile. "You know, Sarah really liked Emily. She's been talking about asking her to be Liam's godmother."

The suggestion stuns me. "Emily? As Liam's godmother?"

Jack nods, his eyes full of understanding. "Yeah. She felt a connection with Emily. She wants someone who feels like family."

I take a deep breath, feeling emotions I've been trying to bury for weeks rise to the surface. Emily as Liam's godmother. I picture her holding Liam, smiling down at him with that gentle look in her eyes, and it's almost too much to bear.

Jack's gaze softens. "I know it's complicated, Andrew. But you both shared something real. Just think about it."

I nod, not trusting myself to speak. Jack gives my shoulder a reassuring squeeze before he heads back to Sarah, and I walk away, Liam's tiny face still etched in my mind.

As I exit the hospital, I can't shake the thought of what might have been, of the life I thought Emily and I would build together.

Sundays are turning out to be my worst days.

It's the day that used to feel like a reset. Making love with Emily in the morning, playing with the dogs in the backyard, then lunch at my parents' with Emily.

Now, it's just another reminder of what I don't have. The house is too quiet. It feels like an abandoned home. Every room reminds me of Emily. The only reason I go home at the end of each day is because of Bruno and Bear.

I haven't moved back into the master bedroom. It's too painful. Too stark of a reminder of Emily.

I head to my parents' house for lunch. I've missed the last two Sunday lunches, using work as my excuse, but now Mom's insistence finally wore me down.

As soon as I step inside, the familiar scent food fills the air. My stomach growls, reminding me that I skipped breakfast this morning. I'm not eating properly, I barely slept. I lied to Jack when I said it's all in the past.

Emily is with me day in and day out. The only time I get a respite from aching for her is the few hours of sleep that I catch at night.

My mother's face lights up as she sees me, though her eyes have a hint of that worried look she's been giving me lately. She and Daniel are in the living room, and they stand up when I enter.

"I've called you twice and you haven't returned my calls," Daniel says.

I sigh, running a hand through my hair. "I've been busy. Renovations at the Lakeside Riviera are all-consuming right now."

He raises an eyebrow, looking unconvinced. "Sure. Because that's definitely what's been keeping you occupied."

It's only been a minute, and he's already calling me out. I force a tight smile, realizing he sees right through me. Honestly, I've barely been functioning, if I'm being real with myself. Work is just an excuse.

Mom gestures towards the couch. "Sit down. We haven't seen much of you."

I sink into my favorite armchair. "Where's Dad?"

"Finishing up some work," Mom says, rolling her eyes. "On a Sunday. I can't wait for him to retire."

"Good luck with that," I retort and she merely smiles back, as if she knows something that I don't.

Her features grow solemn, glancing at Daniel before looking back at me. "You know, I've been thinking a lot lately, Andrew. About how your father and I almost didn't get married."

"What do you mean?" I ask, wondering where that came from.

She chuckles softly, though her eyes are serious. "We had a misunderstanding. A big one. I was so convinced he didn't care about what I wanted. But, well, things were complicated, and I almost left. It took us a while to really talk it out. Almost didn't happen, you know."

I nod, as understanding dawns. She's referring to me and Emily. "It's different for us. Emily lied to me. You don't lie about something so monumental." My words don't have as much conviction as they did in the weeks following our separation.

She nods. "Maybe. But sometimes, when emotions are high, it's hard to see the bigger picture. I just don't want you to give up on something that might be worth holding onto."

Her words settle stir up emotions I thought I had a handle on.

Just then, my father enters the room and breaks the tension. "Alright, enough lingering in here. Let's get to the dining room before the food gets cold."

We troop out and settle around the dining table. Just as we're about to start, Dad clears his throat, a serious expression on his face.

"I wanted to talk to you both," he begins, his gaze moving between Daniel and me. "Your mother and I have made a decision."

Mom looks at him, and I catch the slightest nod of encouragement from her.

"It's time I start stepping back," he continues, his tone steady. "Your mother's been more than patient all these years, with all my long hours and missed dinners. She deserves more of my time now, and I'm ready to give it to her. So, I'll be retiring at the end of the year."

I stare at him, processing his words, while my mother's face glows with pride. After all these years, I'd always seen him as someone who'd never step down.

"Andrew," he says, turning to me. "I want you to take over. To be the CEO of Bennett Developers. You've earned it. I know the company will be in good hands with you."

A flood of emotions surge through me. I've wanted this but never thought it would actually happen.

Daniel claps me on the back with a grin. "Congrats, man. You're going to do great."

Mom reaches across the table, squeezing my hand with a proud smile. "We're so happy for you, Andrew. You deserve this."

I find myself smiling back, trying to express the gratitude I know they expect. "Thank you. It means a lot to me."

Mom stands, her eyes shining. "Well, I think this calls for some champagne."

"Shouldn't we eat first?" Daniel says. "What's happening to my family?"

We all laugh and Mom heads to the kitchen, returning with a bottle and glasses. She pours for each of us, and we clink glasses, and everyone around me is grinning, laughing, celebrating.

But as I take a sip, the fleeting joy I felt evaporates.

I should be ecstatic. This is what I've worked so hard for, the dream I've chased for as long as I can remember. I've finally proven myself, shown my family that I'm capable of leadership, of taking on this role.

Yet, all I feel is a dull ache, a hollow emptiness that I can't shake.

I raise my glass again, taking another sip as everyone continues talking around me, but my mind drifts elsewhere. The taste of victory is bitter, tainted by the lingering absence of the one person I wish could share this moment with me.

Emily.

Even after everything, after the lies and betrayal, she's the one I ache for. She's the missing piece, the one who makes everything make sense. Without her, all of this—the title, the success—it feels incomplete.

I realize with a pang that I've been lying to myself. Telling myself that I could just move on, build this life without her, fill the void with work and titles and ambition.

But it's her I want, her I miss. She's the one who made me feel grounded, whole.

## Chapter 39: Emily

I'm at my desk, struggling to keep my focus, when Amy, our operations director, knocks lightly and steps in.

"Hi, Emily," she says. "I've just come from the Lakeside Riviera. It looks fabulous. You should pop by and take a look."

It's no secret in the office that I haven't gone to see the renovations. I can't bear to see my father's favorite hotel, the first one he ever built, torn and remodeled into something that he would have hated.

I smile politely and nod. "That's good," I say in a voice that sounds as dull as I feel.

Amy watches me for a second, as if expecting more, but when I don't say anything else, she gives a small nod and leaves.

I turn back to my screen, staring at the spreadsheets and emails I've been trying to work on all day, though none of it holds my attention.

It's afternoon, and I can't wait for the day to be over. There's a drinks date with Lisa that I'm holding on to like a lifeline, the one small point of brightness on the horizon.

I try diving back into my work, but my focus drifts. The words on my screen blur, and the numbers lose meaning. Then my phone rings, and I grab it, grateful for the distraction. Sarah's name flashes on the screen.

"Hello?" I say, forcing my voice into something resembling cheerfulness.

"I had the baby boy," she says after we exchange greeting." Sarah's voice is warm and full of joy, and a small smile tugs at my lips in spite of myself.

"Congratulations. That's wonderful." I reach for a sticky note, making a note of sending her flowers.

"Thank you," she says, her voice softer now. "Emily, I was hoping... I mean, I'd really like it if you'd be Liam's godmother."

Her words stop me short. "Me?" My voice wavers, caught between surprise and gratitude. "Sarah, you know Andrew and I are separated?"

"Yes," she says gently. "But I have faith that you'll work it out. I've never seen Andrew look at a woman the way he looks at you, Emily. He adores you."

A knot forms in my throat, and I glance away, swallowing hard. "It's been two months, Sarah," I say quietly. "I think he's moved on."

"He just needs time," she says confidently. "I know him. Andrew's hurt, but he's also the kind of man who sees through to what matters. You're what matters, Emily."

I close my eyes, Sarah's words washing over me like a balm. I want to believe her, more than anything, but I saw Andrew's eyes. He meant it. We're done.

"So what do you say?" Sarah's voice brings me back to the moment.

"I'd be honored," I say. "Thank you."

We exchange a few more words, but I feel the sting of tears and know I need a moment. When we hang up, I take a deep breath, trying to push the emotions back down.

A soft knock on the door interrupts my thoughts, and Catherine peeks in. I fight down my irritation. I can't seem to get a moment alone.

"Matthew's here, waiting to see you," she says.

I take a moment to collect myself, nodding. "Show him in."

Matthew enters, the spreadsheets and financial reports in hand, and begins explaining the latest financial projections.

I know I should be listening carefully, analyzing each figure, but my mind keeps drifting back to Sarah's words, to the baby, to Andrew.

"...and with these adjustments, we're seeing a solid quarter," Matthew finishes, his gaze expectant as he waits for my response.

I blink, scrambling to pull myself back into the moment. "Right. That's good. Thank you, Matthew," I say, forcing a smile.

He hesitates, as if he senses something is off, but he nods and gathers his things, leaving me alone in the office.

I let out a breath I didn't realize I was holding. Relief floods over me as soon as he's gone. I'm barely managing to keep it together, and the meetings, decisions, and updates are only making it harder.

Everything feels heavy—like I'm moving through quicksand.

I glance at the clock, grateful that the day is finally inching toward its end. The idea of escaping into the noisy din of a bar with Lisa feels like the best relief I'll get right now.

***

The evening feels empty as I step into my apartment, a pristine, renovated space that's beautifully put together but lacks any warmth.

It's like a model unit in some upscale brochure, with perfect finishes and coordinated decor, yet it doesn't feel like mine. The walls are silent, cold.

There's no sound of paws skittering across the floor, no Bear and Bruno greeting me at the door, tails wagging. And, of course, no Andrew. No warm embrace, no familiar scent, no one to make me feel like I belong here.

It's thick, almost oppressive, as I move through the place. I shed my work clothes and step into the shower, hoping the water will wash away some of the weariness that clings to me.

When I'm done, I slip into something comfortable but presentable, glancing at myself in the mirror and barely recognizing the woman staring back. I brush a comb through my hair, barely paying attention.

With a deep breath, I head out, hoping the night with Lisa might provide some kind of escape.

In the Uber, my phone rings, and I glance at the screen, surprised to see Daniel's name flash up.

"Hello?"

"Hey, Emily," he says, his voice unusually serious. "Can we meet? Just briefly."

I hesitate. "I'm actually on my way to meet Lisa for drinks."

There's a pause, then he says, "If you don't mind, I'll join you guys?"

I'm curious over why he wants us to meet. "Fine."

I reach the bar first, settling into a booth and ordering a cocktail to take the edge off. A minute later, Lisa arrives, giving me one of her all-seeing looks.

"You look like shit," she says bluntly, sliding into the seat across from me.

I raise an eyebrow, more amused than offended. "Thanks. That's exactly what I needed to hear."

"I mean it," she continues, waving a hand toward my hair and lackluster appearance. "What happened to a bit of makeup and a salon visit? It wouldn't hurt, you know."

I shrug. "I'm just tired, Lisa."

"You have to take care of yourself, Em," she says, her tone softening. "You can't let yourself go."

How do I even begin to explain to my best friend that I've lost interest in everything? That my entire life feels as though it's unraveled in a way I can't seem to stitch back together?

The server arrives with Lisa's cocktail drink. "I know grief is tough," Lisa says, taking a sip. "But you have to try."

I shake my head. "It's not grief, Lisa. I mean, not really." I look down at my glass, swirling the liquid inside. "I think I grieved my father a long time ago. When he went into a coma, a part of me just knew he wasn't coming back."

Lisa watches me, her face soft with understanding, but then she gives me a probing look. "So if it's not grief, then it's Andrew."

Before I can respond, Daniel walks in, spotting us and striding over. He greets us with a small hug, then takes a seat across from me.

“You look as shitty as he does,” he says, and waves over the server and orders water.

I raise an eyebrow at his choice. “Water?”

Daniel nods, looking pleased with himself. “I haven’t had a drink in nine weeks.”

Lisa and I exchange impressed glances, congratulating him. “That’s great,” I say, genuinely happy for him. “How’s work?”

“It’s surprisingly fulfilling,” he says. “I see now why my brother’s a workaholic.”

It’s then that the question tumbles out before I can stop myself. “How is he?” I hold my breath waiting for his answer.

Daniel’s expression softens. “Terrible,” he says bluntly. “He misses you. That’s actually why I wanted to talk to you.”

A wild hope springs up in my chest, hammering against my ribcage. “He misses me?”

Daniel nods. “More than he’ll ever admit. Dad’s retiring, you know. He’s making Andrew CEO, but Andrew’s more miserable than ever.”

A pang comes over me. A bittersweet mixture of pride and sadness. Andrew had worked so hard for this moment, for his father’s approval and trust. He deserves it. I wish I’d been there to share that moment with him.

“But missing me isn’t the same as forgiving me,” I say.

Daniel looks at me thoughtfully. “If it were me, I’d forgive you,” he says.

I meet his eyes. “I know.”

Lisa clears her throat, glancing between us. “I think you two just need to talk. Really talk.”

I shake my head. “There’s nothing left to say. Andrew’s already moved on.” I pause, gathering the courage to voice the part that hurts the most. “He’s even renovating the Lakeside Riviera. The one hotel we agreed he wouldn’t touch.”

I feel the sting of betrayal all over again, like a wound that refuses to heal. “It’s clear that he doesn’t care anymore.”

Daniel leans forward, his voice gentle. “I don’t think that’s true. Andrew cares more than you know. He’s hurt, Em. And sometimes, when you’re hurt, you make decisions out of anger, not logic.”

I grip my glass tightly, the ache in my chest throbbing. “It’s been weeks now.”

Lisa places a hand on mine, her eyes full of empathy. “If he truly loves you, he’ll come around.”

I want to believe them, but doubt gnaws at the edges of my mind. If Andrew really wanted to reconcile, wouldn’t he have reached out by now?

But then again, I know Andrew. He’s as stubborn as he is principled, and once he’s made up his mind, it’s hard to get him to change it.

## Chapter 40: Emily

It's Friday, long past the time I should have left for the office. I step out of the shower and wrap myself in a towel. I head back to the bedroom while toweling my hair.

My phone screen lights up on the night table. A missed call. From Andrew.

My heart leaps, thumping erratically. I stare at the notification, barely breathing. I take a steadying breath and hit "call back" before I can overthink it.

The line rings twice before I hear his achingly familiar voice.

"Hey, Emily," he says. "How have you been?"

The simplest of questions, but I can barely find my voice. "I've been good," I say, the lie twisting something deep inside me. "You?"

"I've been all right." There's a pause, and when he speaks again, his voice is softer. "It's good to hear your voice."

I'm not sure how to respond.

He clears his throat. "Can you meet me at the Riviera Lakeside?"

My heart stumbles. Pain, sharp and visceral, slices through me. He wants me to see it? The place where he's altered everything my father held dear, everything that was part of his vision? It feels like a slap.

I manage to swallow past the ache and keep my voice steady. "I'm busy today," I say, hoping this will put him off.

"Please, Emily," Andrew says, his voice a quiet plea, and something about the way he says it crumbles my resolve.

I let out a slow breath, reluctant but resigned. "Fine," I say, the word heavy in my mouth.

We disconnect, and I stand there, staring at the screen, wondering what I've agreed to. I'll have to face him eventually—might as well get it over with.

I step back into the bathroom, running my fingers through my hair and reaching for my brush. My hands move automatically, pulling myself together piece by piece, forcing composure.

After drying my hair, I put on makeup, the familiar ritual calming me. My reflection looks back, more composed than I feel, but the slight tremble in my hand gives me away.

I pick out a simple outfit—a navy skirt and a white blouse, neat and understated. Nothing too formal, but something that gives me a sense of control.

Finally, I slip on my shoes and grab my keys, the thundering of my heart the only sound in the quiet apartment.

As I drive toward the Riviera Lakeside, I can't stop wondering how it will feel to see him again. To stand in front of him, to look into those familiar eyes that once held such warmth, only to see them cool and distant.

When I finally pull up, the sight of the hotel stops me in my tracks. The building is freshly painted. I step out of the car.

Andrew has kept the same colors—warm, neutral tones that blend with the natural surroundings—but there's a new vibrancy to the place, a feeling that it's somehow been reborn.

My father's hotel, yet different.

Then something catches my eye. My gaze lifts, and I see the name, clear as day, shining above the entrance: The Ace Riviera.

Emotion wells up, thick and uncontrollable, spilling over before I can stop it. Tears blur my vision as I stand there, feeling the enormity of what he's done, of this gesture I never expected.

Footsteps sound beside me, and then Andrew is there. "I thought it was a good way to honor your father," he says, his voice soft, filled with a quiet sincerity that reaches me through my tears.

I try to speak, but no words come. All I can do is nod, my throat tight as I swallow back the overwhelming gratitude, the mix of emotions I can't even begin to name.

"Come on," he says gently. "I'll show you inside. There's no one here this morning—I made sure of that."

I follow him in, each step hesitant as if I'm afraid to breathe and break the spell of this moment.

The lobby is bright, bathed in morning light, and though everything looks new, the familiar warmth and charm are still here, lovingly preserved.

"It's beautiful," I say, my voice trembling. "My father would have loved this."

We walk through the space together, moving from the lobby to the staircase and then upstairs. He leads me into one of the newly renovated rooms, and I pause, taking it all in.

The room is elegant, understated, with touches of modern style blended seamlessly with the old-world charm my father loved.

The colors are soft and inviting, a mix of deep greens and warm wood tones, accented by tasteful art on the walls that echoes the local landscape. It feels like a place to breathe, a sanctuary that welcomes without overpowering.

I turn to Andrew, tears filling my eyes again, overwhelmed by the thoughtfulness of it all. "Thank you," I whisper, my voice breaking.

He looks at me, his gaze intense but softened with an understanding I hadn't expected.

I walk over to the window, trying to steady myself, looking out at the view of the lake, the gentle ripples on the water somehow mirroring the turbulence inside me.

Andrew comes to stand beside me, close but not quite touching. His voice is quiet, almost hesitant, when he speaks. "How are you, really?"

I inhale deeply. It's tempting to give a flippant answer but after what he's done with the hotel, I can't. "Surviving."

"I'm sorry about your father," he says. "I can't imagine how painful that is."

I nod. "It was, still is but I'm coming to terms with it," I say. "I was selfish wanting him to hold on. He would have hated to stay in that coma."

"I'm sorry I wasn't there for you," Andrew says quietly.

My chest tightens. "I didn't give you a chance to be there."

"I keep thinking how tough it must have been for you. Balancing your father's illness with a new marriage," Andrew says. "At first, when I found out, all I could focus on was that you lied to me. I was only thinking of myself."

A sob chokes me. I don't deserve this.

"I wanted to tell you so many times," I say.

Andrew pulls me into his arms and I throw my hands around his neck, loud, ugly sobs ripping out of me.

"It's okay, it's going to be fine," he croons, holding me tight.

It all comes out in the form of tears. The months of worrying whether my father will come out of the coma. The strain of keeping it a secret. The weeks of missing Andrew.

Needing him to hold me the way he's holding me now.

Andrew holds me until my crying stops. Then he draws back and keeping one hand around my waist, he uses the other to gently wipe the tears from my cheeks.

I inhale deeply and try to smile. "Enough about me. How have you been?"

"Not good," Andrew says. "I miss you, day and night, Emily."

My insides turn to water. I hoped for forgiveness but this, I never let myself hope, dream that there was a chance for us.

"I'm sorry, for not understanding. For being too harsh. For not seeing things from where you were standing."

His words pierce through me, and my heart pounds. But I can't let him take all the blame.

"I should have told you," I say, my voice raw with emotion. "I'm so sorry for keeping it from you, for letting it all fester in secrecy. I wanted to tell you so many times, but I was caught between loyalty to my father and my love for you. I didn't know how to bridge that divide."

Andrew watches me, his gaze unwavering, and then he nods. "That loyalty... it's exactly why I fell in love with you. And why I want you as my wife for life." He pauses, and a faint smile touches his lips. "I just wish I'd seen that sooner."

Giddy joy floods me. A happy laugh rises up my chest but nothing can get past the lump lodged in my throat.

Our lips meet, tentative at first, then deeper, our emotions pouring into the kiss. It's a kiss that holds both apology and forgiveness, a connection that reaffirms what we nearly lost.

Andrew pulls me close, his hands trailing down my arms, and suddenly we're caught up in the swell of everything we've been holding back, the need to bridge this distance that's kept us apart.

His touch is familiar, but it feels new, as if we're rediscovering each other with every movement, with every brush of our skin.

We move toward the bed, shedding the last barriers between us as he lays me down, his gaze warm and filled with an intensity that sends a thrill through me.

His hands are gentle, reverent, exploring, and I'm lost in him, in the moment, in the certainty that whatever we've been through, this is where I'm meant to be.

Our breaths intertwine, and every kiss, every caress feels like a vow. A promise to let go of the past, to embrace the future together, no matter what it holds.

Afterward, we lie together, his arms wrapped around me, my head resting on his chest. The room is silent except for the sound of our breathing, and for the first time in months, I feel whole, as if the broken pieces have finally come together.

I lift my head, meeting his gaze and Andrew's hand reaches up, brushing a strand of hair away from my face.

"I love you so much Emily," he says, his eyes brimming with emotion. "I can't live without you."

Tears fill my eyes. Those are the words I've been craving, needing from him. "I can't live without you either."

We lie on the bed, talking and talking, filling the gaps of the time when we were apart.

Andrew pulls my head down and brushes his lips against mine. "I don't ever want to go a day without you. Okay?"

I nod. "Okay."

## Epilogue: Emily

- *Six months later*

"Who stands for this child?" The priest's voice fills the church, warm and resonant.

Andrew squeezes my hand, and I step forward with him, my heart swelling. "We do," we answer together, our voices steady.

It feels like such an honor to stand here as Liam's godparents, promising to be a part of his life and help guide him.

The love and pride in Jack and Sarah's eyes as they look at us are overwhelming, and I feel a rush of gratitude to be part of this family.

We're all bound together in so many ways, and now, Andrew and I are preparing for a new journey of our own.

The ceremony continues, with soft choir music echoing through the church as the priest blesses Liam, dipping his fingers into the holy water and making a small cross on his forehead.

Liam's wide eyes blink up in wonder, his tiny face the picture of innocence.

I feel Andrew's hand on my back, rubbing small circles. There's a sense of calm and warmth around us, a reminder of all that we've built and everything we've gone through to be here.

After the service, we gather outside in the church courtyard, where laughter and joyful congratulations fill the air.

Friends and family gather around, passing Liam from one set of eager hands to another, his little fingers grasping at anything he can reach. Sarah makes her way over to us, a joyful smile lighting up her face.

"Thank you, both of you, for being here and for agreeing to be Liam's godparents," she says, her voice full of emotion. "It means everything to Jack and me."

Andrew pulls her into a warm hug, his voice soft. "We're honored, Sarah. Liam is going to be an incredible little boy."

Sarah glances down at my belly, her eyes twinkling with excitement. "And I can't wait for Liam to meet his future playmate," she says with a knowing grin.

My cheeks warm, and I place a hand over my small but growing bump. It's only been a few months, but the life growing inside me already feels like a miracle.

Andrew's hand joins mine, resting on my belly with gentle pride.

"We're looking forward to that, too," Andrew says, his eyes full of love as he gazes at me. His touch is so protective, so filled with promise, that my heart aches with joy.

If it's a boy, Andrew and I have agreed to name him Ace, after my father. If it's a girl, we'll give her a female variation of the name.

I'm so touched by how determined Andrew is to honor my father. First the Ace Riviera and now our baby.

The hotels have all been renovated and the transformation has breathed new life into each one, blending my father's vision with Andrew's modern touches.

After we exchange a few more words with family and friends, I step aside to watch Andrew as he holds Liam, looking so at ease, so ready for the journey ahead as a father.

The sight fills me with warmth, and I can't help but think of how he will be with our child, his protective nature paired with such tenderness.

My mother has promised to be back in time for our baby's birth. She rekindled her friendship with her old friends and together with two widowed women, they've been cruising the world.

She sounds happy and settled and that makes me happy to see her enjoying her life again.

Barbara has stepped into my Mom's shoes and she's always there when I need her. She'll be a wonderful grandmother. She'll spoil her grandchild, no doubt about that, but I wouldn't have it any other way.

Sarah sidles up beside me, following my gaze. “You two have something really special, Emily,” she says softly. “I could see it from the start.”

I nod, my heart swelling. “We’ve been through so much. And somehow, it brought us here.”

As if sensing my thoughts, Andrew looks over, catching my eye with a smile that’s meant just for me. Then he makes his way to where Sarah and I are standing.

He bends down and presses a gentle kiss to my forehead, his love enveloping me. “To family,” he whispers.

“To family,” I whisper back.

**The End.**

## About the author

Elara Long is a author from Canada. With a passion for storytelling that ignited in her childhood, she crafts tales filled with endearing protagonists and irresistible love interests.

Elara resides in the picturesque town of Kelowna, British Columbia, with her partner, two energetic kids, and her beloved golden retriever, Max. When she's not busy penning her next novel, she enjoys exploring local farmers' markets, indulging in culinary adventures, and soaking up the great outdoors with her family.

Early mornings are her sacred writing time, where, with a steaming mug of herbal tea in hand, she lets her imagination roam free, weaving together stories that resonate with her readers and celebrate the magic of love.

Made in the USA
Las Vegas, NV
18 November 2024

12047747R00142